Good, Ba
Pure Evil...

The Anglesey Mysteries
Book 1

by

Conrad Jones

The Anglesey Murders Series
Unholy Island
A Visit from the Devil
Nearly Dead
A Child for the Devil
Dark Angel
What Happened to Rachel?
Good, Bad and Pure Evil

The DI Braddick Series
Brick
Shadows
Guilty
Deliver Us from Evil
Detective Alec Ramsay Series
The Child Taker
Criminally Insane
Slow Burn
Frozen Betrayal
Desolate Sands
Concrete Evidence
Thr3e
Soft Target Series
Soft Target
Soft Target II 'Tank'
Soft Target III 'Jerusalem'
The Rage Within
Blister
The Child Taker
Unleashed

Chapter 1

Cristy was nervous. Her anxiety levels were off the scale. Shopping in Tesco had never been fun, but when the virus descended, everything became a whole new level of unpleasant. She didn't want to risk catching it, but three of her elderly clients depended on her to get their shopping, so she had no choice but to use the supermarket. Being a carer was hard enough before the risk of catching COVID-19 complicated things. Now it was ridiculously difficult. She adjusted her face mask. It was itchy and uncomfortable, but she felt safer wearing it. Looking around at the other shoppers, it was clear not everyone thought the same. *A lot of people didn't want to wear a mask; selfish shitheads*, she thought. She could see her neighbour, Francis O'Grady, at the fish counter without a mask, breathing her germs all over the haddock. She didn't have asthma; if she was short of breath, it was because she was so fat. If she got the virus, Kentucky Fried Chicken would go bust. Francis, and people like her, were getting around the rules by playing the asthma card. Most of the locals knew each other anyway and being told to go away and mind their own business was part and parcel of working there as the latest lockdown tightened. People were anxious and short-tempered; fear was the new normal.

'Hello, Cristy. Fancy seeing you in here,' a voice she recognised said. It sent shivers down her spine. A cold sweat formed on her brow. The sound of his voice struck fear into her. 'I can't believe I've seen you here. It's been a long time. Seven years in fact.' She felt like her heart was going to explode from her chest. Fear gripped her and squeezed the air from her lungs. 'You look good in those jeans. They cling to you,' he said, lowering his voice to a whisper. 'And I like your hair dark like that. Very sexy.'

Cristy didn't want to turn around, but she couldn't help herself. She had to see if it was him. Surely it couldn't be. He had years left to serve. Her breath came in short gasps, trapped in her chest; her pulse quickened, and she started to tremble. She reluctantly turned to face him. Jon Price grinned at her, his eyes dark and piercing. That look had struck fear into her for years, and it still did. Their relationship had been volatile and unforgettable for all the wrong reasons. She bore the scars to remind her of him whenever she looked in the mirror. Her nose was misshapen, and the cigarette burns on her arms and legs were still red and angry; the years didn't seem to make them fade. Nor did the memories of when he'd inflicted them. He'd held her captive. The last three days of their relationship were etched into her consciousness.

'What are you doing here?' she asked. Her voice trembled. She was glad she had the mask on so he couldn't see her lips quivering. Her knuckles turned white as her hands squeezed the handle of the shopping trolley tightly. She felt weak at the knees.

'Aren't you pleased to see me?'

'No,' she whispered, shaking her head. 'How did you get out?'

'The virus, Cristy,' he said, beaming. 'Early release for hundreds of us. Lucky for me, hey?' Cristy couldn't answer. She was stunned, frozen like a rabbit in the headlights of an oncoming lorry. 'Aren't you going to say hello?' Jon said, frowning. He looked her up and down, like a predator eyeing its prey. Her long black hair was tied up in a ponytail. She looked trim and gym fit. She felt his eyes on her and they were unwelcome. The intensity of his gaze on her body made her feel queasy. 'You look amazing. I've missed you so much, but then prison does that to you. You miss everything, even the shit things, like a cheating, slut girlfriend.'

'I'm not your girlfriend and when I was, I never cheated on you. It was all in your head,' Cristy muttered, her voice breaking. Panic was setting in. She looked around for help, but the aisle was empty.

'So you said, but you're a liar, Cristy. I've had a lot of time to think about the things you said and did.'

2

'I'm not talking to you about it and you're not allowed to come near me,' Cristy said, her voice breaking again. He towered over her. He was tall and lean. It appeared prison had made him bigger. His presence was enough to intimidate most people, but it was way beyond that for her; he struck sheer white-hot terror through her entire being. 'You could be arrested just for coming near me.'

'Oh, you mean the court injunction?' he said, rubbing the dark stubble on his chin. Cristy nodded, feeling the urge to urinate, desperately trying not to piss her pants in front of him. Not again. The last time she'd done it, he laughed so hard she thought he might choke to death. 'Do you think I'm going to do what a crusty old fart in a wig tells me to?' He chuckled, dryly. 'I never have before, I'm unlikely to start now. Besides, you're my baby girl, Cristy. No matter what happens, we always end up back together. How can I stay away from you?' He reached out his hand to touch her face. Cristy instinctively stepped back and flinched.

'Don't touch me,' she hissed, shaking her head. She put the trolley between them. He looked surprised and angry. 'Get away from me or I'll scream the place down.'

'Scream away. I like that.'

'You're sick. I'm calling the police,' she said, taking out her mobile. She clicked off three pictures of him and turned on the video. His face turned to thunder. 'I'm filming you now. Get away from me or I'll call nine, nine, nine, and you'll be back in prison where you belong.'

Jon nodded and a thin smile touched his lips. He held up his hands in apology. 'I'm sorry I came near you. It was an accident,' he said, playing to the camera. 'I didn't know it was you because of the facemask and your hair is a different colour. My mistake. I didn't recognise you. I'll go and do my shopping in Morrisons,' he said, turning to walk away. He winked at her and the smile disappeared. His eyes told her what he was thinking; she'd seen the hate in them a hundred times. He wanted to hurt her for rejecting him. That was how his mind worked. He wanted to hurt her for testifying against him. He wanted to hurt her because he could.

'Say hi to your mum for me. You're still living in her house above Turkey Shore Road, aren't you?' Cristy couldn't speak. 'Harbour View. Of course, you are,' he added. He walked away slowly, a swagger in his step. 'You haven't got the backbone to live on your own.'

Tears rolled down her cheeks, and she felt warm fluid run down her thighs, but she couldn't move. She was frozen in fear. A puddle formed around her trainers.

'I'll see you soon, Cristy,' she heard him shout from the doorway. 'Sooner than you think.'

Chapter 2

Sergeant Bob Dewhurst looked through the passenger window towards Snowdonia. It was late afternoon and warm for October. There was snow on the upper slopes reflecting the watery sunshine; the lower slopes were slate grey all the way down to the tree line. The mountains dominated the horizon against the bright blue sky. It was one of those rare days when the sun and the moon shared the same sky, courting each other above the emerald sea, which separated the island from the mainland. Sergeant April Byfelt was driving the marked patrol car along the narrow back roads towards Church Bay. It was getting towards the end of their shift and this was a mission of mercy.

'What's the name of the house again?' April asked. She looked ten years younger than her true age. Bob, twenty-years her senior, teased that her elfin features and long dark hair made her look like a character from *Lord of the Rings*. April agreed as 'she had pointed ears and hairy feet.

'Heathfield,' Bob said, checking his phone to be sure. He put on his glasses to see the small print. Age was dulling his senses. 'It should be on the left down here.'

'I can't see it,' April said, squinting. She drove on slowly. A hundred yards further on, she saw stone gateposts. They were barely visible, overgrown by unruly hedges and sycamore trees. April pointed to them and slowed down. The name of the house was carved into the stone. The gold lettering was faded and worn by the elements. 'There it is.'

She turned into the gate and followed a winding driveway through a copse of evergreen trees. The house at the end of the drive was quite understated and disappointing. It looked dilapidated and poorly maintained. The window frames were peeling and cracked, and the borders overrun with brambles and weeds. All the curtains were closed.

'This place has seen better days. It looks like the church is running out of money. When was the priest last seen?' April asked.

'We're not sure. The details are a bit sketchy. He's been calling in on vulnerable members of his congregation through lockdown,' Bob said. 'One of them spoke to him on Saturday morning, but no one has seen or heard from him since Sunday. He's tried calling his mobile and his landline and has left messages on his voicemail but Father Creegan hasn't returned his calls, which is very unusual, apparently.'

April stopped the vehicle near the front door and turned off the engine. *Father Creegan*, she thought. The name rang a bell somewhere deep in her memory. Something clawed at her mind, making her feel uneasy.

'All the curtains are closed. It doesn't look like he's up and about, does it?' she said, looking at the windows. 'He might be sick. He could have contracted the virus if he's been visiting parishioners through lockdown.'

'He might be. Let's go and find out,' Bob said.

They got out of the car and approached the front door, gravel crunched under their feet. A crow cawed from the trees and a flock of starlings circled above. April felt a sense of unease, which she couldn't explain. Bob tried to look through a gap in the curtains, but it was dark inside. April knocked on the door. It creaked open slightly. She hesitated, waiting to see if Father Creegan would greet them with a smile, but the door didn't open any further. There was no one behind it.

'It's open,' April said. She pushed it and looked inside. There was a pile of junk mail behind the door. The smell of decomposition hit her like a punch on the nose. 'Can you smell that?'

'I can.'

'That's not a good sign at all,' she said, covering her nose and mouth. She took out a facemask and hooked it over her ears. Bob followed suit. 'We'd better take a look.'

'After you,' Bob said.

'Father Creegan,' April called. There was no reply.

April stepped inside. The air was musty, tainted with decay. It became stronger as they walked down the hall. She flicked on the light. The kitchen was straight ahead. April looked inside. A single cup sat on the stainless-steel draining board and half a crusty loaf was on a wooden chopping board in the centre of a small dining table. The bread was green with mould. A carving knife lay on the table next to it. She moved through the kitchen to the living room door, twisting the brass handle to open it. A two-seater settee was against the wall to her left and a single armchair to her right, next to a bookcase that was full of classics and religious literature. There was no television, which didn't surprise her.

'He must be upstairs,' April said, backing out of the room. 'This place gives me the creeps.'

'It smells like he's been gone a while,' Bob said, leading the way upstairs. He switched on the landing light. The bathroom door was open, revealing an olive-green suite, popular in the seventies. A floral shower curtain hung over the bath. Some of the hooks had been ripped free from the pole. There were dark spots on the curtain and the tiled backsplash. 'That looks like blood to me,' Bob said. He pointed to the bath. Dried rivulets ran towards the plughole.

They moved down the landing, and the stench intensified. The doors were closed apart from one, which was ajar. April pushed each door open and checked inside. Each room was furnished with a single bed and wardrobe. The bedside tables had a lamp, and a bible placed neatly on them. A crucifix was fixed to the wall above each bed. The last door was open. Bob took the lead this time and stepped inside. April followed and recoiled from the hellish scene before her.

'Jesus Christ,' Bob muttered.

'Move.' April gagged before emptying the contents of her stomach onto the Axminster. 'Sorry,' she said, wiping her mouth.

'Are you okay?' Bob asked. She nodded. 'I'll call it in. Although I'm not sure what the hell I'm calling in,' he said to himself.

April composed herself and looked around. The priest was tied to a chair, fully clothed, still wearing his dog collar. His chin was on his chest. Dried vomit stained the front of his shirt. The skin on his hands was white as paper and not much thicker. Dark veins and liver spots mottled them. Sitting opposite him in an armchair was the body of a male. The man was naked. Nothing remained of his head but the tongue and lower jaw; his bottom teeth left exposed. A fan-shaped bloodstain spread up the wall behind him to the ceiling. Stalactites of congealed pink goo clung to the Artex, threatening to drip onto their heads. Between his legs was a double-barrelled shotgun, his fingers still on the trigger.

'He's blown his own head off,' April said, shaking. 'The spatter is congealed. It happened days ago.'

'That's what it looks like to me,' Bob said, nodding. 'I'm getting too old for this.'

April moved closer to the men. The stench intensified. A squadron of bluebottles was feeding on the congealed blood. Blowfly maggots wriggled around the tongue. One of them balanced on the lip and tumbled down the chin. April stepped back and nudged Father Creegan's shoe. The priest made a gurgling sound.

'Did you hear that?'

'Hear what?'

'He just made a noise.' April stopped and listened intently. Father Creegan lifted his head up, opened his eyes, and began to cough.

Chapter 3

Detective Inspector Alan Williams arrived at the vicarage. His detective sergeant, Kim Davies, was driving. Uniformed officers manned the cordon at the end of the driveway, and blue flashing lights illuminated the scene.

'I hate these winter evenings. It's as black as pitch at six,' Alan said, running his hand over his bald head. It looked cold outside, and he wished he'd brought a hat.

'There's a beanie on the back seat,' Kim said, as if reading his mind. They had worked together for years. Early in their partnership she noticed he touched his head when it was cold. Her perception and ability to read people was what made her a good detective. She could have advanced her rank significantly had she transferred to a bigger force, but she had no desire to leave the island. Alan reached into the back and retrieved the hat, pulling it down over his ears without looking in the mirror. The older he got, the more he avoided mirrors; the man he saw was no longer him. 'Shall we go and see what all the fuss is about?' she said, pulling the BMW to a stop.

'I'd rather be going home with a vindaloo and a bottle of red, but if we must, then we must,' Alan said, opening the door. An Anglesey wind blew hard, tugging at his clothes. He pulled the hat down further. Kim tied her long blond hair into a knot on the back of her head. She grabbed a black bubble jacket from the back seat and struggled into it, zipping it tightly to the neck. The vicarage looked dishevelled; the lights burnt behind the curtains. Bob Dewhurst waved from the front door. They walked towards him; hands deep in their pockets. 'It's gone cold,' Alan said to him.

'Bloody freezing,' Bob agreed. 'Step inside. Welcome to the madness of Father Creegan.'

'I think I saw that on Netflix last week,' Alan said.

'I wondered where I got that from,' Bob smiled. 'I thought I'd made it up myself. If it's not a film, it should be.'

'Have you heard how he is?' Alan asked.

'April went to the hospital with him. She rang just before you got here. He's pushing seventy, so it's touch and go. He was tied to a chair for days.'

'Do we know how many?'

'No. We asked him how long he'd been there, but he was incoherent. The doctors said he's dehydrated and in shock. *Severely traumatised* are the words the doctor used. He's been beaten and has a cut on the back of his head, which needed stitches. He's been sedated while they get fluids into him.'

'I want to be told when he wakes up,' Alan said. 'How long until forensics get here?'

'The CSI unit are on their way. They've been working on a suspected murder halfway up Snowdon, apparently. Pamela Stone is on the way, but half of her team are still up there.'

'What, actually up the mountain?' Kim asked.

'Apparently so.'

'What's gone on?'

'A couple in their fifties went walking and only one of them returned. He reported that his wife had slipped and fell. They recovered the body but later on, another group of climbers said they'd been scaling the mountain higher up and seen the husband pull his wife, kicking and screaming, to the edge. Then he threw her off. They called it in as soon as they were low enough to get a signal.' Bob chuckled drily. 'I might take Eileen up there for a walk.'

'There's only one winner there,' Alan said. 'My money is on Eileen coming back down that mountain.'

'Sad but true,' Bob agreed. While they chatted, Alan and Kim followed the sergeant along the hallway and up the stairs. It was like a time capsule stuck in the seventies. The ceilings were high, and the walls covered in textured paper and painted dark green. Random landscapes decorated the walls, some were images of local landmarks, others were places unknown to anyone but the artists who painted them and they were long dead.

'There's blood in the bath,' Bob said. They glanced into the bathroom and then moved on. 'All the action is in the far bedroom, at the end of the landing.'

'It's getting a bit ripe,' Kim said, taking a jar of Tiger Balm from her pocket. She smeared a small amount on her top lip and felt its warmth grow. The aroma of eucalyptus filled her nostrils, almost masking the stench of decomposition. She passed the jar to Alan, who followed suit. Bob gave them a pair of gloves and plastic overshoes and they stepped into the bedroom.

Alan approached the faceless corpse. There was a tattoo on the left shoulder; a ship's anchor and chain surrounded by skulls and roses. A gold chain hung around the neck, encrusted in blood. He spotted a pile of clothes next to the chair.

'Shoes, socks, jeans, T-shirt, hoodie,' he said. 'He must have tied up the priest and then undressed here before he killed himself.'

'Any ID?' Kim asked.

'There's nothing in his pockets.'

Alan studied the body. He tried to gauge the age of the man. His hands were rough and weathered. They didn't belong to a young man, nor a man over sixty. He couldn't narrow it down any further. The fingernails were blackened at the tips. 'He might have been a mechanic,' Alan said to himself. 'Are there any vehicles outside?' Alan asked.

'There's one in the garage. It's a Toyota Prius registered to Father Patrick Creegan.'

'So, John Doe either came here with Creegan or he had a long walk, carrying a shotgun. Unless the shotgun belongs to the priest,' Alan said.

'I've asked Richard Lewis to contact firearms licencing at Chester, but they're closed until tomorrow,' Bob said.

'Okay. Good. We need to know who this is to explain why he tied up Father Creegan, undressed, put a shotgun in his mouth, and blew his brains out.'

'I'm interested in what Creegan has to say about it,' Bob said, shaking his head. 'A naked victim and a Catholic priest. I'm guessing he can tell us who this is. I'm very interested indeed.'

'You're such an old cynic,' Kim said.

'I don't know what you mean,' Bob said, shrugging.

'I'm thinking along the same tracks as Bob,' Alan said.

'Mind reader now, are you?' Bob said.

'You stereotype people. It's part of being our generation,' Alan said, smiling. 'We're old and have preconceived ideas.' Bob tutted but couldn't challenge his point. 'Catholic priest, naked male, suicide, all the ingredients for a revenge attack for historical sexual abuse?'

Bob shrugged but didn't agree or disagree. 'Sounds like a reasonable explanation to me.'

'You think he's a disgruntled choirboy come back to reap revenge on his abuser.' Alan smiled.

'You sound like Poirot,' Bob said straight-faced, but he blushed a little. 'Actually, I wasn't thinking that.'

'It was exactly what he was thinking,' Kim agreed.

'You shouldn't tell lies, Bob,' Alan said. 'It's a sin.'

'I'll add it to my never-ending list of things to improve.'

'How long until Pamela gets here?'

'I am here,' Pamela said, walking through the door. Her bright red curls were contained under a blue baseball cap. She looked at the body and grimaced. 'The cause of death looks clear to me.'

'Really?' Alan asked, frowning.

'Yup. It's a gunshot wound to the head,' she said, putting her case next to the naked corpse. She had a twinkle of mischief in her eyes. Bob grinned and shook his head. He liked Pamela's dark humour. 'I'd stake my reputation on it.'

'But you've only just arrived. I don't know how she does it, do you?' Alan said.

'Shotgun in the mouth, probably suicide,' she added, drily.

'Such a talent.'

'You concur?'

'Yes. We would have worked that one out through a process of elimination,' Alan said, nodding. 'I need to know who he is.'

'Leave him with me and I'll see what I can do.' The smile was gone, and Pamela Stone got to work.

Chapter 4

Jon Price waited outside the Jambo Chinese takeaway. It was in the centre of Holyhead, next to St Cybi's church, which was built on a Roman fort. Locals said the Jambo was built before the Romans arrived, serving crispy duck to the Druids. Jon checked his watch. It was nearly ten o'clock. His concept of time had changed in jail. Time and its passing became all encompassing. Prisoners say, 'they can lock the locks, but they can't stop the clocks.' It was an ode to the long-term prisoner and the anticipation of freedom. Every second that passed was a second served and a second closer to being released. His release had come as a massive surprise. The early release program was supposed to be for non-violent offenders only. Designed to take the pressure off crowded prison populations. Non-violent prisoners. He chuckled as he thought about it. The Home Office had screwed it up so badly. He would be constantly waiting for a knock on his front door and a prison officer to say, 'Sorry, Price, we made a mistake. You're a raving psycho and you'll have to come back to your cell and finish your sentence.'

It could happen if he didn't do as he was told. They explained the rules he had to follow. He had to make the most of every minute he was at liberty. Things needed to be ironed out, then if they rearrested him, it wouldn't matter so much; he would be able to sleep soundly at night. At the moment, things were imbalanced. They weren't how they should be, and that messed with his karma. He was unable to restore things to normal from his cell. Things needed to be put in order quickly in case the Home Office did a U-turn and recalled him. Things were delicately balanced. Follow the rules and don't fuck up. It wasn't rocket science.

Jon watched as the door of the takeaway opened. Two men were arguing inside. One of them pushed the other one to the floor where he rolled around like a turtle on its back. Sutton walked out of the takeaway, oblivious to the scuffle, a bag in each hand. He was still a big lump. Twenty-stone at a conservative estimate. Jon felt his blood boiling. Sutton's evidence had been crucial to putting Jon away, but he'd lied, and Jon wanted to talk to him about that. Sutton got into a waiting vehicle. It was a new Porsche. The driver was a young female who he didn't recognise. She was out of Sutton's league but some women would do anything for a regular supply of whatever drug turned them on and Sutton had the money and contacts to anything and everything. At least he did for now. With Jon in prison, Sutton had manoeuvred himself into the top tier of the criminal network where everything was available. That was about to change.

A knock on the driver's window made him jump in his seat. He looked around angrily. Two uniformed officers were staring at him through the window. One of them he recognised as Colwyn Gallagher. Gallagher was a sergeant and a dick-head of the first degree. He gestured for Jon to wind the window down. Jon rolled his eyes but complied. He didn't have a lot of choice.

'Jon Price. I didn't expect to see your face for a few years,' Officer Gallagher said. 'Did you dig a tunnel under the wall?'

'Officer Gallagher,' Jon said, smiling, although the hate in his eyes was apparent. 'I can't tell you how much I've missed you.'

'I can imagine. The feeling is mutual.'

'You have no idea how many times I've pictured meeting up with you again,' Jon said. 'Just you and me, burying the hatchet. Do you know what I mean?'

'I hope you're not threatening a police officer, Price,' Gallagher said. Jon shrugged; the smile faded. 'Did you hear that?' Gallagher asked his colleague.

'Yes. It sounded like a threat to me.'

'Get out of the car.' Gallagher stood back from the door.

'I'm all right where I am, thanks,' Jon said.

'I won't ask again. Get out of the car or you'll be in the back of the van before you can blink.'

Jon opened the door and climbed out. Gallagher leant into the vehicle and had a brief look around. It was clean and new. He spotted the Hertz sticker in the window.

'This is hired,' Gallagher said.

'Bugger me with a brass trombone,' Jon said, shaking his head. 'Your observational skills are frightening. You are wasted in uniform. Have you thought about becoming a detective?'

Gallagher looked angry. He didn't have the wit or the intelligence to joust with Price, and Price knew it.

'Still a smart-arse.'

'Smarter than you for sure.'

'What are you doing here, Price?' he asked.

'I live here, Columbo.'

'You were sentenced to fifteen years,' Gallagher said. 'Seven years ago.'

'Early release for prisoners with good behaviour. Bet you never thought you'd hear that.'

'We would be informed if you were being released,' Gallagher said, shaking his head. 'They wouldn't just kick you out without telling us.'

'They let thousands of us out. The Home Office had to take the pressure off the con population. The virus is causing havoc. I've been released on licence and I'm back in town, officer Gallagher.'

'Early release?' Gallagher asked, astounded. 'That was for non-violent criminals. Check his story,' he ordered his colleague who used his comms to reach headquarters. 'What exactly are you doing here?'

'I told you.'

'Not in town. I mean here on the high street.'

'I was going for a takeaway,' Jon said. 'It's been a long time since I've had a Chinese.'

'You weren't waiting for Paul Sutton, were you?'

'Who?'

'Sutton. Paul Sutton. He was one of your downtrodden investors who got pissed off with you being a bullyboy and turned evidence against you. Do you remember him now?'

'Sutton?' Jon shook his head. 'Doesn't ring any bells.'

'That's funny because you were watching him when he came out of the Chinese just a few minutes ago,' Gallagher said. 'So much so, you didn't see us coming across the road.'

'Sutton. Sutton. Is he a big fat bloke who always wears tracksuits, despite never having exercised in his life?'

'You think you're smart, Price, but you're not as smart as you think you are. That's why you went down,' Gallagher said. He tapped his finger against his forehead. 'Get this into your head. No one likes you. They never did but you're a bully so people pretended to be your friends until push came to shove and they all turned on you, didn't they?' Jon didn't respond. It was his turn to look angry. 'When all that stuff came out about what you did to Cristy Dennis, you were finished in this town. The big rich businessman who beat the shit out of a tiny little thing like her.'

'So she says,' Jon said, shrugging. His face flushed in anger. 'She likes it rough, what can I say?'

'The cigarette burns on her arms and legs say you're an abuser. Or did she put them there herself?' Gallagher said. He turned to his colleague. 'He terrorised his ex-girlfriend for three days. Locked her up in his flat and tortured her like the proper hard man he is.'

'There are two sides to every story. Don't believe everything you hear.'

'Not in this case. No one likes a rapist.'

'We were in a long-term relationship,' Price said. 'There was no rape. She loved it.'

'There're a lot of people in this town waiting to mark your card, sunshine. Wait until they find out you're out. I reckon they'll be queuing up.'

'Oh, really?' Jon said. He dwarfed both policemen. 'I sincerely hope you're in the queue, Gallagher. I would pay good money to see you try.'

'His story checks out,' the second officer said. 'He was released yesterday.'

'I'll be on my way then, officer,' Jon said, getting back into his vehicle. He started the engine and put on his seat belt.

'What about your takeaway?'

'I've lost my appetite. It must be listening to you talking shite; put me right off.'

'Watch your mouth, Price.'

'You know what? It's all coming back to me now. Paul Sutton. Yes, I remember him. He stood in the dock and lied through his teeth for your lot. He committed perjury. That's a crime, officer, and you know what they say. Justice will prevail.' Jon closed the window and smiled. He flicked his middle finger at the policemen as he drove away.

'I guess he's trouble?'

'He's trouble with a capital T,' Gallagher replied. He had a sinking feeling in his stomach that something bad was going to happen.

Chapter 5

Cristy got out of the shower and grabbed a towel. She patted herself dry, running on autopilot. Her mind was in turmoil. The incident at the supermarket had rattled her badly. Seven years ago, her doctor had diagnosed her with post-traumatic stress disorder following the trial, which saw Jon Price and his associates put away for serious fraud. The seven years Jon was away had allowed her to recover. She'd developed some semblance of normality but seeing him again had set her recovery back by years. Her mother was horrified when she'd arrived at home to shower and change her soiled jeans. She was so upset she could hardly speak. Cristy couldn't tell her what was wrong at first, but eventually she broke down and told her what had happened.

Her mother was heartbroken that the man who had systematically abused her daughter was back on the streets. He'd tormented her for years, but the final assault he'd subjected her to had left her daughter broken, mentally and physically. She knew the emotional and mental impact of seeing him would have a dreadful effect on Cristy. She was so frightened she'd lost control of her bowels. That made her feel sick to her stomach. No mother wanted to think of their child being so afraid they'd wet themselves. Cristy was an adult; it was heartbreaking to think of her being so scared. She wanted to protect her child, no matter how old she was, but couldn't.

'Are you okay in there?' Myra Dennis asked through the bathroom door.

'Yes. I'm okay. I'll be out in a minute.'

'I thought you might have fallen down the plughole.'

'I'm fine, Mum.'

'Your dad is here,' Myra said. 'He's worried about you.'

'Oh my God!' Cristy said. 'I told you not to tell anyone.'

'He's your dad. I had to tell him.'

'Oh no. This is so embarrassing.'

'He needs to know that bastard is out of prison,' Myra said, angrily.

'He would have found out soon enough, Mum, without your help,' Cristy said. 'I just need to calm myself down before I see anyone.' Her mother didn't answer. 'Tell him I'm okay but I want to rest.'

'They want to see you.'

'What do you mean *they*? Who are they?'

'Your brother is here too. He's worried sick about you.'

'Mum! Why don't you phone *The Chronicle* and ask them to hold the front page?'

'I didn't tell him,' Myra said. 'It must have been your dad that called him.'

'I don't want this turned into a massive family drama, Mum,' Cristy said. 'There's an injunction on him. He has to stay away from me.'

'But he hasn't stayed away from you, has he?' Myra argued. Cristy didn't have the strength to complain any further. 'I've put the kettle on. We'll have a cup of coffee and talk about it as a family.'

'I'll be down in a minute,' Cristy said, sighing. There was no point in getting annoyed. The news would be around town that Jon Price had been released early. Her dad and brother would have known within hours anyway. That kind of news travelled fast. She brushed her hair and wrapped it in a towel, glancing in the mirror. The condensation distorted her reflection, but she could still see the bump on the side of her nose. It made her look like a pugilist. Her friends and family played it down and said they could hardly notice it, but it wasn't their face, was it? No. It was hers and for years she felt disfigured. Her doctor had discussed surgery but couldn't guarantee the result would appear natural.

Three years ago, she'd started seeing her brother's best friend, Rowan, who had been in love with her since school. He treated her like a princess and made her feel special; special enough that her broken nose hadn't mattered as much for a long time. She'd hardly noticed it for years until now. Today she saw her reflection and her nose appeared deformed once again.

Cristy got dressed into jeans, pumps, and a baggy jumper. She thought about leggings, but Jon Price had a thing for women in leggings. They would be staying in the drawer for a while. She looked in the mirror again and straightened her hair. Reluctantly, she went downstairs. She took a deep breath before walking into the living room. The first person she saw was her boyfriend, Rowan.

'OMG. What are you doing here?' She tutted and shook her head, glaring at her mum. Her mum looked away, feeling sheepish. 'This is ridiculous,' Cristy said. Rowan was sitting next to her brother Phil and her dad was standing by the door.

'Come here and give your old dad a hug.' Her dad grabbed her and hugged her tightly to his chest. Cristy didn't resist, and the floodgates opened. All the pain and all the guilt he'd felt for not being able to protect her poured out of him. Cristy wept for herself and for her family's pain. Jon Price had caused them all an indescribable amount of grief, and she felt responsible for that. No one spoke until they parted.

'Who wants coffee?' Myra asked, sniffling, and wiping a tear from her eye. Her dark hair was grey at the roots as a result of lockdown. Phil and Rowan declined. 'Cristy. Do you want a brew?'

'No thanks,' Cristy said, wiping a tear away with her sleeve. Rowan stood up and hugged her. 'What are you doing here, did my mum call you too?'

'I was with Phil when she called.'

'She said she didn't call, Phil.'

'I was there.' Rowan shrugged. He was lost for words. They had talked openly about the abusive nature of her relationship with Price, and he was fully aware of the physical and emotional damage he'd inflicted on her. They lived in a small community and he knew it would be difficult for them to avoid Price when he eventually got out of prison, but he didn't think they would have to face it so soon.

'Are you okay?' Rowan asked.

'I'm okay,' she said to him. 'It was just a shock to see him, that's all.'

'How did he get out so soon?' Phil asked. He and Rowan were roofers and had their own business. They played rugby for Holyhead and were both stocky and solid. They had beards, their hair was curly and shoulder length, scraped back into a ponytail. To look at them, they could have been brothers.

'Because of COVID-19,' Cristy said. 'Apparently, the Home Office used an early release scheme to empty the prisons as much as they could.'

'He's more dangerous than any virus. How could they let an animal like that out onto the streets?' Myra asked. 'They should have thrown away the key. He killed people, everyone knows he did, and they let him back out.'

'They couldn't prove it, Myra. They never found any bodies,' Frank Dennis said. 'He was sentenced for conspiracy to defraud.'

'Why are you defending him?' Myra asked.

'I'm not defending him. What I'm saying is he wasn't convicted of murder, so when it comes to looking at parole, they can only look at the fraud conviction. What they think he did is irrelevant.'

'Well, it's all wrong,' Myra said. 'He shouldn't be allowed back onto the island after what he's done.'

'It's all academic,' Cristy said. 'He is here and there's nothing we can do about it.'

'There's plenty we can do. I could kill the bastard,' Frank said. 'That would put an end to it once and for all.'

'My thoughts exactly,' Phil agreed.

'And mine,' Rowan mumbled.

'That's a great idea,' Cristy said, astonished. 'Why don't you all go and kill him together.'

'Someone needs to sort him out.'

'Genius. Jon Price ends up dead and I wonder where the police will look first?' She rolled her eyes. 'My dad, my brother, and my boyfriend would probably be high on their list of suspects. All three of you can share a cell while you serve life.'

'I'll make sure they don't find him,' Phil said. 'No body, no crime.'

'Really?' Cristy asked, shaking her head. 'Is that who you are?'

'It is where Price is concerned. He needs to pay for what he did to you,' Phil said.

'Do you know why I couldn't tell you what he was doing to me?' None of them replied. Phil looked at the floor.

'You should have told me,' her dad said.

'Have a guess why I didn't tell you. One of you, come on.' They stayed quiet. 'I didn't tell you or ask for your help because he's a psychopath. He would have hurt you too.'

'He's just another man,' Phil said. 'Hit him in the right place and he'll break just like anyone else.'

'No, Phil. Listen to me,' Cristy pleaded. 'He has no empathy for anyone. He's a killer and he wouldn't think twice about hurting all three of you just to hurt me.' She looked from one to the other. 'I know you're angry, but you're not gangsters. You're not bad men. You're good men. Violence is not the answer to this because if you go down that road with Jon Price, he'll hurt you at best and do it just for the fun of it.'

'I'd like to see him try,' Phil said.

'He won't think twice, Phil. Those men involved in the fraud case were gangsters from Liverpool and Manchester. They thought Jon Price couldn't hurt them, and now they're gone. No one knows where they are. Don't underestimate him.'

'I don't know how he got away with it,' Myra said. 'How can you kill people and not be convicted of murder?'

'They couldn't convict him of murder because he disposed of the bodies in ways that they'll never be found.' Cristy sat down and folded her arms. She closed her eyes as if recalling her memories. 'During those last three days when I was locked in his house, he told me things that you wouldn't believe. If you didn't know him, you wouldn't believe it was true, but I believed him. I believed every word he said, and that's why I didn't tell you what he was doing to me because I know what he's capable of.' She stood up and tried to smile. 'People always ask me why I stayed with him. I stayed because he wouldn't let me leave. He would have killed me before he saw me with another man.'

'We would have protected you,' Frank said.

'And who would have protected you?' Cristy asked. Frank looked at the floor. 'You couldn't be with me twenty-four hours a day. No one could have stopped him if he wanted to get to me. I knew the police were building a case against him, and I made the decision to bide my time until they sent him away. I know you're just protecting me, and I love you for it, but leave Jon Price to his own devices. Drop the tough guy acts, will you?' An uncomfortable silence followed.

'It's not an act,' Phil said, flexing his biceps. 'I am tough.' He pulled a stupid face.

'You're a clown.' Cristy chuckled. 'Let's have that coffee, shall we, Mum?'

The atmosphere was tense. Frank looked like he was going to explode. Myra went into the kitchen, muttering to herself. Phil may have made light of what she said, but she knew her brother and she could sense he was steaming inside. He always had a slow burn before he exploded. Ever since they were kids, she could spot when to stop annoying him. In contrast, Rowan looked like he was out of his depth.

'I'm going to tell Colwyn Gallagher that Price approached you in Tesco,' Frank said. 'I know you don't want a fuss, but the police need to know. Col is the one they send out when someone breaches bail or an injunction.'

'Col Gallagher is a knob,' Phil said. 'Jon Price won't pay any attention to him.'

'He might be a knob but he has a uniform and a warrant card and I'm sure if Price has been let out on early release, he'll have to adhere to restrictions, especially the injunction,' Frank said. His face was ruddy and lined with deep wrinkles. Frank clipped his grey hair close to his head. Every year at sea on the deep trawlers was etched on his face. 'It's up to the police to enforce it but mark my words, if they don't, I'll have that bastard. I don't care how dangerous he is. He needs to stay away from you.'

'If you tell Col Gallagher, he'll go and warn Jon not to come near me,' Cristy said. 'I know how his mind works. It will be like a red flag to a bull. I don't want him provoked unnecessarily. It's been seven years since he went to jail and I know at least three women from the island who have been visiting him inside and plastered it all over Facebook how much they love him.'

'Bloody idiots,' Myra said.

'I was one of those idiots, Mum,' Cristy said. 'He's a good-looking man and very charming when he wants something. Let them find out who he is in their own time. He will be distracted by them for a while at least. It might have been a genuine coincidence that I bumped into him. He might not give me a second thought.'

Myra came back into the room with a tray of cups. 'I wonder if all the others were released too,' she said.

'Do you mean the ones who went down with Price?' Frank asked.

'Yes. How many of them went down with him?'

'Five,' Phil said. 'I heard they were sent to different jails. Half of them have been accused of grassing on Price and the others were all pointing fingers at each other about missing money.'

'I heard that too,' Rowan said. 'The police reported recovering over three million in money and shares from a bank account in his property business name. Rumours have it there should have been a lot more than that. Someone helped themselves before the police found it.'

'Good. I hope they turn on each other. If they all come home at the same time, there could be fireworks,' Phil said. 'There are some grudges to be sorted out. Paul Sutton and his work mates testified against him.'

'They were all tradesmen, weren't they?' Myra asked.

'Most of them. Some were in the horse trade.'

'A few of Sutton's men were involved in the fraud. Most of them testified against Price to save themselves,' Rowan said.

'I can't see Sutton bowing down to Price,' Frank said. 'I was at sea with his old man. He was as tough as old boots, scared of no man.'

'Maybe Sutton will do the job for us,' Phil said. 'Whatever happens, Price will have his hands full.'

'Let's hope so.' Cristy nodded and sipped her coffee. 'Now, can we talk about something else?' She was projecting the image of a calm exterior, but inside, she was terrified. Terrified for herself and terrified for her family. Jon Price was more dangerous than any of them realised.

Chapter 6

Father Creegan had been awake for three hours, which had gone by in the blink of an eye. The first person he saw when he awoke was a uniformed police officer. The terrible memories were coming back to him in flashes. He wasn't certain what had happened. Alan looked through the glass porthole in the door and noted his eyes were open.

'He's awake,' Alan said. He turned to the junior doctor who was looking after the priest. 'Can we speak to him?'

'He was confused and distressed when he woke up. He'll be a little groggy as the sedative wears off.'

'How is he?' Alan asked.

'When he came to, we put him through a quick MOT and told him that physically, he's fine, but the shock will take time to settle. We need to keep him on a drip to rehydrate him and we need to monitor his heart and blood pressure for a few days because of his age.'

'Has he said anything about what happened to him?' Kim asked.

'Not much. One of the nurses told him that several of his parishioners have called to ask how he is and if they could visit. They've been told they can't because of the virus. Father Creegan was disappointed but said he understood. He also said he was surprised detectives were waiting to speak to him already. He thought you might give him time to recover his composure.'

'We like to get them when they're still groggy,' Alan said, seriously. 'We can get them to admit to all sorts that way.'

'Really?' the doctor asked, frowning.

'Not really. It was a joke,' Alan said. 'But we do need to talk to him.'

'I see. A joke,' the doctor said, smiling.

'Yes. Between us, a joke,' Alan said. He winked. 'You look like the type who can keep a secret. We need to be careful you see.'

The doctor looked confused. 'I've mentioned the bump on the back of his head and explained the symptoms of concussion to him. He'll feel the tug of stitches beneath the dressing but he should be fine to talk to you but not for too long and don't make him anxious.'

'We'll do our best, doctor,' Alan said, opening the door. 'Thank you for your help.' Kim and Alan entered the room and the uniformed officer remained outside. 'Father Creegan,' Alan said in greeting.

'Is there a reason why a constable has been stationed outside my room?' the priest asked, concern in his eyes. 'Am I in danger?'

'A firearm was involved in the incident,' Alan said. 'So, we have to use belt and braces to be on the safe side. I'm DI Alan Williams and this is DS Davies,' Alan said. Alan watched the priest studying them, looking from one to the other. His expression was blank, his eyes furtive and curious. They were watery green and deep wrinkles spread from the corners. His lips were thin and reptilian, and the skin on his neck hung like a turkey's throat. 'We need to ask you some questions about what happened at the vicarage.'

'Yes, of course you do. That's fine. It's to be expected under the circumstances although everything is a little hazy.'

'There's no rush. Take your time.'

'I've been trying to remember things as they happened but it's all such a blur.'

'Let's start with what you do remember,' Alan said. 'How long were you in that chair?'

'How long?'

'Yes. Can you remember what day it happened?'

'Goodness me. Let me think,' Creegan said. He closed his eyes. 'Of course. It was Sunday.'

'You're sure?'

'Yes. Sundays are quite important to a priest, inspector.' Alan smiled but felt the barb in the comment, nonetheless. The priest had taken an instant dislike to him, and the feeling was mutual. 'The church has been closed to my congregation, but not to me. I spent most of the day there and went home to have some tea about four o'clock.' The priest checked his watch, instinctively. 'From what I can remember, it happened shortly after I arrived home.'

'From the church?'

'Yes.'

'Who was he?' Alan asked. The priest looked surprised by the question.

'I have absolutely no idea,' Creegan said. His eyes were difficult to read. 'I didn't see him, you see,' he added. 'Not while his head was intact, anyway.'

'How did he get there?' Alan asked. 'Did you stop anywhere on the way home?'

'No. Not that I can remember.'

'Did you stop or didn't you?' Alan asked. 'It could be important.'

'I didn't stop.'

'Your car was in the garage to the rear of the house,' Alan said. 'Did you park it there?'

'If it was in the garage, I must have, but I can't say I remember doing that.'

'Do you always garage it?'

'Not always. I can't remember putting it away, but we do these mundane things automatically, don't we?'

'We do. Take your time. Tell us what you can remember after you got home.'

'I know I was in the bathroom and there was a noise behind me,' Father Creegan said, touching his bottom lip as if in deep thought. 'Then someone hit me hard on the back of my head and I must have passed out. When I woke up, I was tied to a chair in my bedroom and there was a body sitting in the chair opposite me.' He closed his eyes and shook his head as if the memory disturbed him. 'I've never seen anything like that before. It's all been such a shock. The poor soul had committed suicide right there in front of me.'

29

'Did you recognise his voice?'

'No. I didn't hear his voice.'

'He didn't speak to you?' Kim asked, frowning. 'When he was tying you to the chair.'

'He may have done, but I was unconscious, you see,' Creegan said, smiling as if he was talking to a child. His teeth were yellowed, definitely a lifelong smoker. 'I certainly don't recall him saying anything to me. My memory is a blank.' He looked confused. 'Don't you know who he is?'

'Not yet. There was no ID on him,' Alan said. He sensed the priest was lying. 'DNA and dental records will identify him. We don't have the results back yet.' The priest nodded that he understood. He looked saddened by the news. 'Can you think of anyone who would want to hurt you, Father?' Alan asked.

'No. Absolutely not.' Creegan shook his head. 'I've never given anyone reason to dislike me. I try to help people as much as I can. It's all part of the job,' Creegan said, smiling warmly. Alan didn't like religion, and he didn't like priests. There was something sickly about this one; something fake.

'Think carefully,' Alan said. 'Think back as far as you can. Is there anyone from your past who could bear a grudge against you? Even if you think it might be inconsequential. The slightest thing could help.'

'Someone who could bear a grudge against me personally?' Creegan held his chin between his finger and thumb. 'I can't think of anyone,' Creegan said, shaking his head. 'Could someone have something against the church or God himself, absolutely yes? Hundreds of disillusioned souls bear grudges, but not against me, personally. Surely this is a random act against the church?'

'We don't think this is random. It looks to be more personal than an attack on the church,' Kim said.

'You think it's personal because of what?'

'They chose you and they chose your home to do it, not your church.'

30

'I see. If you look at the hard facts like that, it does appear to be personal.' The priest nodded, deep in thought. 'I'll admit that. I know where this is heading,' Creegan said. The priest wagged his forefinger. His expression became stern. 'I'm not a stupid man. I can see how this looks.'

'How does it look?' Alan asked.

'A Catholic priest, a naked man commits suicide in his bedroom. It all points to me being Jimmy Saville in a dog collar.'

'We're not saying that,' Alan said.

'Really?' Creegan asked. 'Forgive me, but I think you are. Does it look like I was interfering with choirboys when I was younger?'

'We're asking you if there's anyone with a grudge,' Alan said. 'That's all.'

'You think I've done something wrong in my past. *That* is how it looks,' Creegan said, looking from one to the other. 'Be honest with me. To you it does, doesn't it?'

'Sometimes we have to take things at face value. If it walks like a duck, swims like a duck, and quacks, then it's a duck. We have to ask some awkward questions,' Alan said.

'Awkward for who?' the priest asked. 'Not awkward for you, I'm sure.'

'We're not trying to make you feel awkward.'

'Well. You are making me feel awkward. Very awkward indeed. I'm not a closet paedophile nor a closet anything else for that matter,' Creegan said, growing frustrated. 'I can assure you there are no sexual skeletons in my closet. You need to look elsewhere for the reason that man chose to end his life the way he did. He was clearly deeply disturbed.'

'Disturbed people are rarely so organised and dramatic,' Alan said.

'I'm not sure I follow.'

'Disturbed people throw themselves under trains or off motorway bridges with no regard for the painful death they'll endure. There is rarely such a level of planning, or paraphernalia involved.'

'You've lost me.'

31

'Do you own a shotgun, Father?'

'Good heavens, no. Why on earth would I want a shotgun?'

'Sport,' Kim said.

'Football is sport. Shotguns are designed to kill. I would question the reason why anyone wants to own one.' The priest shook his head in disgust. 'There must be something wrong with them mentally.'

'I have two,' Kim interjected.

'I mean no offence.' The priest held up his hands in apology. 'I'm tired and not a fan of guns.'

'A lot of people in rural communities and farming areas own them. There are thousands on this island.' The Father looked shocked. 'I use them for clay pigeon shooting. Sport.'

'I see. Please accept my apology. I meant no harm.'

'Apology accepted,' Kim said. 'The gun used in your house doesn't belong to you or anyone you know?'

'No. Of course not.'

'If it isn't yours, it's paraphernalia, Father Creegan.'

'What is paraphernalia?' Father Creegan asked, shaking his head. 'You're referring to the shotgun?'

'I am. A complete stranger made his way on foot to your home, broke in, and attacked you in the bathroom, tied you up, undressed, and blew his brains all over your bedroom wall.'

'That would appear to be a reasonable summary of events.'

'He had to have the gun with him when he arrived. Hardly a simple thing to achieve bearing in mind where you live. It would take a level of planning beyond the capabilities of someone suffering a breakdown,' Alan surmised. 'You can see where I'm coming from, Father?'

'Yes. I can, but there are other possibilities.'

'Such as?' Alan asked, but the priest remained silent. 'You want us to consider this very deliberate act was carried out by a complete stranger who just happened to stumble across your house?' Alan asked.

'He may not be a stranger but that doesn't mean I know him and he may have arrived by bus or taxi or parked nearby and walked to the vicarage.' Creegan grasped for an explanation. He was becoming annoyed. 'How would I know?'

'He got a bus carrying a shotgun?' Alan asked, smiling. 'We haven't recovered a gun case of any kind at the scene and I'm certain most bus and taxi drivers would be extremely reluctant to pick up someone carrying a gun, case or no case.' He paused to let the priest think. 'The local taxi companies have no record of anyone being dropped off in your part of the island and it is pretty remote, to say the least.'

'Meaning what?'

'Taxi drivers would remember dropping someone off in the middle of nowhere.' Alan shrugged and watched Creegan's expression change. He looked genuinely confused. 'Especially carrying a shotgun.'

'Yes. I can see how that would be memorable,' Creegan mumbled.

'We've canvassed most of your parishioners and no one has reported or noticed anyone missing from the community.' He left another pause. 'There are no abandoned vehicles nearby, so we're back to the original question, which is why would a stranger kill himself in your home?'

'I simply can't answer you, detective,' Creegan said. His eyes held Alan's. He reached for a cup of water and sipped it. 'And I might add that I'm not happy with your tone or your insinuations.'

'That's unfortunate, but a man has blown his head off in your bedroom and he wanted you specifically to witness the act and the aftermath.'

'I can see how it looks like that.'

'I can't apologise for doing my job, Father Creegan.' Alan shrugged. The priest nodded that he understood. 'So, I'll be straight with you.'

'Please do.'

'In my book, you know who this man was.'

'You're very wrong.'

'He targeted you specifically.'

'You're saying he wanted me to witness it. Me specifically?'

'That's exactly what I'm saying.'

'That's pure speculation.'

'Really?' Alan asked. 'He definitely knew who you were or why would he target you as his audience?'

'Because I'm a priest.'

'In which case he must have known you're a priest. He wasn't wandering aimlessly around the island waiting for someone wearing a dog collar to go by.'

'Maybe he wanted one of God's servants to witness his death.' Creegan suggested. 'I can't tell you the answer,' he added with a narrow smile. 'And I can't tell you who he was. I didn't see him.'

'Did you witness his death, Father Creegan?' Alan asked.

'What?'

'Did you actually witness his death?' Alan repeated. 'Only earlier you said he was already dead when you came around.'

'Yes. He was already dead.'

'Did you hear the blast?'

'I've had enough of this.' Creegan sighed. 'I'm not sure being attacked and tied to a chair and left to starve to death is actually a crime or have I missed something?' The priest frowned. 'Why do I feel like you think I've committed a crime?' Alan and Kim remained silent. 'I'm the victim and I'm very tired and you're confusing me,' Father Creegan said, folding his arms. 'If you have any more questions, I suggest you arrest me for something, and I'll bring the Church's solicitors with me. They're very experienced at dealing with slander and false accusations.' The priest looked at them defiantly. His eyes challenged them. 'Now, please leave me alone. I'm not saying anything else to you.'

'Okay, Father Creegan,' Alan said. 'I understand you're frustrated. We'll leave it at that for now.' Alan gestured to Kim that they should leave. As they reached the door, he turned back to the priest. 'Just one more question.'

'What?'

'How do you think your attacker got into the vicarage?' Alan asked. Father Creegan looked stumped. His face blushed a little. 'There's no sign of a break-in, you see.' The priest shrugged but didn't answer. 'Do you think you might have left the front door open by mistake?'

'I have no idea how he got in,' Creegan said. His lips narrowed and the muscles at his temple twitched. 'You're the detectives. Go and detect.'

Alan nodded and smiled. 'We will do that,' he said. 'I hope you're on the mend soon.'

****

Luca counted his takings. He had sold enough cocaine to pay Sutton what he owed him and a bit more on top. That was a relief because Sutton was becoming oppressive to work for. He was taking too much of his own gear and becoming a paranoid prick. One day he would push someone too far and get a good hiding. He wasn't as hard as he thought he was. It wasn't that long ago that Jon Price destroyed him and sent him to Ysbyty Gwynedd in the back of an ambulance. He did use a baseball bat, but that didn't matter; a win is a win. At the time, Sutton was pushing his weight around and he got slapped into place for it. That was in the good old days when Price was top dog on the island and Sutton was just the fat boy who dealt from an ice-cream van on the council estates. The same thing would happen again if he didn't take a chill pill and stop giving everyone a hard time. He needed to realise there's always someone who can beat you, especially if they bring a weapon to the party. His phone rang. Talk of the devil. It was Sutton.

'All right, mate,' Luca said. 'What's up?'

'Have you heard about Price?'

'No. What about him?'

'He's out, man,' Sutton said. He sounded worried. 'I need you to keep your eyes and ears open and if you speak to him, I want to know about it.'

'How can he be out?' Luca asked, incredulous but excited too. 'He's only done seven years.'

'Some crazy shit to do with the virus. They released all of them.'

'That's madness. Fucked up.' Luca fist bumped the air. Jon Price would wipe the floor with Sutton's head and then stick it up his arse. 'I'll keep my ear to the ground. Don't worry. You can count on me.'

'I'm not worried. Call me if you hear anything,' Sutton said bluntly before he rang off.

Luca wanted to call his contacts to see if anyone had spoken to Jon, but decided to let others do the gossiping. Sutton would be watching like a hawk. He would be looking for dissent in the ranks and there would be plenty. It all started going wrong for Sutton when he began screwing Hayley Longhurst earlier in the year and things went downhill from there. Granted, she was good looking enough and half Sutton's age, but she was also a raging cokehead with a volatile temper and a jealous streak the size of an elephant. She had Sutton partying till all hours in the morning for days on end, sniffing the uncut gear they kept for themselves. No wonder he was losing his grip. His brains were fried.

Luca felt his mobile phone vibrate. It was a text message from a withheld number asking for an ounce. He sent a message back with his location and instructions. He was near Penrhos Beach, but not on it. He could see customers arriving without being seen himself. It was an excellent vantage point. The view from the hospital car park was ideal. His exit route was perfect too should the dibbles or a rival try to set him up. This would be his last customer of the night, and then he was going home. His missus had left him again and taken the kids. She was kicking off about him dealing, but how else did she expect him to pay the bills? He was doing his best. The mortgage was covered, Sutton was paid, and he had enough gear left to clear a few grand by the end of the month to keep her happy. She might come home if he could persuade her. He couldn't wait to tell her that Jon Price was out.

A vehicle pulled onto Penrhos and flashed its headlights three times. That was the signal he gave to all his clients. A hundred yards of low sand dunes lay between him and the car park, the sea to his left. He stashed his money and the rest of his stock under the driver's seat and put an ounce down the back of his boxer shorts, which had a secret pocket stitched in them. Luca opened the door and climbed out, heading to a dark spot in the dunes. He saw his client heading towards the meeting place from the direction of Penrhos. A cigarette burnt in his hand; orange embers flickered in the wind. They reached a dip in the sand and faced each other. Luca couldn't make out his client's features. His mouth was covered with a facemask.

'All right. How much did you say you wanted?' Luca asked. It was a final check that this was who had messaged him. If he said anything but an ounce, the deal was off.

There was a flash of dull steel to the left of his blind spot. Luca stepped back, but it was too late. The crowbar struck him above the left ear, splitting his skull before becoming embedded in the brain cavity. Luca fell onto the sand, twitching uncontrollably. He felt his attacker putting his foot on his back so that he could tug the bar free from his head. The pain was blinding. Lights flashed behind his eyes as the blade was tugged free. He heard a whooshing sound as the crowbar fell again. He felt a devastating crack against his neck and freezing cold air rushing into his lungs as his windpipe was severed; then he felt nothing.

Chapter 7

Cristy was tucked up in bed with a cup of hot chocolate and a biscuit, watching *Prison Break*, which seemed ironic. She was three seasons in and hooked. Jon Price was not going to ruin her binge watching. She had told her boss she would be all right to work the next day, which her mum disagreed with completely, but the world would keep spinning regardless of where Price was. Cristy wanted to carry on as normal. She had to if she were to remain sane. Hiding in her bedroom dwelling about what had happened seven years ago would do no one any good. He had broken her then and turned her into a hermit, frightened to be around other humans. She wasn't going to let it happen again.

Her mobile rang. The screen said it was Karen from work. She was worried when she'd called in earlier, distraught, saying she had to go home. Karen had been a friend and colleague for years, and she knew all about Price. The entire town knew, as did most of the island too. His notoriety for domestic abuse was legendary. A string of ex-girlfriends recounted the same pattern of behaviour, yet it didn't stop him charming others into his web. In hindsight, Cristy couldn't fathom how she became ensnared, but it didn't matter now. She had fallen in love with a bad egg, and now she had to deal with the consequences.

'Hello, Karen,' Cristy said. 'I'm really sorry to let everyone down.'

'Don't be sorry. You haven't let anyone down. I can't believe they let him out. Are you all right?'

'I'm fine. It was just a shock. I panicked but I've calmed down now.'

'Good. It must have been a huge shock for you. I can only imagine how scary it must be to know he's back,' Karen said. She seemed hesitant. 'I don't want to frighten you, but does he know you're a care worker now?'

'I don't know, to be honest, why?' The question caught her off guard a little.

'Someone called me earlier and asked me if you worked here,' Karen said. 'I said I'd never heard of you and they hung up. It was a man, and he was local.'

'It must have been him,' Cristy said. Her heart was beating like a drum again. She felt sick to her stomach. 'Why can't he just leave me alone?'

'If you need to take some time off, just ask,' Karen said. 'I will completely understand.'

'I feel sick,' Cristy said. She thought for a few seconds. 'I'm not letting the bastard scare me into giving up my job. I'll be in tomorrow. He's not controlling me again.'

'I could swap you and Tracey over so you can work in the nursing home and she can take the home visits for a while. At least you'll be safe inside surrounded by other people.'

'Thanks, Karen. I'd really appreciate that,' Cristy said. 'I'll go straight there in the morning. Will you tell Tracey she's got my round?'

'I'm with her now,' Karen said. 'It was her idea. She says hi.'

'Tell her hello from me and thank you. I'm really sorry about this. I was reluctant to get the police involved, but I may have to. He ruined my life once, he won't do it again. I'm not going to let him interfere with our routines at work.'

'We can be flexible until you sort him out. I wonder how he knew to call here?' Karen asked. 'Do you think he's asked people about you to find out what you're doing?'

'Probably. It wouldn't take long, would it?' Cristy said. 'Some of his cronies are still out there. They would know where I work. You know what town is like. Everyone knows everyone's business. I'm sorry he's bothered you. I feel so embarrassed about the whole thing. He's haunting me.'

'You don't need to feel embarrassed around us. We're your friends and we're here for you, Cristy. We'll help in any way we can. Men like that need their bollocks cut off and I'm quite happy to do it. Pass me the scissors and make sure they're blunt,' Karen said. Cristy chuckled despite being frightened. 'That's better. You nearly laughed.'

'Nearly,' Cristy said. 'Thank you again and I'll see you in the morning.'

'Good night, Cristy,' Karen said. 'Try not to worry too much. Easier said than done, but you know what I mean.'

'Yes. I do. I'll try. Good night.'

Cristy lay back on the bed and took a deep breath. She was tired and frightened and angry and frustrated and a dozen other things too. She wanted to tell her mum and dad that he might have contacted work, but she couldn't yet. There was no point in them not sleeping too. She would tell them in the morning and let her dad call Col Gallagher. It couldn't hurt. Price was clearly not going to let her live her life. She wondered if he knew about Rowan yet. It wouldn't stay hidden from him for long. The first questions Price would ask would be who she'd been with while he was away and who she was with now. Rowan was fit and strong and could look after himself, but Jon Price was evil. Her phone beeped. It was a text message.

Night, night, Baby Girl. I'm thinking of you naked on your knees. You like that. See you soon. X

Cristy reread the message. It was from a withheld number. There was only one person who called her that. Price. Another message arrived.

You're a total slut, but I forgive you. x

The psychopath had her number. She felt vulnerable. Another message beeped.

Your friend Karen at work lied to me. She's a little liar just like you. I'm going to fuck her before I drown her.

Cristy dropped the phone. He had reached into her safe place. Her bedroom was sacrosanct to her state of mind and emotional stability. It was a place even her mum didn't enter. Price had violated her yet again.

Chapter 8

Penrhos beach was cordoned off in its entirety, angering the local dog-walking community, but they hung around anyway, waiting for the latest gossip. When Alan arrived, a black Audi was being winched onto a tow truck. Kim was waiting for him in the hospital car park. Her hair was blowing across her face in the wind. She looked cold. Alan handed her a large latte from McDonald's and sipped on his.

'I thought you would want one,' Alan said. He needed the caffeine to seep into his system to jump start his brain. The sun was only just up, and an icy wind blew off the sea. An Irish ferry was manoeuvring around the lighthouse at the end of the breakwater, leaving a foamy white wake. 'It's too early for anything complicated. What have we got?' Alan asked.

'The victim is Luca Bay, age thirty. He's originally from Cemaes and has been a low-level dealer since leaving school,' Kim said, heading in the direction of the dunes. 'That's his vehicle on the flatbed. We've recovered cash and cocaine from under the driver's seat. It looks like he stashed it, locked the car, and headed into the dunes, probably to make a deal.'

'But he met his attacker?' Alan said. Kim nodded. 'How much cocaine are we talking?' Alan asked.

'Not enough to warrant a crowbar to the head,' Kim said. They reached the dip in the dunes and were instantly sheltered from the wind. Luca Bay was lying on his back, arms folded across his chest – hands on his shoulders as if he were hugging himself. The sand around his head was deep red. His eyes were wide open, staring at the low grey clouds which skated across the sky. A long crowbar was buried deep into the skull, almost splitting it into two halves – the metal teeth were positioned in the centre of his forehead a few inches above his nose. The handle pointed towards the derelict Tinto factory. It had been shut down for years, but the chimney was still standing, looming like a sentinel overlooking the Holy Island. 'Meet Harry Rankin,' Kim said, greeting the CSI working the scene. 'This is DI Williams, better known as Alan. He'll be the SIO on this.'

'Nice to meet you at last, Alan,' Harry said. He shifted his considerable bulk to face Alan. 'I've heard a lot about you from Pamela.'

'Where is Pamela?' Alan asked, disappointed. He was a creature of habit. Kim Davies was his partner, and Pamela Stone processed their crime scenes. Anyone else was an intruder.

'Self-isolating,' Harry said. 'She has a temperature and developed a cough overnight. She asked me to step in while she gets tested.'

'Oh dear,' Alan said, even more disappointed. 'If you're going to be in the driving seat, you might as well start with a bang.' Alan gestured the victim. 'What can you tell me?'

'Three blows,' Harry said. 'One to the side of the skull above the left ear, another to the side of the neck here, and the final blow to the centre of the forehead where, as you can see, the weapon remains. My guess is he was probably dead before the last blow was delivered and the position of the body is staged. He has a white-gold wedding ring on, a gold neck chain, and a gold identity bracelet on his right wrist. His wallet, keys, and phone are in his pockets.'

'Are there any drugs on him?' Alan asked.

'I haven't found any yet, but I can't search his clothing properly here. He may have them hidden on him somewhere,' Harry said.

'How much coke was in the Audi?' Alan asked, frowning.

'A couple of ounces at most,' Kim said.

'This is total overkill for a heist of that size. The killer left all his belongings on him,' Alan mused. 'This is personal.'

'Have you read your emails this morning?' Kim asked.

'What do you think?' Alan said.

'I think there's a first time for everything,' Kim said, shaking her head. 'You should read them over breakfast.' Alan raised his eyebrows. 'You know, breakfast? Grapefruit, melon, yoghurt.'

'Don't be disgusting. My eyes aren't the best first thing in the morning.' Alan offered as his best excuse.

'I was going to tell you on the way back to the station,' Kim said.

'Tell me what?' Alan asked.

'The Home Office let Jon Price and his crew out on early release,' Kim said.

'When?'

'It was a staggered release which began last week. Price was released the day before yesterday.'

'Has he come back to the island?'

'Yes. Col Gallagher spoke to him outside the Jambo yesterday. It was the first we knew of it.'

'You are kidding me?' Alan said. 'This has to be a huge mistake.'

'Apparently not. They emailed us this morning to let us know officially.'

'Who did Luca Bay work for,' Alan asked, looking down at the victim. 'Tell me it's Paul Sutton.'

'Correct,' Kim said. 'If I remember rightly, he worked for Price on a building site before he went down.'

'Was he involved in the trial?'

'Not that I can recall. He was pretty low down the pecking order. I think he kept himself to himself. He certainly didn't appear on our radar.'

'I don't recall him,' Alan said. 'His name didn't come up in any of my cases.'

'I dealt with him a few times when I was in uniform,' Kim said.

'Does he have a family?'

'Yes. A wife, Janine, and two kids under five, William and Charlotte,' Kim said.

'Jesus. This is not good. How many of Price's crew did they let out?' Alan asked.

'All five of them.'

'We need to get everyone up to speed with the fact that they're back in circulation. The island is struggling. Lockdown has strangled the life out of the tourist trade. There are no jobs and not much money about – they'll be looking to get back into business as soon as they can and this could be the start of removing the opposition.'

'Whoever did this didn't take the drugs or the money,' Kim said.

'He might have been disturbed,' Alan said. 'That's what's so weird about it. Arrange for an MIT meeting in the operations room in an hour. This might be nothing to do with Price being released, but the chances are it is. Sutton might see this as a direct attack on himself. If he does, this could spiral out of control very quickly.'

'I'll organise it now,' Kim said.

Chapter 9

Cristy hadn't slept well. Her dreams were filled with disturbing images of the past. Jon Price had invaded her mind once more. After seven years of recovery, the overwhelming feeling of fear that she once lived with day and night, had descended on her again. It was suffocating, crushing the life from her like a ton of bricks on her chest. Her eyes felt like she had grit in them, and a dull headache was forming at the back of her head, threatening to spread and become more intense as the day went on. She opened the curtains and looked out over the harbour. Two huge ferries were docked at Salt Island and the street lights of Holyhead burnt yellow in the darkness. The port was busy working while the town slept. She had made up her mind that she was going to call the police. It was seven-thirty when she showered and donned her uniform. The green smock was two sizes too big for her. After a quick check in the mirror, she went downstairs into the kitchen and switched the kettle on. Myra walked in from the living room.

'Are you okay?' her mum asked, yawning. She fastened her dressing gown around her as she spoke. 'I fell asleep on the settee again,' she said.

'Too much rum?' Cristy asked. Myra nodded.

'I don't like going to bed alone since your dad left,' Myra said.

'That was five years ago, Mum. Do you want coffee?'

'Yes. A gallon will do me. Did you sleep okay?'

'No. I've hardly slept a wink. I've made my mind up. I'm going to call the police before I go to work,' Cristy said. Myra looked surprised at the change of heart.

'What's made you change your mind?'

'Someone called work last night asking if I worked there or if they knew me. Karen said she'd never heard of me and they hung up. They didn't give a name, but I know it was him.'

'What is he playing at?' Myra asked, angrily. 'I'll strangle him with my bare hands!'

'And he sent me a load of text messages,' Cristy added. 'I haven't slept a wink thinking about it, but I'm not going to let him terrorise me again. I'll stop it before it starts this time.'

'Give Col Gallagher a ring now,' Myra said. She went into the living room and returned with a business card. 'Your dad left his card here for you in case anything happened.'

There was a knock on the front door. Cristy checked the clock on the wall. It was too early for the postman. He was like clockwork. Myra went to the door and opened it. There was no one there. She looked down the road but couldn't see anyone. It was still dark, and a van went by. Its headlights illuminated the street. Myra waved at the driver; he was a plumber who lived at the end of the road. Something caught her eye, and she looked down. There was a single rose on the doorstep, wrapped in lace. She picked it up and took it inside; her stomach twisted in knots.

'What is that?' Cristy asked, frowning. She backed away, instinctively. Her mouth open in shock.

'It was on the doorstep,' Myra said. 'A red rose wrapped in lace.'

'It has to be him.'

'Who else would it be?' Her mum agreed. 'He's crossed the line knocking on my door.'

Cristy pulled herself together and took the rose from her mum. She unwrapped the lace material and held it up. It was torn down the centre. Cristy felt her knees trembling. She grabbed the kitchen table to stop herself from collapsing. Her head began to spin.

'What is it?' Myra asked. She took it from Cristy and looked closely. It was a pair of black lace knickers ripped at one side.

'They're mine,' Cristy said. 'I was wearing them the night he attacked me.'

Chapter 10

Father Patrick Creegan signed himself out of hospital after the doctor had checked him over again. He took a taxi from the rank outside the reception area. The driver didn't stop talking from the time he got into the vehicle until he got out. His facemask made understanding him difficult. The one-way conversation was painful, and the ride home cost him an extortionate amount of money. He arrived at the vicarage just after ten o'clock, tired and sore. His muscles were bruised, and his joints were stiff from inactivity. It was damp and gloomy, and he wanted to get inside and put the heating on. He needed a decent cup of coffee. The offerings in the hospital were weak and barely warm.

The police had brought his keys to the hospital; they still had a plastic tag on them with his name scribbled on it. He pulled it off and squashed it in his hand and then pushed it into his pocket next to a nearly empty packet of mints and his pipe. He had the urge to fill it with Pure Virginia tobacco and smoke it, but he would have to wait. There was too much to do. He noticed the doorframe and wood around the lock were coated in fingerprint dust, which he thought was odd at first, but then he realised the police weren't taking anything for granted. They were checking to see if his attacker was an invited or uninvited guest. The DI had asked how he thought his attacker had got in. They were searching for prints to see if the man had pushed the door open or used a key or not touched the door at all. If there were no prints, they would ask if he was invited in. That would cast aspersions on his version of events. His paranoia intensified. As far as men of the cloth were concerned, the police were as bad as the rest of society – Guilty until proven innocent. Not that he could blame them. The historical cover-up of institutional abuse over decades had rocked the Catholic Church to its foundations. Father Creegan knew it wouldn't recover its reputation any time soon, certainly not in his lifetime.

He opened the door and kicked all the post out of the way. Nothing that came through the letter box was any use to him. He'd thought about sealing it up completely. The smell of death and decomposition still lingered in the air. He wedged the door open with the junk mail and then went through the kitchen to the back door and repeated the process, using a chair to wedge it. He searched the cupboard beneath the sink for cleaning products and found a bottle of bleach and a tin of air freshener. Both were nearly empty. He took them up the stairs and squirted the bleach into the bath. The dried blood had been hosed away, but he rinsed it with the shower. The stench remained. He went from bedroom to bedroom, opening the windows and doors to purge the stale air. His own bedroom was last on the list. He was very apprehensive about going inside, which was irrational. His attacker was as dead as a dodo, and the only thing to fear was the smell. Yet he was frightened. The image of the dead man in the chair opposite him was etched into his memory. He had called for help until his voice was hoarse and his throat was sore, but no one had heard him. Watching the blood trickling down the wall was surreal yet somewhat satisfying. He should be ashamed to feel that way, but he wasn't.

His hands were shaking, and after much mental debate, he opened the bedroom door. When he went inside, he wasn't sure what to expect and it was a relief to see the police had sent in a clean-up team. The blood and brains had been cleaned from the walls and ceiling, and the chair his attacker had sat on had been removed. A dark watermark on the carpet told him they'd attempted to clean it. The results were cosmetic at best; it would have to be replaced. He wasn't sure if his insurance would cover it. Was there a clause in the policy that covered suicide and the damage it caused, or would it come under an act of God?

What would be, would be, and whatever happened next, it was better than he expected it to be. The odour of decomposition mingled with the sharp smell of disinfectant. He opened the window in a bid to dissipate the stench. A breeze flowed through the vicarage. It brought the smell of fallen leaves turning to mulch. The fresh air cleansed the air as it travelled. He looked at the spot where his attacker had pulled the trigger and he closed his eyes in silent prayer. He didn't offer forgiveness or pray for his soul, instead he wished that he'd had the chance to curse him before he died and he hoped the horrible bastard was rotting in hell, where he belonged.

The police said his suicide was dramatic. His death had been dramatic indeed. A single second of devastating power as the trigger was pulled and his head exploded into a cloud of red mist. His life was over in the blink of an eye. The damage caused to a human being by a shotgun blast inside the mouth was beyond catastrophic. Barely anything recognisable remained. It was effective, but it was all too quick. He deserved to suffer much longer than he had. Hell would welcome him with open arms if there was such a place. Father Creegan wasn't sure it existed in the afterlife or if he was there already. His belief was in tatters. Good and evil were at war for his soul.

Chapter 11

Harry Rankin sipped his tea and read the report twice. He took a bite of his tuna sandwich and frowned. It was dry without mayonnaise, but his wife had put him on a diet. Low fat and reduced sugar were the new normal. She said he needed to lose weight, lower his blood pressure, and cut his alcohol intake to below two units a day. All from the mouth of a woman with an arse the size of Saturn. He took off his glasses and went to the fridge. He took out a squeezy bottle of full-fat mayo and doused his tuna in it. With his karma restored, he went back to his reports.

The DNA test results from the vicarage had come back, and he was trying to make sense of it. He was the new boy and didn't want the Anglesey detectives to think he was incompetent. Professional respect had to be earned, and that takes time. The detective inspector from Holyhead wasn't happy that Pamela Stone hadn't processed the murder site at Penrhos. It was a complicated scene. The victim, Luca Bay, had been brutally murdered in the sand dunes, which are notoriously difficult to work in; recovering uncontaminated samples was nearly impossible. Harry sensed the DI wasn't happy that he was in charge. That was blatantly obvious. He had hardly tried to hide the fact. He seemed to be a straightforward type – not afraid to say what he was thinking. Pamela had worked with him for a long time and she had a lot of respect for him, so he had to give him the benefit of the doubt. Some people get set in their ways and don't like change. Harry knew it was all about doing his job properly. Give the police the correct information quickly, efficiently, and at a competitive rate, and the cases would keep coming. All he had to do was process them. Pamela ran an outstanding lab, and Harry was delighted to have been hired by her. He thought about calling her to run the report by her. It was unusual, but the information was clear enough. All he had to do was communicate it to the police. He typed an email and attached the report and then sent it. *How hard could it be?* he thought, finishing his sandwich. There was a secret Twix bar in his jacket that had his name all over it.

****

Sergeant Colwyn Gallagher was sitting in the kitchen at the Dennis residence. His ginger hair was unruly and needed cutting, but the barbers hadn't reopened yet. He'd known Frank Dennis since school, and while they weren't close friends, they'd socialised as part of a wider circle. It was a small community and difficult to deal with issues like rape and domestic violence at the best of times, but it was compounded when those involved were known to him. Meeting people's expectations was impossible sometimes.

He put the underwear and the rose into evidence bags and asked Cristy to sign for them and to sign her statement. He put the paperwork into a file and finished his cup of tea. Myra and Cristy were waiting for some words of reassurance. They wanted to hear that Price would be rushed back to prison and locked up for good.

'I'll be straight with you, Cristy. There isn't a great deal that we can do,' Col said. 'The incident in Tesco is a breach of the injunction as are the call to your employer, the text messages, and the delivery of the rose.'

'And the underwear,' Myra added. 'That's a threat if ever I've seen one.'

'The underwear is just sick, but this is Jon Price we're talking about. The man is an animal,' he said, tapping the evidence bag with his forefinger. He looked at Cristy. 'I remember you giving evidence at his trial. It's one of the bravest testimonies I've witnessed.'

'Thank you.'

'The problem we have is these offences are impossible to pin on him. We can't categorically prove he sent the text, made the call, or knocked on your front door this morning.'

'Someone did, obviously,' Myra snapped.

'Obviously. But it wasn't him. I can guarantee it. He could have told one of his minions to make the call or drop off the rose, and we have no proof either way.' Myra was going to argue, but he stopped her. 'I know what you're going to say. Cristy has him on camera in Tesco.'

'She does. Surely that's proof.'

'She has him on camera, apologising for approaching her. He clearly says it was a mistake because she was wearing a facemask and you've changed your hair colour. He says he didn't recognise you.' Col held up his hands and shrugged. 'No judge is going to send him back to jail on that evidence.'

'He's stalking Cristy, and that's a crime,' Myra said, angrily.

'He is, and you've made a formal complaint. No one wants to put that man back behind bars more than me, believe me. But we have nothing we can prove.'

'So, you're going to do nothing?' Myra asked.

'I'll be going from here straight to his house and I'll tell him in no uncertain terms that he needs to leave you alone. You can rely on that happening, one hundred per cent. What I can't do is lock him up. Not until he does something we can prove and then he'll go back to prison and he'll have to finish his sentence. Until then, you need to speak to me every day for an update and we'll record everything that happens. Any more mysterious calls, texts, or packages sent to you will be added to this evidence until he makes a mistake and buries himself. Trust me, I'm right here if you need me day and night. We will not let this man terrorise you. You're not alone in this.'

'Okay,' Cristy said, nodding. 'I understand you can't prove anything.' She paused. 'Will you call me once you've spoken to him?'

'Yes. I will. I'm going to see him right now.' He checked his watch. 'I'll call you before lunchtime.'

'Thank you,' Cristy said.

Col Gallagher left the house and walked down the path to his vehicle. A sea mist hung over the harbour. The jib of a crane reached skyward through the haze as if suspended by the cloud. Col mulled over what had happened. Jon Price was playing his mind games again. He'd done it over and over again, yet females were attracted to him and people fell for his business scams. Some women like bad boys but Price was beyond bad. He was the epitome of a fatal attraction. Cristy Dennis was a beauty; most men would crawl over broken glass to be with a woman like her. Price had raped her, beaten her, and treated her like she didn't matter at all, as if she were worthless. It baffled him how many good men struggled to find a good woman like Cristy, when men like Price had a queue of them. He knew that if he could find the answer, he could write a book and be a millionaire. He called the DI to bring him up to date.

'Morning, Col,' Alan said. 'How did it go?'

'Not good, Alan,' Col said. 'Cristy Dennis was approached by Price in Tesco. She was obviously scared, so she filmed him, but he apologised on camera, saying he didn't recognise her. She was wearing a facemask and changed her hair colour.'

'He's slippery,' Alan said. 'Too smart for his own good. What else did she say?'

'Last night she received a batch of text messages from an anonymous number and someone called her boss asking if she worked there.'

'He isn't being very subtle.'

'That's not all. To top it off, someone delivered a red rose to the front doorstep this morning. It was wrapped in black lace knickers, identical to the pair Cristy was wearing the night he raped her.'

'What?'

'Exactly.'

'Jesus. He's pushing his luck,' Alan said. 'Sick bastard. Is there anything we can pin on him?'

'Nope.'

'I thought not.'

'I'm going to his house now to have a word with him,' Col said.

'Take Bob with you,' Alan said.

'Is that a good idea? Bob hates the man.'

'Exactly. Have a conversation with him and find out where he was last night.'

'Last night? Are you fancying him for the Luca Bay killing?'

'I haven't made my mind up yet,' Alan said. 'I think it's a nasty coincidence that he's back in town the day it happened. My instinct is he has more than Cristy Dennis in his sights. He's been stewing in a cell for seven years, plotting and planning payback for anyone he feels turned on him. Rattle his cage and warn him Cristy Dennis is out of bounds.'

'I will. I'll pick Bob up from the station, but you realise I'm not responsible for his behaviour.'

'No one is responsible for his behaviour. Bob Dewhurst is a force of nature' – Alan paused for thought – 'Ask Price if he's had any contact from the others who were released. He's unlikely to tell you the truth but gauge his reaction and get back to me.'

Chapter 12

Detective Sergeant Richard Lewis opened an email from the forensic laboratory. He didn't recognise the email address. Pamela must have been hiring. He sneezed, and his jowls wobbled for a few seconds. The sneeze drew disapproving glances from some of his colleagues. Despite it being winter, his hay fever was back, which wasn't making him popular with the COVID-19 panic squad. Any sign of a cough or sneeze would drive some individuals to douse him in Dettol and make him self-isolate for a decade. He ignored the frowns and read on. The email had a report attached which held the results of a search of the DNA database on a sample from the vicarage. He read the results and shook his head. The results left him with more questions than answers. There was no meat on the bone. Some vital background information was missing. He picked up the phone and called the lab. The receptionist transferred him to the technician who had sent the report.

'Harry Rankin,' he answered, his mouth full of tuna.

'Hello. This is DS Lewis from the MIT at Holyhead,' Richard said. 'I've just received your report on the Father Creegan case.'

'Good. I'm glad it arrived safely,' Harry said, taking off his glasses. He rubbed his eyes. They were tired and itchy. 'How can I help you?'

'The report says the DNA taken from our John Doe, matches DNA found during a cold case review, which was run by Merseyside four years ago?' Richard said.

'Yes. That's correct. Is there a problem?' Harry asked.

'Yes, there is. It doesn't tell me who it matches or what the cold case was investigating or what the case review number is,' Richard said.

'I need to know the answer to those questions, or the information is no use to me.'

'Ah, I see,' Harry said. He brought up the case notes on his screen. 'Here it is. The DNA matched samples taken from an item of clothing that was retrieved from an evidence box by the Merseyside force in twenty-sixteen.'

'That's what I have written here in your report,' Richard said. 'But who does it match up to?'

'No one,' Harry said.

'No one?'

'It matches a sample discovered on an item of clothing, but the person is unidentified. Your suicide victim is not in the system.'

'Bugger,' Richard muttered. 'Okay, that explains it. Can you give me the case review number please?' Richard asked.

'I can do one better than that,' Harry said. 'I'll email the case notes to you.'

'That would be helpful,' Richard said, shaking his head. 'Thank you very much for your help.' Richard hung up. 'You should have done that in the first instance,' he muttered to himself. He opened a bottle of water and sipped from it while he waited for the email to arrive.

'Are you playing five-a-side tonight?' one of the detectives asked.

'I'm playing on Tufty's team,' Richard answered. 'Are you playing?'

'I'm in Jacky's team. You lot are too old. We'll run rings around you.'

'I'm old enough to have heard it all before. We'll see how quick you are tomorrow,' Richard said, rubbing his arthritic knee subconsciously. 'I find a swift kick in the shins slows most people down,' he muttered beneath his breath.

The envelope icon appeared on his screen. He opened the email and downloaded the report. It had been compiled by a detective superintendent by the name of Ian Osborne who was stationed at Canning Place in Liverpool. Richard had attended a course there a few years before. It was in the heart of the city centre overlooking the river. He remembered the attendees walked to the Albert Docks for lunch that day and had a pint at the pierhead when the course finished. Richard recalled Ian Osborne because he was nearly seven feet tall. He had to duck underneath doorframes. The report stated the DS had been investigating a cold case from the early nineties. Richard read the report twice and then called the DI.

'DI Williams,' Alan answered.

'Alanio,' Richard said. 'Have you got a minute?'

'Yes. I'm on my way back to the station. We need a briefing on the Luca Bay murder and about Jon Price being released.'

'Kim called me earlier to let me know,' Richard said. 'I'm compiling a list of who was released and where they are now.'

'Good. What's up?' Alan asked.

'I've got the DNA report for the Creegan case. It's interesting reading. I've sent it over to you, but I wanted to run it by you.'

'Okay,' Alan said. 'Carry on. Kim is with me and you're on speaker.'

'Hello, Kimio,' Richard said.

'Hello, Richard.'

'Okay. If you're sitting comfortably, I'll begin. The DNA has matched a sample taken from an item of clothing found during a cold case investigation run by Merseyside four years ago.'

'I can feel a *but* coming,' Kim said, looking out of the window as they drove over station bridge. A train was leaving the station, heading for London.

'But we don't have a name for our John Doe. He's not in the system.'

'That's not ideal,' Alan said, disappointed.

'It's not, but there are some interesting connotations in the cold case.'

'Okay. Run it by me anyway.'

'In July of ninety-four a thirteen-year-old boy called Chris Deeks was reported missing by his parents. He'd gone on a day out with his friend, Ewan Birley, also thirteen and never returned. Birley was in care at the time and wasn't reported missing until the next day. They both lived in the Prestatyn area.'

'What were their names again?' Alan asked. The cogs in his brain were turning.

'Christopher Deeks and Ewan Birley.'

'I remember the case vaguely,' Alan said. 'It was in the local papers but didn't get much national coverage.'

'The fact is, the teenagers simply disappeared, never to be seen or heard from again,' Richard said. 'Merseyside were involved because Birley was from Toxteth. His parents were dead, and his aunt campaigned for months for them to open an investigation into his disappearance. They were slow to respond.'

'Because North Wales were dealing with it?'

'It would appear so. Deeks had told his parents that they were going on an organised canoeing trip arranged by the county council for the kids in care and their friends, but Birley told the carers at the home he was going with Deeks and his parents to Beaumaris Castle. The parents denied that any trip had been planned or even spoken about. Both boys had lied. Deeks had withdrawn all his savings from his Post Office savings account and it was suspected Birley stole a sum of money from the home's petty cash tin.'

'How much did they have?' Kim asked.

'The estimate at the time was about fifty-pounds between them.'

'They weren't going far on that,' Alan said.

'Exactly my thoughts. The investigation was dead in the water from day one. No one knew where the boys had actually gone, so there was no crime scene, no bodies, no eyewitnesses, and zero evidence. After months of campaigning in the press for information, a jacket was recovered from the British Rail lost property department at Bangor. It had a camouflage wallet in the lining, which had been missed when it was found. It was identified as belonging to Ewan Birley. His carers confirmed it was his. There was no record of where or when the jacket was found and handed in. The jacket sat in an evidence locker for twenty-two years before the cold case was opened. They discovered DNA on the sleeve.'

'What type of DNA?' Alan asked.

'Semen,' Richard said. 'The DNA matched the sample taken from the vicarage.'

'So, the man who committed suicide in front of Father Patrick Creegan secreted semen onto the sleeve of a teenager who went missing in nineteen-ninety-four but we don't know who he is,' Alan surmised.

'In a nutshell, yes,' Richard agreed. 'I was on a training course with the DS who ran the cold case investigation. Do you want me to give him a bell?'

'Yes. Do that.' Alan thought for a moment. 'I'm convinced the John Doe lived on the island. He couldn't have travelled far with a shotgun. Run it by him when you speak to him.'

'What are you thinking?'

'There may have been sightings of the boys on the island that were disregarded at the time. The jacket was found in a railway lost property so, it's probable the teenagers got a train to somewhere and if the jacket was sent to Bangor, then they probably came this way. If they went the other way, the jacket would have been sent to Chester.'

'Agreed. That makes sense.'

'Give Osbourne a call before the briefing and then we'll have another conversation with Creegan. He knows more than he's telling us. This information might loosen his tongue. Something needs to.'

Chapter 13

Jon Price owned a house in Trearddur Bay, overlooking Porth Diana. It was renovated the year he went to prison and still looked like new. Panoramic windows and glass balconies gave the front elevation stunning views over the bay. Col pulled the vehicle to a stop outside the house and watched the waves crashing onto the rocks across the bay. Price had a prime spot, that was for sure. His home was huge.

'Look at the size of the place,' Col said, shaking his head. 'We're on the wrong side of the fence, Bob.'

The wrought-iron gates were closed. Bob looked at the property and strung together a sentence comprising totally of expletives. Col chuckled as he climbed out of the car although it did rankle that the property was paid for with the proceeds of crime.

'I don't know how he got away with keeping this place when he went down,' Bob grumbled. 'What happened to seizing their assets?'

'A thousand-pound a day barrister and some creative paperwork involving an umbrella company,' Col said.

'Which doesn't belong to him.'

'Yup.'

Bob pressed the button on the intercom, which was fixed to a brick gatepost. A fisheye camera loomed above them. There was no reply. He pressed it again, but this time kept his finger on it to increase the nuisance value. After a few minutes, the speaker crackled.

'Take your finger off the button!' Price growled. 'What the fuck do you lot want?'

'Open the door,' Col said. 'We need to speak to you.'

'I'm busy,' Price said. 'Make an appointment.'

'Open the gates or we'll be back in under an hour with a warrant for your arrest,' Col said.

'For what?'

'Breaching an injunction for a start,' Col said. 'Judge Channing is a particularly good friend of Myra Dennis. She's not a big fan of yours. I have her number in my phone. Open the gate or I'll call her, and you can listen to the conversation.'

'Wanker,' Price moaned. The gates opened slowly. A carport to the left of the house sheltered a Tesla, which was attached to its charging point. A hire car was parked next to it. They walked along a pressed concrete driveway towards the front door and Price opened it, wearing a dark Armani tracksuit, his chest bare. He stepped back to allow the officers in. 'It's too cold to talk on the doorstep. Go through into my office.'

They walked beneath an open staircase, crafted from teak, which spiralled up to the living room on the first floor. The ceiling was angled glass, which made a bright atrium. The bedrooms were on the ground floor to their left. A young woman walked naked across the hallway, her long blond hair hung down her back. She waved at the policemen and smiled.

'Hello,' she said, cheerily. Bob instinctively waved hello, trying not to stare at her behind.

'Don't speak to them,' Price said, dumbfounded. 'They're not here on a jolly, you muppet.'

'I was just being nice,' she said, frowning. She looked like a little girl scolded for something she didn't understand.

'Well, you can stop being nice and get back in the bedroom. I won't be long,' Price said, scowling. She tutted and stormed off down the hallway. Price went into his office.

The office was bright and airy with white walls and patio doors which looked over the sea. Grey laminate flooring and wicker furniture gave it a contemporary feel. Black and white prints of boxing champions and topless models adorned the walls. The policemen stepped inside, and Price went behind his desk. It was chrome and glass

– on top were three laptops and an iPhone. He turned his back to the police officers, looking at the view.

'Do you want me to make coffee for everyone?' a female voice asked.

Bob and Col turned towards the voice. A brunette with long wavy hair was standing in the doorway. She was wearing boxer shorts and a baggy T-shirt. Both appeared to belong to Price.

'Don't be fucking stupid. Why would I give them my coffee?' Price said. The woman looked hurt. 'What's wrong with everyone? Can't you see they're dibble and they're not welcome. Go back to the bedroom. I won't be long.'

'Fine,' the woman said, frowning. 'I was trying to be helpful.'

'Stop trying, idiot.'

'I see you've not lost your charm,' Bob said. He could feel his blood boiling.

'I've always had a silver tongue.' Price grinned. 'They love that.'

'Yes. Just like a snake,' Bob said.

'Let's not waste time,' Price said. Anger flashed in his eyes. 'I haven't had a shag for seven years so, I'm a bit busy. If you know what I mean?' He smiled. 'Actually, you two probably don't know what I mean.' The policemen didn't rise to the bait. 'What do you want?'

'You approached Cristy Dennis in Tesco yesterday,' Col said. 'That's in breach of the injunction against you.'

'It was an accident. I didn't recognise her.' Price shrugged and sat in a leather swivel chair. He put his feet on the desk and crossed his legs. 'She's changed her hair and was wearing a facemask. It was an easy mistake to make.'

'Last night, her boss received a call at work from a male asking if she worked there,' Col added. Price cocked his head and stared through him, but chose not to respond. 'She also had a batch of text messages from someone calling her 'baby girl', which she recalls clearly as the pet name you had for her. It also threatened to drown her employer. A lady named Karen?'

'Did she give you the number it came from?'

'It was withheld.'

'Shame. She's got a poor memory. I never called her baby girl. Slut, slag, whore, empty head, were more likely.' The policemen remained deadpan. 'I shouldn't call her a slut, but she couldn't keep her legs closed.' Price shrugged again. 'I haven't sent any text messages to Cristy Dennis. Do you want to check my phone?'

'We'll be checking via the network providers,' Bob said. 'Things have moved on. Withholding a number doesn't mean we can't trace it.'

'Crack on. Do I look bothered to you, Officer Dewhurst?'

'Not yet,' Bob said. 'But you will.'

'This morning there was a rose delivered to her house, wrapped in lace underwear.'

'That's a lovely touch. Nice to see romance isn't dead,' Price said. His eyes sparkled with mischief.

'I don't think it was romantic,' Col said. 'I think it was sent to frighten her.'

'Why would a pair of knickers frighten her?'

'Who mentioned knickers?' Col asked. 'I said underwear.'

'Lucky guess. Cristy couldn't keep her underwear on. That was the problem. She probably left them on someone's bedroom floor.'

'Really?'

'Yes, really. She'd be better off not wearing any knickers. It would save her time. Cristy-bury-me-in-a-Y-shaped-coffin, I used to call her.'

'They were identical to the pair Cristy Dennis was wearing the night you raped her,' Col said, ignoring his remarks. He stared into his eyes.

'Allegedly raped her,' Price said, shaking his head. 'The rape was never proved.'

'Maybe not, but we all know it happened,' Bob said, coldly.

'That could be deemed as libellous, but I don't have the time or the inclination to call my lawyer,' Price said. He stared at Bob. 'The truth is, she likes it rough. Little Cristy Dennis isn't the angel she makes out she is. The rougher the better.'

'There's rough and then there is rape and torture,' Bob said. 'It would appear you can't tell the difference.'

'Some girls like being tied up. Cristy did at first, but then she decided she didn't, when it suited her.'

'That might have been about the time you burnt her with a cigarette,' Bob said. A flash of anger crossed Price's face again. 'It might have turned her off a little?'

'Nope. It was when I caught her cheating on me. I had a go at her about it and suddenly she turned on me and started chatting shit to you lot.' He paused to calm his nerves. Talking to the police wound him up no end. 'She's a Judas bitch, but I haven't so much as given her a second thought.' He pointed in the direction of the bedrooms. 'As you can see, I've got my hands full. I can see what you're thinking.' Price grinned.

'Enlighten us,' Bob said.

'You're wondering if they're hookers. They're not. Part of an ever-growing fan club.'

'There's no accounting for taste,' Bob said.

'Whatever. The last thing I need is a woman with an attitude. Cristy Dennis is not even on my radar at the moment. There're plenty of women who are happy to have a fuck without any strings attached. Right now, that's all I'm interested in. Ex-girlfriends are not on my list of people to look up.'

'I know who sent the rose and you know who sent the rose, Price,' Bob said. 'You've had your fun, but if you continue to play games, we'll have you.'

'This is really boring,' Price said. 'I need you to go.'

'Where were you last night?'

'Have a guess, Columbo,' Price said. 'Feel free to go and ask the ladies what time they arrived. I've been remarkably busy banging the back out of them since they got here.'

'They'll say whatever you tell them to say,' Bob said. 'You can play your games, Price, but if you don't leave Cristy Dennis alone, we'll be jumping all over you.'

'Really?'

'Yes, really. If you give us the opportunity to send you back where you belong, we'll be only too happy to oblige.'

'Okay. You've said what you need to say, and I've got the message,' Price said, pointing to the door. 'Now you can fuck off and leave me alone. I've got a lot of catching up to do.'

'Talking of catching up, have you been in contact with any of the others who were released?' Col asked. Price shook his head slowly; a thin smile touched his lips.

'None of them?' Col pushed. Price remained tight-lipped.

'Did you hear about Luca Bay?' Bob asked.

'Who?' Price feigned interest.

'Luca Bay.'

'I've never heard of him.'

'He worked for you.'

'It must have been a long time ago. I don't recall the name. Now, will you please fuck off and die…'

The policemen looked at each other and headed for the door. Price picked up his phone and headed down the hallway to the bedroom. Bob closed the front door behind them. There was a sick feeling in the pit of his stomach. Just being around Price sent his blood pressure rocketing.

Price watched them leave through the gates. He clicked a remote, and the gates closed slowly. He watched them through the railings. The policemen approached the vehicle and realised all four tyres had been let down.

'I don't believe this,' Bob said, fuming. He looked back at the house and saw Price smiling at them through the window. 'That scumbag is asking for it.'

'I'll call recovery. He was in the house with us all the time,' Col said, shaking his head. There was nothing they could do, and they knew it.

'I'd love five minutes alone with that bastard,' Bob said.

'Five minutes wouldn't be anywhere near enough for me,' Col said.

Price closed the blinds. He took out an encrypted mobile, scrolled through his contacts, and selected the one he wanted.

'Have they gone?'

'No. They've had a puncture.'

'Shame that.'

'Yes, it is. Apparently, she loved the rose.' Price chuckled. 'You know what to do next.'

'Leave it to me.'

Chapter 14

The Major Investigation Team was assembled in the operations room at Holyhead Police Station. Forty detectives were already working on the Luca Bay murder. Images from the scene were displayed across three digital screens positioned on the walls, so that they could be seen from anywhere in the room. The chatter of voices filled the air. Alan walked to the front of the room and the officers quietened. He scanned the team and was happy with the quality of the detectives he'd been sent. The days of other stations sending their dross when support was requested were gone. Only the best people were sent to investigate a major incident on neighbouring turf. The big city forces could afford dedicated teams, but rural forces had to firefight with seconded detectives from within their force. Silence settled and Alan pointed to an image of the body.

'Luca Bay, thirty-years of age, originally from Cemaes Bay but moved to Holyhead aged sixteen. He lived with his wife and two children on Richmond Hill. He was lured to the dunes at Penrhos Beach to conduct a drug deal, we think. The activity on his mobile confirms our theory. When he got there, he was attacked with a crowbar,' Alan said. Images of the injuries appeared on screen. 'He was hit three times around the head and neck. We can have no doubt his attacker intended to murder him.' He looked to Kim to continue.

'He was a dealer, mostly cocaine and ecstasy. We know his supplier was Paul Sutton, who allowed him to buy wholesale and sell to his own customers. Bay is low level, and his drugs and money were still on his body, as was his wallet, watch, and jewellery. There's a wider investigation into Paul Sutton and his network, which we need to be sensitive about. Drug Squad is running a coordinated operation with the NCA focusing on some big hitters from Liverpool and their County Line networks. We don't want to tread on their toes.'

'It's like a huge whack-a-mole game,' Alan said. 'We knock one out and another pops up.' There were nods of agreement around the room. Drug supplies could be interrupted but never completely stopped. 'We know Bay worked for Jon Price on one of his building sites before his operation was shut down seven years ago, but he was never indicted or interviewed in connection with the fraud investigation.'

'Price was released on the day Bay was attacked?' a detective from Caernarfon asked.

'Yes,' Alan said. 'He could be taking out anyone who worked for him. We cannot rule out Price and his crew coming back to the island and setting up where they left off. The tourist economy is screwed, which means the chances of them finding jobs and going straight are slim to zero. Where are they, Richard?'

Richard Lewis blushed and straightened his jacket. He didn't like the limelight in MIT meetings. 'Price was one of five convicted of conspiracy to defraud and money laundering. For clarity, only four of his associates have returned to the island. Two of them to Holyhead, one to Llangefni, and one to Menai Bridge. They all have to report to a probation officer once a month for the next six months, and the meetings will be virtual because of COVID-19.'

'They might as well send them a letter telling them to behave,' Kim said.

'Exactly. They are out on license in theory, but we can consider them back in circulation,' Richard said. 'They're registered as going back to their permanent addresses but we have no way of verifying that and unless they re-offend, we can't just knock on their doors to see if they're behaving. That is the remit of the probation service and they get shirty if we interfere with their clients.'

'Let's add their names, addresses, and mugshots to the case wall. I want a team on each one of these men and their wives, girlfriends, brothers, sisters, and anyone else they see on a regular basis. Check the visitor logs from prison. That will narrow down who they remained in touch with. I want any new names and faces added to this wall and uploaded to the system, so we can cross reference in real time.'

An increasingly large section of one wall was being covered with maps, photographs, and notes. Alan walked to the compilation of information, impressed with the amount already gathered.

'The scene was worked by a new CSI, Harry Rankin.' Alan paused to check the report. 'I wasn't sure about him at first, but I'm beginning to see why Pamela Stone hired him. He photographed multiple sets of footprints, which led from the car park at Penrhos to the scene of the murder and back to the car park. There are other sets of prints leading to different spots in the dunes but only six going to the spot where Bay was murdered.' The image on the screen changed. 'In his opinion, the set which matters is this set here.' He pointed to a deep print in the sand. 'This is a clear print from a moulded sole that would be found on a boot.' He looked around. 'Harry Rankin knows his boots,' Alan said. Several of the faces were smiling. 'This particular sole belongs to a Dr Marten's boot, size ten, and could be any of these particular styles.' A series of boots flashed on the screen.

'Why has he singled out that print?' a detective asked.

'Because there's blood in some minute particles of sand and because of the stride pattern.' Alan nodded, knowingly. 'We all know how important stride pattern is.' There were more smiles. 'This set of footprints shows the owner walked normally to the scene. You can see measured steps all the way, then there's a flurry of activity around where the body was found and then the stride pattern back to the car park is much wider and the weight is on the front of the boot.'

'He was running,' Richard said, nodding.

'Sprinting, actually,' Alan said. 'Whoever killed Luca Bay sprinted back to his vehicle. You, me, and any half decent criminal knows that running looks suspicious to an eyewitness. Anyone driving past the entrance to Rio Tinto, either heading to or from Valley, could have seen someone on the path leading to the sand dunes and not thought anything about it, but if they were running, that's a different story. Witnesses always remember someone running. We're going to put out an appeal on *Mon FM* and the local news.' Alan paused and raised his hand. 'The fact he was sprinting back to his vehicle gives us the advantage.'

'Meaning?' someone asked.

'Meaning that our killer panicked.' Alan looked around the room. 'Killers that panic don't interview well. If we get close to him, he'll panic again. When we start talking to this man, formally or informally as part of the investigation, it will be written all over his face and detectives of your quality will spot it a mile away.' Enthusiastic nods agreed with him. The team was champing at the bit. 'So, we can't bother Price and his associates officially, but we can bump into them and ask them a few questions as part of a murder inquiry. Keep your eyes and ears open. There's a killer out there and we need to find him, quickly. You know who your teams are, let's get on with it and debrief at 10 p.m. sharp.' The team broke into their operational groups. Richard approached Alan. 'Did you speak to your contact in Liverpool?' Alan asked.

'No. I'm afraid DS Osbourne died in a car crash last year,' Richard said. 'I've been given the contact details for DS Alec Ramsay. He's a bit of a legend, apparently, retired but still consults on old cases from his time in MIT. I've left a message on his voicemail. Hopefully, he'll come back to me. Do you want me to speak to Creegan, anyway?'

'Yes. Let's do it formally. Ask him to come in and bring his solicitor with him,' Alan said. 'I want him to know this investigation is far from over.'

Chapter 15

Cristy had made it to lunchtime with no issues. Her phone was turned off, and she didn't intend to turn it on until her shift had finished. There was no way for Jon Price to reach her via her mobile, if she kept it turned off. Price could go and boil his head, the loser. She was hoping he would get bored with tormenting her and go away; changing her working conditions was an upheaval for everyone concerned. The nursing home was a depressing place to work. It was the reason she chose to do home visits. At least she could enjoy the fresh air between clients, winding the window down and turning the stereo up. The roads were exhilarating to drive on and the views cathartic. The island had a magic about it which was difficult to put into words, but it was undeniably there. Millions of visitors felt it, and it wasn't lost on the locals. Driving the length and breadth of the island was no burden. She loved being out and about. In contrast, the nursing home was claustrophobic. Most of the patients didn't know their own names or the names of their family members who infrequently visited. It was society's solution to the aging population. Put them away somewhere where we don't have to see them deteriorate or watch them lose their faculties. Avoid the crushing guilt by making sure they're warm and safe and fed by someone else. Put them somewhere we can visit and then walk away when things get too much. For Cristy, it was too emotional to work there day in and day out. It was like staring mortality in the face every day.

Cristy looked at a bald lady dribbling on her smock. She'd had no visitors for six months because of the virus. Her name was Mo, and she had six children and twenty-two grandchildren. Yet nobody had called in to see her on Christmas Day. A bunch of flowers was delivered on her birthday in January and one of her sons came to see her the day after the event, not that she knew anything about it. Her family were living the lives that she gave to them, forsaking what remained of hers. There seemed to be no gratitude from those who owed her life itself. Without her, they wouldn't exist, yet they prioritised themselves over what little life she had left.

Was that all there was to this life? Cristy used to dwell on that question. Get married, break your back to do the best you can for your children – and their children – and then when the money runs out and your health spirals downhill, end up in a place like this. God's waiting room where the food is mush and everywhere stinks of piss. Cristy couldn't work there full-time. It was too depressing.

She needed to sort out Jon Price and get back on the road.

'That's for you,' Karen said, approaching the nurses' station. Karen had her hair pinned to her head, stiffened with gel. She used hand sanitiser and pointed to the telephone. The hold light was flashing. 'How are you getting along?'

'It's like riding a bike,' Cristy said, trying to smile. 'Who is it?'

'Rowan,' Karen said.

'He knows better than to call me at work,' Cristy said, blushing. She rolled her eyes. 'I'm so sorry.'

'Don't be sorry. He's probably worried about you,' Karen said. 'Love's young dream.'

Cristy chuckled and picked up the phone. 'Hello,' she said.

'Why aren't you answering your phone?' Rowan asked, abruptly. 'I've been trying to get hold of you.'

'I'm at work, Rowan,' Cristy said. She felt annoyed he needed to ask. 'Do you have your phone on when you're up a chimney?'

'I'm a roofer, not a steeplejack,' Rowan said. 'Listen. Something has happened that you need to know about, and I would rather you heard it from me. It's all over Facebook.'

'What is?' Cristy asked. Her stomach was tied in knots. She felt sick again. Price sprang into her mind immediately.

'My ex has uploaded some videos,' Rowan said, sheepishly. 'They're from years ago, way before we started dating.' Cristy didn't speak. She couldn't think straight let alone find her voice. 'I thought she was okay, but she's clearly nuts. Are you there?' Cristy didn't reply. 'Look, I've found out she's been going to see Price in prison and I'm sure he's got something to do with it. She wouldn't do that off her own back. It's just not like her.'

'What's on the videos?' Cristy asked, quietly. She really didn't want to know. Wasn't it obvious? Rowan's ex had uploaded videos of them having sex. She felt sick. Rowan was silent. 'Tell me what's on the videos.'

'Bad stuff but we can work through this.'

'Are they sex videos?'

'Yes,' Rowan said. 'They're from way before we started going out, Cristy. It's Price. He's trying to split us up. They don't matter.'

'I think they probably do matter, Rowan. If they're online, they matter a lot.'

'It was way before we started, Cristy. We're not children. We both had previous partners. Price is twisted. I know what he's doing.'

'What do you mean? You said it was your ex?' Cristy asked confused. 'Why are you bringing Price into this?'

'How else would she get hold of them?' Rowan asked.

'I don't understand. What do you mean, *how else would she get hold of them?*'

'The videos. Price must have given them to her?'

'I'm confused. Are the videos of you and your ex?' she asked.

'No, Cristy, not me.' Rowan sighed, audibly.

'What are you talking about?'

'The videos are you and Jon Price having sex,' Rowan said.

'Oh my God, please no,' Cristy said. She froze to the spot. Her stomach contracted and made her feel sick. 'Where has she uploaded them to?'

'Everywhere,' Rowan said. 'She's put them on porn sites and then put the links on Facebook.' He waited for Cristy to speak, but she was gone.

Chapter 16

Father Creegan opened the back door and walked towards his garage. He pulled up the collar of his trench coat and hunched his shoulders against the rain. Leaves blew across the lawn and the trees swayed in the wind. To the rear of the garage was a lean-to, which housed a small workshop. It was once his refuge from the pressures of the world. His hobby was working with wood he found. He would walk on the beaches and find driftwood to shape into mirror frames and table lamps. Many years ago, he'd built a greenhouse to grow tomatoes and onions, a kitchen table, and a rocking horse for his niece. The rocking horse was a replica of a Victorian design, and it was a work of love. Everyone that saw it said it was stunning. He was enormously proud of it and his niece adored it and insisted it stayed in her bedroom, kissing it goodnight before bedtime. She was eighteen now, and the rocking horse was a childhood memory. Now and again, he would open the workshop and look inside, searching for the creative spirit he once had. It was long gone, and the thoughts of shaping something beautiful from wood once again were nothing more than a pipedream. It saddened him that his hopes and positivity had been sucked from his soul, leaving a shell filled with loneliness and bitterness. His pursuit of good had made him vulnerable to the powers of evil. Unfortunately, evil was more fun. He'd fought the temptations dangled in front of him, but he was weak. Where was God when evil was grooming him, stalking him, setting him for a fall from grace, a long deep fall into the chasm of darkness? Where was he then and where was he now? Nowhere. He'd forsaken him a long time ago.

He went to the workshop and unlocked the door. It was dry inside and he could still smell sawdust. He switched on the light and took a spade from a rack on the wall. A half-finished coffee table was sitting on the workbench, crying out to be completed. He picked up a piece of sandpaper and rubbed the corner of the table until it was shiny smooth. It felt good to his touch, silky beneath his fingertips. Maybe one day he would finish it, but it wouldn't be today.

He closed the door behind him and headed along the garden path into the dense woodland, which meandered for miles down to the sea. Most of the trees were deciduous and bare, their leaves rotten on the ground, returned into the soil. Nature's wheel turned endlessly; never stopping to mourn the demise of any living thing, be it man or beast or plant. She created, and she destroyed. The only certainty for any living thing was death. Creegan felt no sorrow for what he was about to do, nor did he take any pleasure from it. It evoked memories he'd tried to bury in the bowels of his mind. There was nothing but revulsion and fear when he remembered those times. The memories had been dragged to the surface kicking and screaming and he wanted nothing to do with it or them. He had to make sure nothing had been disturbed. It had been a necessity all those years ago, and it was a necessity again. All his instincts told him to leave things be, but he couldn't simply ignore them. The idiot might have defiled the site before he blew his head off. Selfish bastard that he was.

Creegan reached the spot where he'd been told to make a mark on a tree many years before. The sycamore tree was fully grown now. Moss covered the lower limbs, but etched into the bark above his head was the symbol he'd carved. It looked like an umbrella blown inside out and then turned upside down, the handle pointing skyward. He remembered its meaning and its significance, and it filled him with unease. This was the place, yet it looked so different.

Creegan surveyed the area. It was once a clearing covered in grass where bluebells and snowdrops grew in the spring. Now it was a wilderness covered in saplings and briars. The brambles were dense, their tendrils thick with thorns an inch long; it was impenetrable. A living breathing barrier between the living and the dead. He sighed and wiped a thin sheen of sweat from his brow. There was no way he could make his way through the dense vegetation before darkness fell; that was a good thing. It meant no one else could either. He would have to wait until sunrise tomorrow to make sure they'd not been disturbed, and everyone was where they should be.

Chapter 17

Richard contacted Father Creegan and made formal arrangements for him to attend an interview. The priest didn't sound happy at all, but refrained from threatening to sue, which was the usual reaction from most interviewees who had something to hide. There was something in his voice that Richard couldn't put his finger on. Resignation or exhaustion or acceptance of the situation; he couldn't nail it down. Creegan had repeatedly asked if there had been any new developments but Richard couldn't disclose that. He was jotting down his thoughts on how the interview would go when his mobile rang.

'DS Lewis,' he answered.

'Hello. This is Alec Ramsay. You left a message for me to contact you,' Alec said.

'Thank you for calling me back, sir,' Richard said, sitting up in his chair as if a superior had walked into the room. He straightened his tie. 'I'm a detective sergeant with NWP, based in Holyhead. I'm sorry to disturb your retirement, but I was given your contact details in regard to a cold case from the early nineties.'

'That was my era,' Alec said. 'It was a cold case, you said?'

'Yes. It was reopened by DS Ian Osbourne a few years back. Do you recall it, sir?'

'Yes, please call me Alec. I haven't been a sir for a long time.'

'Okay, Alec.'

'Osbourne was a top man. His death was a loss to the force,' Alec said. There was a pause as if he was thinking or about to say something else. 'This is about the Deeks and Birley misper case, isn't it?'

'Yes, that's the one. I wanted to pick your brains if possible.'

'Why?' Alec asked. 'What's happened.'

'Sorry,' Richard said, confused.

'Why would a detective from Anglesey want to talk to me about a cold case from the nineties?' Alec asked, jovially. 'Something must have happened to bring this to your attention.'

'Yes, something has,' Richard said. 'We had a call out to a vicarage on the island. The parish priest was reported missing during lockdown. No one had heard from him for a number of days, anyway, to cut a long story short, we found him and he'd been attacked in his home. He was tied to a chair in his bedroom, starving and almost dehydrated to death. His attacker had stripped naked, sat in a chair opposite him, and blew his brains out with a shotgun. His DNA matches a sample taken from the evidence Ian Osbourne found in the misper case.'

'Does it match the semen on the sleeve?' Alec asked.

'Yes. But we have nothing else on him.'

'What's the approximate age of the John Doe?'

'Between thirty-five and forty-five. Further tests should narrow that down significantly,' Richard said. 'He would have been a teen to early twenties when the boys went missing.'

'And you say the John Doe killed himself in a vicarage, in front of a priest?'

'Yes. It was dramatic.'

'But the priest can't ID his attacker?'

'Can't or won't,' Richard said. 'We're not sure on that one.'

'What is the priest's name?'

'Father Patrick Creegan.'

'Creegan?' Alec said. 'Creegan, Creegan. It rings a bell in the back of my mind, but not in connection with this case. I'll have to have a think about that one' – Alec paused – 'Osbourne identified a number of priests he wanted to speak to but most of them are dead now. Creegan wasn't one of them from what I can remember. I can tell you what I know, but I can't prove a thing,' he said.

'I'm listening,' Richard said. He felt the buzz of anticipation when a new piece of the puzzle was revealed. It might not fit yet, but it might make sense later. 'Whatever you can tell me will help.'

'The early days of the investigation turned up nothing. It was a difficult case from day one. The detectives didn't know where to start. My feeling is because Birley was in care, the consensus was they were runaways, and they would turn up sooner or later … but they never did. Deeks' parents made an unholy row, and more officers were thrown at the investigation. Following an appeal, there was an unconfirmed sighting of two young boys at Bangor Station,' Alec said. 'It wasn't given much credence by the investigating officers because of the delay in it being reported. The lady was on a train bound for Chester and she could see the approach road to the station. The eyewitness said the boys she saw appeared to be waiting for someone.'

'*Appeared to be waiting?*'

'Yes. There were taxis at the rank and a bus had just left but they remained on the approach road as if they were waiting for someone. She saw an older man in his fifties approach them with a younger man and they started chatting to him. Then the train pulled out of the station and the eyewitness lost sight of them. She didn't think anything of it at the time but reported it years later following an appeal on *Crimewatch.*'

'That's not much to go on.'

'It's nothing. There were no bodies, and no one knew where the boys had gone to, so there was no starting point and no evidence a crime had been committed. There was nothing for the investigation to follow. Another telephone appeal was launched on *Crimewatch* and they received a few hundred leads but none of them gave anything of substance. The investigation met dead end after dead end. No one had any enthusiasm for the case, except for an ex-copper turned gumshoe, who eventually contacted the investigation team in Liverpool because no one else was listening to him. He'd been pestering the NWP for years, but they ignored him.'

'Pestering them about what?' Richard asked.

'It's a long story but I'll give you the edited version.'

'Thank you, it's much appreciated.'

'No problem. He was an ex-sergeant stationed at Bangor. He was a copper for thirty-years. His record was impeccable until the last ten years of his career. He left under a cloud and retired early following a string of complaints from clergy and community leaders across North Wales.'

'Complaints about what?'

'It appeared he was convinced there was a paedophile ring being operated by members of the church and certain community leaders. He raised the issue dozens of times, escalating it to the top brass whenever he had the chance, but he was quashed each time and reprimanded. Eventually he retired.'

'Forced to retire by the sounds of it?'

'No doubt about it—'

'Sorry to interrupt, but what was his name?' Richard asked, making notes.

'Don Shipley,' Alec said. 'Ian Osbourne followed up on some of his complaints, bearing in mind none of them led to an investigation back then.'

'Why was there so much friction against him?'

'He was accusing clergymen, scout leaders, football coaches, and schoolteachers of being involved. They were upstanding pillars of the community on the face of it and Shipley was smearing their characters.'

'Did he go public with his theories?'

'Yes. The local press lapped it up. His accusations ruined careers, split families, and allegedly caused several suicides.'

'Suicides,' Richard said to himself. 'Is Shipley still alive?'

'No. At least, I don't think so. No one knows for sure,' Alec said. 'He took early retirement from the police. He jumped before he was pushed. Reading between the lines, it only added fuel to the flames. He became more focused on building awareness to the alleged abuse and set up a gumshoe agency in Bangor to cover the bills and set about uncovering the paedophile ring. When he wasn't bothering people, he was tracking unfaithful husbands, long-term disability fraudsters, and some debt recovery work. He continued to make allegations until he disappeared in ninety-seven.'

'He disappeared?' Richard asked.

'Yes. His car was found near Bangor Station with the keys in it. His bank account was emptied the day before but was never touched again. His clients paid some large amounts of money into his account after his disappearance, but it was never touched.'

'That's a bad sign,' Richard said.

'We both know what it means,' Alec said. 'The investigation into his disappearance was half-hearted, and they suspected suicide or a complete withdrawal from society because of the number of people who threatened to kill him. His case was never closed, just suspended.'

'What did Osbourne think had happened to him?'

'Don Shipley wasn't the type to drop out of society. Ian Osbourne made enquiries into the homeless communities across North Wales, but he drew a blank. He said the chance of Shipley pushing around a shopping trolley full of his belongings was unfathomable. He thought he'd been murdered.'

'That would be my guess.'

'What other conclusion is there?' Alec agreed.

'What about the accusations Shipley made?'

'Osbourne thought Shipley had poked the wasp's nest once too often and got stung.'

'It's understandable. Shipley must have been sure he was right to have persisted as long as he did?'

'He was absolutely certain. Some of the men he accused at the time, have since been convicted of abuse on historical evidence given by adults who were groomed and sexually assaulted in the nineties.'

'So, Shipley was on to something?'

'Definitely,' Alec said. 'Ian Osbourne was convinced that the Shipley files needed to be reopened and a thorough investigation carried out, but he was shut down by Westminster.'

'Westminster?'

'Yes. The Home Office stamped on it before it started. It would appear that some of the people he was investigating, still have influence.'

'The church?' Richard asked.

'The church, the politicians, the list of possibilities goes on and on. The fact is, there was no appetite to rake it all up again. It appears that politicians on all sides wanted this quashed before it could get off the ground.'

'That must have been discouraging for Osbourne,' Richard said.

'He appealed the decision as far as he could. His superiors got tired of telling him to shut it down. When the cold case was halted, he was given a desk job collating traffic statistics, which he hated. He saw it as a punishment for asking too many questions. He continued to follow up the leads on his own time up until the crash. His death put an end to it until now. Make of that what you will.'

'Are you insinuating the crash was not an accident?'

'It was investigated and deemed to be driver error,' Alec said. 'I'm not a copper anymore. Who am I to question that?'

'This puts a different perspective on the case. I'm going to run this by my DI,' Richard said, hearing a subliminal message in the tone of Alec's voice. 'I'm assuming Shipley's case is a matter of public record?'

'Ian Osbourne compiled files of a detailed investigation into the evidence and the reports available to him. I can send them to you,' Alec said. 'When Ian unopened those files and began to ask questions, he hit a wall of silence, especially from the clergy.'

'No surprise there,' Richard said.

'I'm glad you're cynical,' Alec said, 'because all the original files are now missing or destroyed.'

'What, you're kidding?'

'Nope. They were destroyed by a fire at the storage facility in Caernarfon. The fire burnt most of them and the sprinkler system did the rest. All that remains are the files Ian Osbourne kept.'

'That's enough to make me cynical even if I wasn't before,' Richard said. 'Thank you, Alec. Is it okay if I call you once I've spoken to my DI?'

'Of course,' Alec said. 'Keep me in the loop on this one.'

'I will, thanks again for your time.'

Chapter 18

Cristy and Sharon were sitting in the office searching for the offending videos online. Sharon had drafted in extra staff on overtime, so she could help Cristy request the removal of the videos from social media. Facebook was automated, so the response was robotic, but they removed the videos within a few hours. Cristy felt it was too little too late. The damage was done. She was devastated and in no fit state to drive home. Sharon phoned Myra, and she said she'd be there as soon as she could be. Rowan called back, but Cristy didn't want to speak to him. She didn't want to speak to anyone. The videos were pornographic, filmed by Price when she was drunk and completely unaware she was being filmed. When they were filmed, she was in love with him and her enthusiasm showed. The passion was transferred to the screen. The likes, comments, and shares on the video posts were degrading at best, soul destroying in truth. Hordes of men made comments, some suggestive, most of them disgusting. Her inbox was filling up with crude messages and her friend requests climbing. Once again, Price had found a way to violate her in public. To say she was distraught was an understatement.

'That's the last of them,' Karen said, looking at Facebook. 'But we can't get them taken down from the porn sites until they've been through the security process to make sure it's you in the video. The police are dealing with them.' The phone rang, and she answered it.

'I can't believe he's done this. This is so cruel even for that bastard. This is the worst day of my life,' Cristy said. 'It was bad enough when he raped me, but this is worse. It's like being raped in public.'

'The police are on the way,' Karen said, hanging up. 'That was Colwyn Gallagher. He said you need to stay here until he gets here. They need to speak to you face to face.'

'I'm not in a rush to go anywhere,' Cristy said. 'I'll never be able to show my face in public again. I need to move abroad.' She looked at her Facebook profile. Her inbox was crammed with messages of support and dozens of sexual advances. She had over thirty friend requests all from men she didn't know. 'How sick are these people?' Cristy said, shaking her head. Tears streamed down her face. She clicked on her status and deactivated her account. It felt like slamming the door in the face of a storm. It gave her some small peace of mind. 'That's all I can do for now. I don't want anyone mithering me, especially perverts. The world seems to be full of perverts. What am I going to do?' She sobbed. 'He calls me a slut all the time and now everyone will think I am.'

'You are not a slut because you had sex with Jon Price. You were a couple, two young people in love.'

'People won't see it like that, will they?'

'Most of them will. There will always be idiots. Those videos were of two adults having consensual sex,' Sharon said.

'I can't believe he filmed us.'

'So, what, we all have sex. It will feel like the end of the world right now, but it isn't. You've done nothing wrong except trust your ex-partner. How were you to know the bastard was filming it?'

'I didn't. I swear to God I didn't. That kind of thing is weird.'

'He's the weirdo, not you. There's no shame on your behalf.' Sharon touched her hand. 'It won't feel that way for a while. You need to keep your head up and don't let that man grind you down.'

'I don't know if I can up after this.'

'You must. Carry on as if nothing can shake you. That will piss him off more than anything else. Show him that nothing he can do to you will frighten you.'

'I'm not so much scared as embarrassed. I feel sick.'

'You had sex with him, so what?'

Cristy listened to her words and steeled herself inside. Price would be waiting for her to implode. He got off on hurting her, he always had. If she could find the strength to walk tall, he would give up in the end, surely, he would. There was a knock on the door. Sharon opened it and Col stepped in, flanked by another uniformed sergeant. April Byfield. April walked across the office and bent to give Cristy a hug. That set Cristy off again.

'I'm sorry. I can't stop crying.'

'It must have been a shock,' April said. She waited for Cristy to settle. 'Did you know he had the videos?'

'No,' Cristy said, trying to catch her breath. 'I had no idea he'd filmed us in bed. I never would have done that.'

'Then you didn't consent to being filmed?'

'God no,' Cristy said. 'I'm too shy. I don't even walk around naked. Please tell me you can take them down.'

'It might take a while, but because the videos encroach on an injunction, they'll have to eventually,' April said. 'The good news is, Melanie Brooks doesn't know how to access the dark web, so they haven't been posted there. Anything posted there, is there forever. Thank heavens for small mercies.'

'Is that her name?' Cristy asked.

'Yes. Melanie Brooks,' April said, nodding.

'Why would she do that to me?' Cristy asked.

'Rowan said it's his ex?' April asked. 'Jealousy, I assume.'

'I don't know her. He went out with her years ago. Not long after we all left school. She was in the year above us, so I never knew her. Is it definitely her that uploaded them?'

'Yes. She's been arrested.'

'Already?' Cristy said, looking shocked. 'Wow.'

'Yes,' Col answered, smiling. 'Rowan called me straightaway. She tagged him in the posts to make sure he saw them. As soon as I was alerted, we got a warrant.'

'Thank you for acting so quickly.'

'My pleasure. She was working on the checkout at Home Bargains when we arrested her. There was a long queue at her till when she was cuffed and taken away. She was crying like a baby,' Col added.

'Oh, that's terrible,' Cristy said. 'I almost feel sorry for her.'

'You shouldn't. She's sweating in a cell for now until I get back to the station to interview her. We needed to speak to you first to make sure you didn't consent to being filmed.'

'I would never do that. I can't understand why anyone would,' Cristy said.

'Only Price can tell us that. I'm afraid,' Col said. 'We'll need to investigate how Melanie Brooks came into possession of them.'

'He won't be arrested, will he?' Cristy asked. April's face gave her the answer. 'Because he didn't upload them?'

'Without your consent, making them in the first place is a crime,' April said. 'But that will take time to prove.'

'Why?' Cristy asked.

'Unless we can find the original source, he can say he didn't film them and he didn't upload them,' Col said. 'She can say she didn't know who the people in the video were, she just likes porn. I don't think she's smart enough to think of that. I saw her being brought into custody. She was terrified. It won't take me long to get the truth out of her. Once she talks, I'll speak to Price. He's burying himself in circumstantial evidence. Eventually, he'll drown in it.'

'I've told Cristy if she looks like she's not fazed by his antics, it will piss him off,' Sharon said. 'He might get bored and leave her alone.'

'I agree,' April said. 'The videos are more damaging to him than you. In the long run,' she added. 'In the meantime, let us give you a lift home.'

'I've called her mum,' Sharon said. 'She's on her way.'

'Okay,' Col said. He squeezed Cristy's shoulder. 'Don't worry. We're right on top of this. Let's go and speak to Melanie Brooks,' he said, turning to April.

'I'll call and see you at home later,' April said, smiling. There was worry in her eyes. Worry and concern. 'Just to make sure you're okay.'

'Okay, thank you,' Cristy said. The phone rang and Sharon answered it. She looked confused and then annoyed, and then she nodded and said goodbye. Her eyes met Cristy's. Cristy instinctively knew the call concerned her. 'What is it now?'

'Your mum's car has a puncture,' Sharon said. 'She's waiting for your brother to go and change the tyre.'

'It looks like you'll be needing that lift, after all,' Col said. 'Grab your coat and we'll take you home.' Cristy looked at Sharon for permission. Sharon nodded and smiled.

'Go home and we'll see you when you're ready to come back to work,' Sharon said. 'Call me later if you need a chat.' Cristy hugged her and put on her coat.

The officers and Cristy left the nursing home. She breathed in the fresh air and savoured it. They walked around the side of the building to the visitors' car park. Cristy was quiet, and the officers seemed preoccupied. They were focused and determined to protect Cristy Dennis from Jon Price. Col broke the silence.

'If there's one thing I hate, it's a bully,' Col said. 'Price makes me want to puke. We'll nail him for this.'

'Oh, he's so much more than a bully,' April said. 'He's in a class above that. He's a complete sociopath. And he's genuinely disregarding the law. I'm worried about how he's manipulated this Melanie Brooks character,' she added. 'I'm worried she's been bullied into uploading the videos.'

'Don't be worried just yet. We'll ask her and see what she has to say,' Col said. 'If she's been threatened, she's got NWP right behind her.' He stopped in his tracks. 'Oh, for fuck's sake,' he shouted.

'What's wrong?' April asked. Col pointed to their vehicle. All four tyres had been deflated.

Cristy could see slash marks in the tyres.

'Jon Price did that,' Cristy said.

'We don't know that,' Col said, flushing red with anger.

'Who else would do that to a police car?' Cristy mumbled. She knew he didn't care about the police, and this was his way of letting her know he could reach her at any time. Ice-cold fear tickled Cristy's neck and made her skin crawl. She wanted to cry and beg him to stop, but she'd done that before and it didn't work. He was cruel. She looked around to see if one of his cronies was filming their reaction. There were empty vehicles in the pub car park across the road. Despite not being able to see anyone, she had the feeling she was being watched.

Chapter 19

Father Patrick Creegan was sitting in an interview room with his solicitor, recommended to him by the diocese. His name was Sean Bannon, and his practice was retained by the Church for everything from property conveyancing to representing employees in dire straits, when need be. The company, which was based in Chester, had represented the Catholic Church in North Wales since before the Great War. Its countrywide expansion over the decades was partly due to the church coffers, which were once bottomless; millions had been made from estates bequeathed by wealthy parishioners, and millions squandered protecting the institution's reputation. Bannon was a specialist in defending priests who found themselves in trouble for whatever reason. His cases ranged from speeding tickets, drunk driving offences, and paternity suits, to more complicated charges such as sexual assaults. He called himself the tow truck. If he couldn't pull you out of deep shit, nothing could. His win rate was impressive. He was five feet two inches tall and wider at the hip than he was at the shoulder, giving him a Tweedledee shape. His hair was combed over his bald head in a vain attempt to hide his hair loss, and it was too black to be natural. His hands were dumpy, and his fingers were reminiscent of uncooked sausages adorned with too many gold rings. Father Creegan had spoken to him on the telephone at length the evening before, but got the distinct impression that Bannon was convinced he was guilty of something. What that was, he could only guess. He felt an instant dislike for the man, despite his fearsome reputation and the fact he was representing him.

DI Williams and DS Davies walked into the room. A mixture of Fahrenheit aftershave and Armani drifted in behind them. They explained the interview was under caution, although he wasn't under arrest, and that the proceedings would be recorded on camera. The priest agreed to the conditions, and the detectives settled down ready to begin with their questions.

'Father Creegan, have you remembered anything about your attack since we last spoke?' Alan asked. He noted that Creegan was sitting back, arms folded defensively across his chest. His eyes darted up and left. He was possibly creating an answer. Whatever he was doing, the answer wasn't given instinctively. Alan knew considered answers were generally the currency of liars or people with something to hide.

'No, nothing of interest. Everything is still a blur,' Creegan said, shaking his head. His eyes looked bloodshot, as if he'd been drinking. Alan got a whiff of malt whisky. It was faint, but it was unmistakeable, especially to a hardened whisky drinker like himself. 'May I enquire why you've asked me to come here with my solicitor?'

'Yes. Of course,' Alan said, locking eyes with the priest. Creegan diverted his gaze. He was hiding something. Alan was sure of it. 'We tested the DNA of your attacker and we found a match.'

'That's good news, isn't it?' Creegan asked. He looked at his brief, but Bannon looked surprised.

'I haven't been made aware of this,' Bannon complained.

'That's because I didn't have a clue who you were until this morning,' Alan said. 'When did you start representing Father Creegan?'

'My services were enlisted yesterday.'

'Late yesterday,' Kim interrupted. 'In fact, you sent a request for information at nine o'clock this morning. What we have is being compiled and will be sent to your office via email at some point today or you can take a copy with you when you leave if you prefer. And we can give you copies of what we have here as we proceed, if you like,' she added.

'Thank you. That will be sufficient for now,' Bannon muttered. He looked embarrassed by her cooperation. 'It has been a bit of a rush.'

'It's not a problem,' Alan said.

'Can you enlighten us about the DNA match, please?' Bannon asked.

'We can,' Alan said, nodding. He smiled at Bannon, not wanting to antagonise him more than necessary. 'The sample taken from the vicarage matches DNA found during the review investigation into two missing teenagers in nineteen-ninety-four.'

'A review investigation?' Bannon asked, frowning. Alan nodded. 'A cold case?'

'Yes. Ewan Birley and Christopher Deeks were thirteen years old at the time they vanished.' Alan looked at the priest for a reaction. He was stony-faced. Was there a hint of recognition in his eyes? 'Do those names mean anything to you, Father?'

Father Creegan shook his head and was about to speak, but Bannon held up his hand to stop him.

'Wait a minute. Don't answer that question,' Bannon said. 'I'm failing to see the relevance of a misper case from the nineties.'

'There is a relevance,' Alan said, nodding.

'My client suffered a serious assault in his own home.'

'The DNA match is the relevance between the misper case and the assault on Father Creegan.'

'You're stretching, but I'm prepared to listen to the details,' Bannon said. 'Give us the shortened version.'

'Okay, thank you. As I said, Ewan Birley and Chris Deeks were thirteen years old at the time they vanished. The investigation was floundering due to a lack of evidence. Following an appeal for information in the local press, a jacket was found in the lost property department at Bangor station,' Alan said, ignoring Bannon's stare. 'It belonged to Ewan Birley. During a cold case review four years ago, semen was recovered from the sleeve of the garment and the DNA matches your attacker.' Alan stared into Creegan's eyes. 'That makes it very relevant to the attack on your client. It could even be the reason for the attack,' Alan pressed. Creegan looked down at the table.

'How can you make that connection?' Bannon looked incensed. 'If the boys went missing in ninety-four, when was the semen recovered?' Bannon asked.

'Four years ago,' Alan said. He knew they were reaching, but he wanted to see Creegan's reaction. So far, there was nothing he could read. He passed the details in paper form to the brief. Bannon read the details and shook his head.

'The garment wasn't found for years and since then it has been sitting in evidence for twenty-four years?'

'Yes,' Alan said, nodding.

'Twenty-four years. The chances of contamination are huge,' Bannon said, frowning. 'I'm a reasonable man. Let's say there's been no contamination. Who does the DNA belong to?'

'Father Creegan's attacker,' Alan said. He knew how feeble that sounded, but it was all they had. He was shaking the tree to see what might fall out.

'You don't know who it belongs to, do you?' Bannon said, talking like a teacher would to a naughty schoolboy.

'Not yet, but we're working on it.'

'Why is my client here?' Bannon asked, smirking. He thought it was over before it had begun. 'This is ridiculous. Father Creegan was attacked and almost died, and you're drilling him for information about a misper from the nineties. Even if there is a connection, he isn't guilty of anything but being in the wrong place at the wrong time. Father Creegan is the victim here.'

'Of course, he is,' Alan said, sighing. It was time to change tack. 'We have a few questions, nonetheless. Father Creegan could be able to help us identify his attacker and in doing so shed light on a historic case. Surely, you don't object, Father?'

'You can ask your questions,' Creegan said, shrugging. 'It can't hurt, I suppose.'

'Thank you, Father.' Alan took a document from his file. 'Have you ever heard of Don Shipley?' Alan asked. There was a reaction in his eyes. Creegan knew the name, Alan was certain of it. 'He was a police officer from Bangor, who turned private detective in his retirement?'

'Yes. I've heard of him,' Creegan said. Alan was almost disappointed he admitted knowing of him. His solicitor whispered in his ear. The priest shook his head and patted Bannon's arm as if he was a child. He sat up and looked at Alan. 'It's fine. Don Shipley is a name from way back in time. It must be over twenty-years since I've heard that name.' The priest leant forward and relaxed a little. 'In fact, it's well over twenty-years. What on earth has he got to do with this?'

'We're trying to join the dots, Father,' Alan said, scratching the pea-shaped growth on his forehead. It was red and angry today. 'Don Shipley was adamant there was institutional sexual abuse happening in the church and the wider community in the late eighties and early nineties.'

'Oh yes. I remember his reckless accusations.'

'He did make accusations, and he was right in some cases.' Creegan didn't answer. Alan waited, but he didn't speak. 'The two boys who went missing may have been seen at Bangor station talking to a man in his fifties, who may have been a priest.'

'He *may* have been a priest?' Bannon mumbled. 'What have you got to suggest that?'

'The eyewitness said the man she saw may have been wearing a dog collar underneath his jacket, but she wasn't sure.'

'When did she make this statement?' Bannon asked, frustrated.

'Following an appeal a few years after the disappearance,' Alan said.

'A few years after and she wasn't sure?'

'The boys were never seen again, but the man who attacked you left semen on the sleeve of Birley's jacket.' Alan stumbled on, trying to ignore the solicitor. There was another uncomfortable silence. The priest sat back and folded his arms again. He was being guarded once more. 'Don't you find it uncanny that the man who secreted semen onto that boy's jacket committed suicide in your bedroom?'

'Uncanny? I'm not sure what I'd call it,' Creegan said. 'It's an unfortunate coincidence although an unfortunate coincidence does not describe how upsetting this is. It was bad enough before you found the DNA match. Now we know my attacker was involved in the disappearance of two young boys. I'm very disturbed by the entire episode.'

'I'm sure you are, Father' – Alan paused – 'Let's see if we can find any pieces of the puzzle that might explain the connection. Where were you in ninety-four?' Alan asked.

'I can see no reasonable explanation why my client is being asked these questions,' Bannon said, interrupting. 'He hasn't committed any crime, in fact, there has been no crime committed that I can see.'

'The chances are Ewan Birley and Chris Deeks were murdered,' Alan said, sighing. 'That is a crime. You may inadvertently know something about it,' Alan said. 'It's a simple enough question to answer. Where were you in ninety-four?'

'Let me jog your memory. You were a priest in Dolgellau,' Kim said before he could answer. She was tiring of the game. Alan was laying out the bait, but Creegan wasn't biting. She decided to speed things up. 'Our Lady of Seven Sorrows to be exact.'

'Our Lady of Seven Sorrows,' Creegan said, nodding. A smile touched his lips. 'That takes me back. I loved my time there. There was a real sense of community back in those days. I wasn't there long. It was a wonderful church and a wonderful community. It's a beautiful building. Have you seen it?'

'We've seen pictures of it,' Alan said. 'Earlier this morning.'

'Of course, you have,' Creegan said. 'You've been doing your homework.'

'There were sixty-two Catholic churches in the diocese then. Shipley raised issue with sixteen of them,' Kim said. 'You were not on the list compiled by Don Shipley,' she added. Father Creegan nodded and smiled. Bannon seemed to breathe a sigh of relief. 'That must have been a worrying time. Do you remember the people he accused of being part of a paedophile ring?'

'Oh, my goodness, yes,' Creegan said. He closed his eyes as if the memories were too difficult to recall. 'It was a terrible time. People's lives were destroyed by that man.'

'Children's lives were destroyed by the men who abused them,' Kim countered.

'I'm not denying that, of course, I'm sickened by what happened but not everyone was guilty. Shit sticks they say and they're right, it does.'

'I'm sure it was disturbing for the innocent men accused, but nine of the people on his list have since been prosecuted, six of them convicted and jailed,' Alan said. 'I'm not saying Shipley was right about everyone but he was right about some of them and if the church had been more open to investigation instead of slamming the doors closed, more of the perpetrators could have been identified and the innocent men redeemed. There was definitely no smoke without fire.'

'No one was more disgusted about what was going on than me,' Creegan said. 'Men I'd known since I entered the priesthood, men I respected and admired were being accused of the worst possible crime. Abusing the innocent is unforgivable in my mind, but so is accusing the innocent. Of course, we were all tarred with the same brush and still are to this day. I don't see that changing anytime soon.'

'Does that make you angry?' Kim asked.

'Yes, detective, it does,' Creegan said.

'Maybe it made others mad. Mad enough to attack you,' Alan said, shrugging. 'Can you think of anyone from that time who might have a reason to seek you out and attack you?' Alan asked.

'No. Not at all.'

'Were you involved in any of the internal investigations?' Alan pushed. 'I'm assuming there must have been some?'

'Any investigations were held way above my humble position, inspector,' Creegan said.

'This is a fishing expedition,' Bannon said. 'I'm going to advise my client not to answer any more questions. He's been more than helpful.'

'We're asking Father Creegan for his help to identify the man who attacked him,' Kim said. 'There is clearly a link between his attacker and what was going on in the nineties. Father Creegan was there when all this was going on. We're not accusing him of anything, simply asking for him to cast his mind back and think about the men who were accused. There were a lot of them, and someone might stand out to you. Someone who didn't like you?'

'I can't think of anyone who would hold a grudge against me,' Creegan added. He closed his eyes again. His breathing was deep and measured, as if he was trying to maintain his calm. 'There were plenty of angry priests around, there still are but their anger wasn't aimed at me. I was one of them. An attack on one member of the diocese was an attack on all of us, especially when it came to accusations of child abuse. It was one size fits all then and it still is. The world and his wife were convinced that every choir member and altar boy were being groomed.'

'They were different times, father,' Kim said.

'In what way?'

'Society was different. Racism was amusing to the masses and the sexual exploitation of women was rife. It has been proven beyond a doubt that children were being abused and those who were accused would have been vilified, innocent or not. As you said, shit sticks.' Kim sat forward, her voice calm. 'Think back, it's a long time ago but can you remember anyone who may have had it in for you, Father,' Kim asked. 'Maybe someone resented the fact that you weren't on the list of accused.'

'I can only repeat what I've said.' Creegan sighed. 'I have no knowledge of anyone who would have a problem with me, then or now.'

'Did you help the diocese investigate Shipley's accusations?' Alan asked. Creegan shook his head. 'Did you interview any of the men accused?'

'You do not need to answer that question,' Bannon said, closing his laptop. 'We're going around in circles and getting nowhere. Unless you're going to charge my client with something, this interview is over.' He looked from one detective to the other. 'Are you going to charge him with something?'

'No,' Alan said. He sat back and let out a deep breath. 'You're free to go, father but if you do think of anyone who may have been around in the nineties, who stands out in your mind, please call me anytime, day or night.'

****

Melanie Brooks was sitting in a cell, wondering what was going to happen to her. She was cold and hungry. Her grey hoody was zipped up to the neck. Her matching leggings were thin and didn't offer much in the way of warmth; nor were they flattering around her curvy behind. She was desperate to look at her phone and tell the world how she'd been wrongfully arrested but they'd taken it from her when she was booked into the custody suite. They had said she was in breach of the law for possession and distribution of non-consensual pornography, which sounded far more serious than she'd expected. Jon Price had told her she might get a bollocking from the police, but he'd never mentioned being arrested. She'd seen the look on her supervisor's face at the time of her arrest. She looked like a bulldog chewing a wasp at the best of times. To say she looked pissed off was an understatement. She was beginning to realise she'd made a huge mistake. The door clanged open and the custody sergeant led her to an interview room, where the duty solicitor was waiting.

'Hello, Melanie,' the solicitor said. She was in her thirties and her spectacles made her eyes look magnified. Her brown hair was scraped into a ponytail. 'I'm Mandy Dickson. I'll be advising you today although if the police decide to press charges, you will need to employ someone to defend you properly.'

'Charge me,' Melanie repeated. 'Surely they'll see it as a joke?'

'I don't think they've seen the funny side,' Mandy said. 'If indeed there is one.'

'Oh, my God. Do you think they will?'

'Revenge pornography is a serious offence. Judges are clamping down on social media crimes.' Melanie shook her head but didn't speak. She pulled her sleeves over her hands like a tortoise withdrawing into its shell. 'Did you upload pornographic videos of your ex-boyfriend's partner?'

'Yes,' Melanie said, quietly. 'Sort of. I think I've been tricked into doing it.'

'You think you've been tricked?'

'Yes.'

'Tricked how?'

'Jon Price, the bloke in the videos, did it on my laptop.'

'But you knew he was uploading pornography?'

'Yes. But it was just his ex. He said it was just a wind-up.'

'I don't think that's going to wash as a decent reason to upload images of an innocent party having sex to Facebook, do you?'

'Probably not, with hindsight,' Melanie said, feeling ridiculously stupid.

'My advice would be to cooperate with the police and hope they believe you've been manipulated. They may feel sorry for you,' Mandy Dickson said. Two uniformed officers walked into the room. The three stripes on their uniforms indicated they were sergeants. They looked at Melanie with a mixture of annoyance and disdain.

'I'm Sergeant Colwyn Gallagher and this is Sergeant April Byfelt.' They sat down and explained how the interview would be conducted. Melanie went from concerned to terrified in sixty-seconds. 'Okay, Melanie. Let's begin by confirming that two pornographic videos were uploaded from your laptop to Pornhub, Bluetube, and Facebook late last night,' Col said. Melanie nodded almost imperceptibly. 'Is that a yes?' he asked.

'Yes,' Melanie said.

'The videos are Jon Price having sex with Cristy Dennis?'

'Yes.'

'Cristy Dennis was unaware that Jon Price had filmed them having sex, which makes them non-consensual. Do you understand?'

'Yes. I think so.'

'You either do or don't, which is it?'

'She didn't know Jon was filming them,' Melanie said.

'Which makes the content illegal,' Col said. 'She didn't consent to having sex on film and she certainly didn't consent to them being shared online,' Col added. 'Can you tell us why you uploaded them?'

'It was a wind-up,' Melanie muttered. She blushed and put her hands between her knees.

'A wind-up?'

'Yes.'

'Can you explain that to us?' Col asked.

'My friend, Jon Price, said he was trying to wind-up his ex, who is in a relationship with my ex,' Melanie explained. Tears filled her eyes. 'He said it was just a joke because they were together now.'

'I'm failing to see the funny side,' April said. 'Can you imagine how embarrassed Cristy Dennis is?'

'Not really, no,' Melanie mumbled. 'I was drunk, and he said it was just a laugh winding them both up at the same time.'

'The humiliation you've caused is cruel,' April said. 'How you can say you thought it was a joke is beyond me.'

'I'm sorry,' Melanie said, crying. 'Jon sent the videos from his phone to my email address, and then he grabbed my laptop and shared them on my Facebook page. I was drunk and didn't think about what we were doing.'

'Did you think that was okay?' April asked.

'I didn't think about it properly,' Melanie said. 'Jon tricked me.'

'He tricked you?' April asked.

'Yes. By using my laptop.'

'It doesn't help your situation that they were uploaded from your device.'

'I feel stupid now, but I was just going along with what he wanted to do. I like him, or at least, I did.'

'Did you visit him in prison?' Col asked.

'Yes. A few times,' Melanie said.

'How many?' April asked.

'I don't know for sure.'

'We can check the visiting logs,' April said. 'Roughly, how many times?'

'Every month or so,' Melanie said, embarrassed.

'Are you in a relationship with him?'

'Sort of,' Melanie said. 'I thought we were.'

'Can you explain what you mean?' April said.

'He said when he got out of prison, we would see each other,' Melanie said.

'Okay. Carry on,' Col said.

'He called me when he got out and came to my flat. We were drinking vodka and then we started to mess about on my laptop. He said he wanted to see what people were up to on Facebook and then one thing led to another.'

'Did you have sex with him?' April asked.

'Is that relevant?' the solicitor asked, frowning.

'Yes.' April didn't avert her gaze. 'Did you have sex?'

'Yes,' Melanie said, quietly.

'Before or after you uploaded the videos?'

'Both.'

'Explain that to me.'

'He uploaded them to Facebook before we had sex and then he told me to upload them to the porn sites after,' Melanie said. She started crying. 'I thought we were going to be together, but I haven't heard from him since. He said it was just a wind-up.' She wiped her nose on her sleeve. 'God, I feel so stupid.'

'You've caused Cristy Dennis and her family a lot of distress,' Col said. 'The distribution of non-consensual pornography is a serious crime. It seems to me that you were a willing participant in the distribution of this material, Melanie, and as such, I'm going to take this to CPS with the recommendation they press charges.'

'Oh, my God,' Melanie sobbed.

'We'll bail you for now and contact you when we need to talk to you again.'

'Am I going to go to jail?' Melanie asked.

'That's not for us to decide,' April said. 'But I certainly wouldn't rule it out.'

Chapter 20

Edward Speers was scouring Facebook for information on what had happened to Luca Bay. There were few facts and much speculation, but what he could gather was someone had bashed his head in with a crowbar. The information on the Net was vague and didn't specify what he was doing at Penrhos Beach in the dark. Edward suspected Luca had been dealing drugs for years although he always denied it. Edward warned him time and time again that it was a short-lived career and would end in tears. Dabbling in a small community was a risky business. There was always someone who would take umbrage. It wasn't clear what the motive was as his money was in his wallet.

That meant the attack could be personal as if it was a punishment for something he'd done.

Edward had worked as a gofer for Paul Sutton, and he'd also worked for Jon Price years ago on one of his building sites. Price had concocted a property scam, worth tens of millions, buying land via umbrella companies, acquiring planning permission for holiday apartments, and selling them off plan once the foundations were laid. He employed dozens of locals to add to the illusion of an established property development company. The entire operation was a front for his other shady businesses. When the Serious Fraud Squad pounced, they forced many of his employees to give evidence against him. Luca didn't go to court, but Edward always worried Price would get out one day and cut any loose ends. He was out much sooner than expected and he may be making his presence known. Price and Sutton were capable of taking someone out without blinking an eye. They were both incapable of giving a shit about anyone else; two of a kind. Neither of them was likeable, not that they would be in the slightest bit arsed about what people thought. Their egos and greed overshadowed anything else.

Edward liked Luca and was godfather to his kids. He'd spoken to his wife, who was completely devastated. She'd gone to stay with her parents on the other side of the island, somewhere near Newborough. He wished he could pack a bag and leave too, but he needed to work. No one else would pay his bills. His bedsit was a shit-hole, but the rent needed to be paid, nonetheless. The landlord had bought several houses on London Road and turned them into flats. At first, they looked nice, modern, and well-built but as time went by, the cracks started to appear. The builders had cut corners and their workmanship was substandard. Despite his constant complaining, the shower leaked, the heating didn't work properly, and there was damp in the bedroom which was making his clothes go mouldy. His wages didn't stretch to saving a deposit for a different place. He needed his original deposit back so he could move. Luca had offered to loan him the money the day before he was murdered. In hindsight, he should have taken it there and then, but he couldn't have predicted someone would cave his skull in. Luca's death had made him nervous. Edward suspected drugs could be involved. He used on occasion, but it was infrequent. He'd seen too many friends and acquaintances screwed up or dead because of drug abuse. It wasn't a world he wanted to be a part of. He feared Luca took his chances in order to make an easy living were as Edward got out of bed at six in the morning and didn't get back home until six in the evening. His job on the railway was safe despite COVID-19.

Maybe killing Luca was just a message. Price and his mob were back in town and they were bad news for everyone, especially the people who had taken their places when they were sent down. They were nasty, and they were bullies, and there would be trouble. Sutton and his cronies would be on red alert; they were equally bad news. It was a perfect storm just waiting to happen.

A knock on the door disturbed him from his Internet search. He checked his watch. It was too late for a parcel delivery. The next-door neighbours often knocked on his door to borrow milk or bread or money or toilet roll. Toilet roll. At what point did they realise they'd run out, before or after? It didn't bear thinking about. He walked to the door and opened it, wondering if they thought he was Bob Geldof or Mother Teresa.

It took a millisecond to realise the hooded figure in the hallway wasn't a neighbour. Edward saw movement and sensed danger but couldn't move in time to avoid the hammer. It landed on his forehead above his right eye. The blow was concussive, and he dropped to the floor like a felled tree, cracking his skull on the terracotta tiles. His attacker struck him again, shattering his cheekbone and fracturing his upper jaw. Edward felt blinding white heat through his brain before he slipped into the fog of unconsciousness.

Chapter 21

When Cristy finally arrived home, her father was holding a double ladder while her brother was fixing a fisheye camera to the wall beneath the upper window ledge, which would cover the front of the house. Rowan was up a second ladder at the side of the house, fixing another camera to cover the driveway and the access to the rear garden. Her mother was standing in the doorway, supervising proceedings with a coffee mug in hand. She saw the patrol car slowing and waved. Cristy felt a pang of guilt run through her.

'I can't believe they slashed my mum's tyres too,' Cristy said. 'In the middle of the daytime. He doesn't have any fear, does he?'

'He's arrogant, but arrogant people are blinded by their own self-importance,' April said. 'He's using other people to do his dirty work at the moment. The last time he did that, they all testified against him and he went to jail. He's playing with fire.'

'I hope you're right.' Cristy sighed.

'It looks like the family are gearing up security,' April said, pulling to a stop. 'Not a bad thing, though, Cristy. It's nice to know they're looking after you.'

'I shouldn't need looking after at my age,' Cristy said, shaking her head. 'My mam will be going ballistic they slashed her tyres. She's pissed off already. All this because I chose to go out with a bad boy. It's a joke.'

'We've all loved a bad boy at some point in our lives.'

'Really. It's not just me?'

'Nope. A bit of rough, my mam used to say.'

'I haven't heard that for a while.'

'Realising bad boys are a waste of space and a mistake is called growing up,' April said, smiling.

'I can't for the life of me think what I saw in him,' Cristy said. 'He's just playing around and messing with me, but look at the effect he's having on everyone. He thinks this is funny. The man isn't right in the head. Why can't you arrest him just for being a twat?'

'There'd be no room in the prisons if we did that.'

'I suppose so.'

'No, he isn't right in the head. He'll make a mistake and when he does, we'll be there,' April said. 'Price and his crew are all under surveillance. One wrong move and they're back in prison, one by one if we need to.'

'Thanks, April,' Cristy said. 'I'd better go and face the music. There will be a family summit, which will involve my dad and my brother turning into terminators, while I try to calm them down and my mum swears like a trooper.'

'I'd like to be a fly on the wall.'

'I don't even know what to say to Rowan. Every time he looks at me from now on, he'll see me in those videos.'

'He'll get over it, I'm sure,' April said.

'I'm not sure I can handle the sympathetic look in his eyes at the moment. He looks at me like I'm a wounded bird that will never fly again.' Cristy shrugged and choked back a sob. She clenched her fists and shook her head. 'Right. Get a grip, Cristy,' she said to herself. She took a deep breath and opened the door. 'Thanks for the lift,' she said, climbing out. April waved and pulled away, turning the vehicle around at the end of the cul-de-sac. Cristy watched her drive down the road and steeled herself to look her family in the eye. She felt more ashamed than words could describe.

****

Father Creegan arrived home in the dark. The winter nights were growing longer every day, and the temperature was dropping. He parked the car at the front of the house and walked quickly to the door, letting himself in and closing it behind him. He closed his eyes and leant against it as if it was a shield against the outside world. The vicarage had been his sanctuary in the early years of living there, but that was before he'd encountered evil face to face. Not evil as it's portrayed on television or in movies, but real, ice-cold, heart-stopping, bone-shaking, mind-numbing evil. Its presence was debilitating. His home was his castle until the first encounter. After that, there was no escaping the evil that stalked him and sucked him in. That type of evil can follow and track you down wherever you may be. There's no hiding from it. It can pervade the bricks and mortar of your home and wait for you to be at your weakest before it crept inside your mind and saturated your soul. It could worm its way into your bones and infect your being. There's no escaping evil once it set its sights on you. No matter how strong you are, it will get you in the end. He had eluded its grip for so long; he thought it might have set its sights on someone else and forgotten about him. Chance would be a fine thing. Evil had come knocking on his door to remind him of the debt he owed. He had danced with the devil for a while and reached the highs evil could take him to, but those highs came at a price and it seemed the time to pay was near. He thought time had saved him by blurring the memories of those involved. Most of them were dead now, burning in hell … where they belonged. *Why now?* he wondered. Why were they raking up the past and risking exposure? They had dabbled with the dark side and got away with it, hadn't they? Why rake it all up now? Was he being paranoid or was his past coming back to make him pay? His bones ached, and he didn't want to play that game again, not even for a moment.

He felt old and tired, too tired to run and hide, too tired to fight or complain. There was no point in praying. God had forsaken him decades ago. His faith and position as a priest were nothing but a sham. He was a shaman among men; a wolf in lamb's clothing, but now the rest of the pack were coming to bring him to task. Maybe he could reason with them, explain himself, the reasons why he'd made the choices he had. His path had taken him from one extreme to the other.

He morphed from being a shepherd tending his sheep, to a predator feeding on them. At some point, the dark pleasures stopped feeling as magical as they once had. The darkness became too dark; fear and terror haunted his imagination night and day. He'd seen things no man should see; heard things no man should hear; and the memories were like photographs on his mind. They never blurred or faded. Innocent faces looked at him in his dreams, asking why they'd done those things to them and he couldn't answer them. They asked what they'd done to be chosen for such a terrible thing. Why did it have to happen to them? Only God knew the answer to that question, and he couldn't hear him anymore. He tried to recover his faith, his belief in God, but the darkness sucked him back like a shark dragging its prey beneath the waves. The realm of Gods and demons was fantasy to most, but he knew better. Heaven and hell were concepts thought up by tortured minds trying to control the masses, yet no one could deny that good and evil coexist on planet Earth. The constant daily struggle between light and dark was exhausting, and years ago when it all began, he almost gave up. That was until the day he met Don Shipley, the man who changed his mind about everything.

Chapter 22

Bob Dewhurst closed the ambulance doors, and the vehicle sped away, sirens blaring. The traffic was light, and it was out of sight in minutes. Uniformed officers were knocking on doors and taking brief statements from neighbours. Harry Rankin was working the scene inside the flats. The crime looked to be an overwhelming assault carried out at lightning speed on the doorstep of the victim's home. There were no eyewitnesses, so the search for forensic evidence was vital. The slightest thing could help.

Bob looked down London Road, towards the bridge and the railway station. There was a pedestrian crossing a few metres away. The camera footage could be vital. The road was jammed with boat traffic as an Irish ferry had just docked and unloaded. The traffic lights on the bridge became less than coordinated. A hundred metres from the junction, Alan's BMW pulled into the car park behind the Boston pub. A group of nosey teenagers were gathering in front of the Craig-y-Wylan chip shop on the next block. Lockdown had little effect on their pack mentality. The chippy was closed, but it didn't stop them hanging around outside. It was their hangout, open or closed. Alan and Kim came into view and were inundated by questions from the youngsters as they walked by. Their unwillingness to answer their questions resulted in a barrage of abuse, mostly aimed at Alan and his sexuality, while Kim's desire to participate in anal sex was also questioned. Bob heard the barracking and summoned a couple of constables to move the teenagers on. They received a similar response.

'Everything okay?' Bob asked as they approached.

'Apparently, I'm a bender,' Alan said, greeting Bob. 'Although I don't feel very bendy.'

'Nor me. I struggle to bend my knees nowadays,' Bob replied. 'I can't touch my toes anymore.'

'I can if I sit down,' Alan said.

'Count yourself lucky,' Bob said. He turned to Kim. 'What did they say to you?'

'Nothing that could be broadcast before nine o'clock,' Kim said. 'A very vivid imagination, if not a little disturbing.'

'What have you got so far?' Alan asked.

'Edward Speers. A thirty-one-year-old male, attacked on his doorstep probably with a hammer,' Bob said. 'There are two blows to his face, one above the eyebrow and one to the cheekbone. Both look bad to me. He was bleeding from the ears. The paramedics said he had depressed fractures and needed immediate surgery if he had any chance at all.'

'Edward Speers doesn't ring a bell. Who is he?' Alan asked.

'He's never been of interest to us, has no criminal record to speak of. The reason I called you, is his next-door neighbour mentioned Luca Bay.'

'In what context?'

'Edward Speers is godfather to Luca Bay's children. Apparently, Luca was a regular visitor to the flats,' Bob explained.

'The neighbours are aware of his murder?' Alan asked.

'Yes. That's why she mentioned it,' Bob said. 'She was fishing for gossip. That aside, he is mad on photography, has no connection to anything illegal, works on the railway, and has the odd pint in the Boston on his way home after his shifts. He called in at the chippy most nights. His neighbours say he's a normal guy and can't do enough for people. He's not the type of man people attack on the doorstep with a hammer.'

'So, you think his attack is connected to Luca Bay's murder?' Alan asked.

'If it isn't, it's a huge coincidence,' Bob said.

'I agree,' Kim said. 'This isn't random.'

'Get a warrant and search the place,' Alan said. 'If we find anything incriminating, it needs to be legit. Put someone on him at the hospital in case the attacker fancies a go at finishing the job. I've got a funny feeling about this.'

****

Cristy walked into the house and went straight upstairs. She could hear her mother following. Her hands were shaking, and her knees felt weak, but she was determined to remain in control. Myra walked into her bedroom and held her without speaking a word. They stayed like that until it felt okay to let go. Cristy felt stronger for it.

'I'm sorry about your tyres, Mam.' Cristy sniffled.

'You didn't burst them. That arsehole did it. Don't you go worrying about what that arsehole uploaded,' Myra said, holding her face. 'You weren't doing anything everybody else hasn't done at some point in their lives. We've all had sex.' Myra thought for a moment. 'You wouldn't be here otherwise.'

'Good point.'

'Everyone has sex, no matter what anyone says,' Myra said, nodding.

'Maybe not as publicly, Mam,' Cristy said, trying to lift her mood.

'Granted, we haven't all filmed it, but everyone has had sex at some time. No one in this house will judge you, nor will your family and friends.' She held her again. 'Not your real friends anyway. Let's go and have a cup of coffee,' she said.

'That's your answer to everything,' Cristy said. She hung her coat up and looked in the mirror. Her eyes were red from crying and she dabbed a little foundation underneath them. 'Come on then. Let's go and see what the men of the house have got to say.'

When they walked into the living room, Rowan was sitting on the armchair next to the door. He reached for her but Cristy moved away from his touch. Her dad tried to hold her gaze but couldn't. Phil was sitting on the settee, checking his phone, pretending to be distracted.

'Let's get one thing straight,' Cristy said. 'I'm sorry you had to see me in those videos like that. I know you're embarrassed for me, especially you, Dad. No father wants to see his daughter like that, nor does a boyfriend want to see his girlfriend having sex with another man. I understand how you're feeling and I'm sorry this has happened.'

'You don't need to apologise to me,' Rowan said, although his eyes said something else. There was pity in them. Pity and contempt. 'I told you when I first saw them, it was a long time ago and it doesn't affect us as a couple.'

'That is a lovely thing to say, but we both know it's total bullshit,' Cristy said. She touched his cheek with her fingers. 'No one could watch their partner having sex with someone else and not be revolted by it. You wouldn't be normal if you weren't angry with me.' Rowan looked away. He couldn't deny how angry he was. There wasn't a word for how he felt. 'I was in a relationship with Jon Price when he filmed those videos. The relationship was quite normal at that time and I had no reason to suspect he was filming us having sex, so I can't take your embarrassment away but I can tell you that no one is more embarrassed than I am.' She looked at them all, one at a time. 'Now, I don't want to hear another word said about the videos or that man again.' No one challenged her. Phil looked at Rowan and they exchanged a silent message. 'Am I making myself clear?' she asked. Everyone nodded. 'I will not let our lives be tainted by that bastard. I'm prepared to get on with my life and I want you all to as well.'

'Well said,' Myra said, nodding. 'I'll put the kettle on.'

☐

Chapter 23

Melanie Brooks was distraught. Her supervisor had called to tell her she needed to go into work for a chat about what had happened. They knew she'd had issues with her mental health since having her children. She said they were concerned about her welfare. That was a lie. They'd been looking for a reason to lay-off staff since lockdown was mentioned. This was the opportunity they needed to get rid of her and her wage burden. COVID-19 was on the march, and jobs on the island were at a minimum. The tourist trade was non-existent, and if she lost her job, she wouldn't get another while the holiday makers were banned from Wales. There were none.

The police were going to recommend she was prosecuted. That would make getting a job even harder. If she had a criminal record, she would have no chance at all. Not that Jon was concerned. He wasn't answering his mobile. She was beginning to think Jon Price had taken her for a ride. She wanted to speak to him face to face. He'd taken advantage of her feelings for him, feelings that she couldn't deny. Yes, he was a rogue, but she loved him. Their relationship had blossomed through their correspondence, and absence had truly made her heart grow fonder. She'd fallen for him hook, line, and sinker.

She drove to his house and parked outside the gates. It was getting dark when she arrived, and a security light illuminated the intercom as she approached. She pressed the button and waited. The butterflies in her stomach had turned into elephants. She felt like a love-struck teenager, which was madness. Jon Price had a hold on her, which she wasn't comfortable with. It left her feeling incredibly vulnerable. The intercom buzzed.

'Melanie Brooks has got the looks. Her big ass is first class and I'm a poet and don't know it,' Price said, his voice slurring. 'What a lovely surprise.'

'Are you drunk?' she asked.

'I wouldn't say drunk,' he said. 'Totally fucking hammered is more like what I am.'

'Have you been drinking all day?'

'Melanie. I've been in jail for seven years and now I'm not, so I'm relaxing at home.' He hiccuped. 'What do you want?'

'I need to talk to you,' Melanie said. She was angry but kept it in check.

'Now is not a great time for me.'

'Open the gates. The police have had me in the cells for hours. They might charge me for uploading the videos.' She waited for him to show some concern, but he just chuckled. 'It's not funny, Jon. I could lose my job. At least let me in so we can talk about it. You need to help me.'

'Stop whining,' Price said. The gates whirred into motion. 'Come in. Quickly before I change my mind.'

Melanie walked between the gates and jogged up the drive. The front door was open, and she stepped inside and closed it behind her. She felt excited to be in his house, but anxious too. Music drifted to her from upstairs. He was listening to Snap. They had a mutual love of nineties dance songs, which they talked about endlessly in their letters. He'd been so different in those letters. She felt that she'd made contact with the real Jon Price. People said she was deluded, that he was intrinsically bad, but she felt he was a gentle and loving man, not the violent thug everyone said he was. They didn't know him like she did.

'Jon?' she called. She didn't want to walk around his home uninvited. 'Where are you?'

'Upstairs,' he shouted. 'Come up.'

Melanie climbed the stairs. The living room was a mezzanine structure overlooking the hallway below. The far wall was glass from floor to ceiling, giving a panoramic view of the bay. Plasma screens dominated the walls. Most of them were showing mixed martial arts fights, the others were playing music videos with the volume turned down. The floor was grey laminate, and a huge L-shaped settee was the dominant piece of furniture in the room. Sheepskin rugs and goat hides covered most of the floor. Jon was sprawled between two females, who looked to be late teens at best. Both were half-dressed and appeared to be unconscious. He looked at Melanie and smiled.

'This is Pinky and this one is Perky,' he said, grinning. 'They're just hanging out for a while.'

'What is going on, Jon?' Melanie asked. She felt like she'd been kicked in the stomach.

'Like I just said, I'm hanging out with friends.'

'They're young enough to be your daughters,' Melanie said, shaking her head. 'Did the other night mean anything to you?'

'Don't be so dramatic. I'm catching up on seven years of being in an eight by six concrete box surrounded by other men, Mel. What's your problem?' He sat forward and lit a cigarette. 'A man needs to do what a man needs to do. I'm not getting married to them.'

'Were all those things you said in your letters just lies? I thought you wanted to make a go of it when you got out?' Melanie said. She felt stupid. Price drew on his cigarette and made smoke rings as he exhaled.

'You're making a big deal out of nothing. It's just a fuck.'

'You said you wanted to settle down.'

'I do at some point, just not tonight.'

'I feel like you've been stringing me along.'

'I'm just enjoying my freedom. It's been a long time coming,' Price said, irritated. He shrugged and frowned. 'And if I'm honest, the other night was more necessity than anything else.'

'A necessity,' she asked. 'What does that mean?'

'I really needed to unload.'

'Oh my God, that's disgusting,' Melanie recoiled. She felt hurt. Shocked that he could be so blunt. 'Why would you say such a thing?'

'Come on, Mel. You've been teasing me for years in your letters and texts, so when I got out, of course I came to your house and took what was on offer.'

'Took what was on offer?' she repeated, angrily. 'You make it sound like it was nothing!'

'You were gagging for it, don't lie,' Price said, laughing.

'I was pleased to see you out of prison.' Melanie shook her head. 'I don't know why you're being like this.'

'It was a bit disappointing to be truthful.' Price shrugged.

'What was?'

'You're a bit chubbier than you look when you're dressed.'

'Oh my God,' Melanie mumbled to herself. 'I don't believe this.'

'My mum always said clothes hide a multitude of sins and she was right. You look much better with your clothes on.' He gestured to the sleeping girls. 'Take these two as an example. Everything is tight and pert and where it should be. There's no low hanging fruit, if you know what I mean.' He chuckled. 'They haven't had kids yet. That's what does the damage.' He stubbed out his cigarette. 'You've got two, haven't you?' he asked.

'You know I have,' Melanie mumbled. She wanted to walk away but couldn't. It was difficult to attribute his words with the man she'd corresponded with for so long. His words were cruel and stung. 'Chloe and Corrin, remember? You asked how they were in all your letters.'

'Yes. I remember now. They have different dads, don't they?' he said, shaking his head. 'You give it away far too easily.'

'What?' she asked, stunned.

'I shouldn't complain. When you haven't had a shag for seven years, any port in a storm. I was grateful at the time but don't read too much into it. We're not dating or anything.'

'I can't believe you're saying that,' Melanie said, filling up. 'I thought we had something. You were using me all along.'

'Are you still here?' Price said. His eyes were piercing and cold. 'I think you should fuck off before you bore me to death.' He pointed behind her. 'The stairs are there. You know the way out.'

'Don't worry. I'll go and leave you with your little slappers,' Melanie said, feeling anger rising. She reached the top of the stairs. 'And you're right about the other night. I've never been so disappointed in all my life.'

'Really?' Price frowned. Anger flashed behind his eyes.

'I've had a sneeze that lasted longer than you did. Those young girls are young and won't know the difference between you and a decent fuck yet.'

Price reached for the ashtray and hurled it at her, but his aim was off, and it shattered against the wall. Fag stubs, glass, and ash exploded across the wall. He stood up and staggered towards her. His expression was a mask of hate. Melanie saw the anger in his eyes and bolted down the stairs. She could hear him clattering across the living room after her. He bellowed a stream of insults after her, but she was through the door and down the driveway before he reached the stairs. She could hear him swearing like a demon. The security lights came on and illuminated the front lawn. She ran as fast as she could, desperate to be in her car driving home, away from him. Tears ran down her cheeks. She'd been a fool, and she knew it. Halfway down the drive, she heard the gates whirring into life and her heart stopped a beat as she realised they were closing. There was no way she could scale the walls, and she stopped and dropped to her knees. Price started to laugh like a man possessed as he walked across the lawn towards her.

Chapter 24

Alan arrived home at the bungalow. The lights were on in the living room and the curtains were open, which meant the dogs were able to see him. Henry, the aging Jack Russell, was trying to compete with Gemma, the much younger shepherd-cross, for window space. They scratched at the patio doors on hind legs, barking and salivating, then they did a full circuit of the hallway before returning to the same spot to start again. It was the same routine every night. Alan wondered who was at home. His eldest son Kris was loved up with his new girlfriend in their new house, the youngest, Jack, was in Vietnam exploring, so he guessed it was Dan. Dan called in regularly on his way home from work in Bangor to make sure the dogs were fed. It didn't seem that long ago his ex-wife Kath and the boys were living there with him, although it was actually thirteen years since she'd left. He still felt her loss like a dagger through the heart. The pain was dulled by time, but ever present. He opened the door and picked up his shopping from the Spar in Trearddur Bay. Two bottles of McGuigan's black label and a Cumberland pie, which would take twenty-minutes in the oven. It was his go-to tea.

Dan opened the door before he reached it. The dogs ran out and mobbed him. Alan stumbled over Henry but managed to hold on to the bag. He ushered the excited animals inside and felt relieved to be home. The bungalow felt like a deserted ship sometimes, but it was his ship, and he was the skipper. Dan gave him a hug, and they went into the kitchen. Alan opened the sliding doors, and the dogs hurtled off into the darkness of the farmer's fields for their daily run. They would return muddy and exhausted when they were ready. Dan had already filled their bowls with food and fresh water, which saved him a job.

'I heard Jon Price and his friends are back in town,' Dan said. 'I guessed you might be late home.'

'That's very perceptive of you,' Alan joked. 'You should have been a detective.'

'One policeman in the family is enough,' Dan said. 'How did they get out so soon?'

'You can blame COVID-19 for that. The prisons are overcrowded, and the virus will wreak havoc. They had to let some inmates out early,' Alan said. He shook his head. 'Clearly, whoever decided Price was eligible for release is a complete imbecile and has no concept of who constitutes a danger to society. Jon Price and his type are far more dangerous than a virus.'

'I heard Eddie Speers was attacked,' Dan said. He made himself a coffee as he spoke.

'News travels fast,' Alan said.

'What happened?'

'We don't know. He was attacked on his doorstep, probably with a hammer.'

'He's an all right guy. Can't see why anyone would want to hurt him.'

'Do you know him?' Alan asked, pouring himself a whisky. He opened a bottle of red to allow it to breathe. The whisky would help him to unwind and the red wine would accompany his meal. It was a civilised concept which enabled people to drink without the guilt.

'Sort of,' Dan said. 'He's a friend of a friend. I've met him a few times at weddings and christenings and the like. He's big into photography, very quiet and isn't into drugs. In fact, he isn't into much but his cameras. I can't see why Price would have a problem with him.'

'Who says he has?' Alan asked, frowning.

'I'm putting two and two together,' Dan said. 'Price gets out and all kinds of trouble begins in town.'

'What are people saying?'

'What they see on the Internet. First, Luca Bay is killed, then Eddie is attacked' – Dan paused to sip his brew – 'Those two are best buddies.'

'We're pretty sure Bay was dealing,' Alan said.

'I heard as much,' Dan said, sipping his coffee. 'People are gossiping about Price uploading revenge porn to Facebook.' Alan nodded and let him talk. Hearing what was being said by the public helped put things in perspective. 'I saw the videos of his ex-girlfriend, Cristy Dennis.'

'That was cruel.'

'Cruel doesn't touch it. That is brutal. She must be going ape-shit.'

'She's being looked after. He won't get away with it,' Alan said.

'I bet Rowan's up for killing him.'

'Who's Rowan?' Alan frowned.

'Keep up, Dad. Cristy's current fella,' Dan said. 'He's a roofer. He plays rugby for Holyhead. Her brother does too. Price will have his hands full with the rugby lads.'

'I'm not so sure Price thinks like that.'

'He should do. I've seen them when they're out on the town. They're nuts. I saw them turd-tapping in the Blossoms once. It put me off playing rugby.'

'I imagine it did,' Alan said, sipping his Scotch.

'They would give Price and his goons a run for their money,' Dan said.

'I wouldn't be so sure.'

'They're all big guys, Dad.'

'Maybe so and I'm sure that helps when they're playing rugby,' Alan said, shaking his head. 'The problem is one group is good at sports and drinking games and the other group has people killed and makes them disappear. Men like Price don't square up to people.'

'I suppose you're right,' Dan said.

'Being able to drink a pint of spirits from the top shelf in one go doesn't arm you to take on dangerous criminals, unfortunately. They're a bit more subtle.'

'I suppose not.'

'They're underhand and you can't fight what you can't see. You can ask Luca Bay and Edward Speers how it feels.'

'Okay. I get the point.'

'I doubt if their ability to down a pint in one gulp would have helped then.' Alan emptied his glass and refilled it. 'Have you heard anything about Price being involved?' Alan asked.

'No.' Dan shook his head. 'Rumours are rife. Everyone wants someone to knock Price off his perch. You know how it is.'

'I do,' Alan said. He nodded and sipped the fiery liquid. 'Someone will eventually. I'm worried what happens between now and then.'

Chapter 25

Col Gallagher was on his way into work on the early shift when he heard the report about an abandoned vehicle on the comms. It made him question his interview technique. He headed straight for Porth Dafarch beach. When he arrived, a marked patrol car was parked on the hill facing down the slope. He pulled behind it, taking in the scene. A feeling of anxiousness laid heavy in his guts. Self-doubt was creeping through his veins.

'Has the owner been confirmed?' he asked, climbing out. A uniformed officer nodded. 'Who found it?'

'The taxi driver who reported it was on his way to the Trearddur Bay Hotel to pick up a fare to the early ferry. He was running late, so he didn't stop but called it in straightaway. We got here at six-fifteen and found it like this.'

The red Mini was parked on the grass verge, lights on and driver's door open. The keys were in the ignition and music was playing on the radio. Col looked towards a stile which breached the wall into the fields beyond. The fields bled onto the gorse-covered headlands above Porth Dafarch. Steep cliffs ran along the coastline to Porth-y-Post.

'Have you checked the headland?' Col asked.

'We've done a quick scout along the cliffs, but it's too dark to see much further than the edge. Once we've got daylight and more officers, we'll do a thorough search along the coast.'

'Okay,' Col said, feeling concerned. 'Have the lifeboat been contacted?'

'Yes. They're out there already.'

'It's rough out there,' Col said. He called the station on the comms. Bob Dewhurst was running the early shift. 'Morning, Bob.'

'Morning,' Bob said. 'Any progress?'

'The abandoned vehicle belongs to Melanie Brooks, Vulcan Street, Holyhead,' Col confirmed. 'The lifeboat is out there, but we need officers to search along the headland. It doesn't look good.'

'Melanie Brooks?' Bob said. 'Why does her name ring a bell?'

'I interviewed her yesterday regarding the Price videos,' Col replied, feeling a twinge of guilt. He wondered if he'd pushed her too far. 'She uploaded them on his behalf.'

'Jon Price. I keep hearing his name. Why does it stick in my throat so much?' Bob asked.

'Because he's an arsehole and you hate him,' Col said.

'That's true. We've got eyes on his house, haven't we?' Bob said. 'I'll ask them if there's anything to report from last night.'

Chapter 26

Father Creegan woke up in a cold sweat. His nightmares were becoming increasingly disturbing. It was as if the victims were haunting his sleep. He could see their faces clearly now, whereas they'd been blurred for decades. It was as if he was there among the writhing mass of bodies, each one inflicting pain on the next, all overseen and encouraged by him. His facial features were the only ones he couldn't distinguish, yet he knew it was him. The eyes were like black jewels set against his alabaster skin. An aura of evil surrounded him like a mist. The malevolence radiated from him like heat from the sun; the closer to it, the more deadly it became. Each time he looked at him, his gaze zeroed in on him. The intensity becoming more powerful.

The dreams had started a week before the visitor arrived with a shotgun in his hand. That was no coincidence. A feeling of dread had descended on him like a cloud that wouldn't shift. He couldn't escape the sense of despair he was feeling.

His bones ached as he dragged himself from his bed and headed for the shower. The water was boiling hot and soothed his aging joints for a while. He washed himself with simple soap and brushed his teeth with a Braun. There was a bitter taste in his mouth, which he couldn't shift no matter how many times he cleaned them. He dressed in clean clothes and donned his dog collar. His church was where he needed to be. Maybe God would be there today. Maybe he would intervene on his behalf. Maybe he would realise what he had done, had to be done. Maybe he would realise he'd had no choices in the decisions he'd made. Maybe he would forgive him before they came for him because they surely would and surely, it would be soon. Maybe God didn't give a shit what happened to him.

Creegan made toast and spread butter and Marmite on it. He washed it down with weak tea and half a glass of orange juice. It was just after nine o'clock and the daylight was weak and dull. The temperature was barely above freezing. He pulled on walking boots and a long wax jacket, which protected him from the Anglesey winds. It felt warm and comfortable when he zipped it up and buttoned it down. Buttons and a zip, double protection. He needed all the protection he could find.

The drive to the church was non-eventful. He parked up at the rear and watched the rain running down the windscreen. Leaves blew across the car park like tumbleweed in the desert. He didn't want to open the door and leave the comfort of the car, yet the sanctuary of the church called to him as it hadn't done for years. Something inside him yearned to feel that peace of mind once again. He opened the door and pulled up his collar against the wind. Head down, he ran to the arched wooden doors. He unlocked them with a key that was as old as he was; the mortice snapped back with an audible crack. The hinges creaked as he pushed them open and stepped inside. A gust of wind howled around the building. It whistled through the belltower above him as he struggled to close the door. His foot touched something on the bristle mat. He looked down and saw a large brown envelope. A bolt of fear and anticipation streaked through him. He picked it up and turned it over. It was addressed in neat handwriting to Father Patrick Creegan. He recognised the handwriting immediately. It was his. He'd found him. Things were worse than he thought. He opened the envelope and pulled out the contents. Photographs. They were old and black and white. He flicked through them. His knees folded, and he leant against the doors. Tears streamed from his eyes and his vision blurred as he looked at each one in turn. Each one took him back to a time he needed to forget. Each image was more depraved, and the memories clambered for space to be seen. He closed his eyes to escape the horror, but it followed him into the darkness of his mind, the images as clear as if he was seeing them for the first time, first-hand. Father Creegan curled up on the mat with his knees to his chest and cried the tears of the damned and begged forgiveness from a god he didn't believe in.

Chapter 27

Richard Lewis was searching through the information DS Ian Osbourne had gathered during his cold case review. The files were extensive, too vast for a single brain to analyse in detail. He was skimming over files looking for something which caught his eye, then he would read further and gauge if there was any substance to it. One thing was linked to another like the branches of a spider's web. The leads spread in all directions, but most were dead ends. To compound issues, the years had ticked by and the people Osbourne wanted to speak to had moved on or died or their memories were jumbled or non-existent in some cases. According to Osbourne's notes, there was a lot of convenient memory loss. The sad fact was the speculation and accusations could not be corroborated. Don Shipley had gathered extensive notes from his investigations but couldn't substantiate them.

It appeared some of the people accused simply pointed their fingers at others, muddying the waters and making it impossible to see things clearly. Deflection had become a martial art. Many of the avenues of investigation had been quashed by powerful people. There was no appetite for a public enquiry into the systematic sexual abuse of minors. Nobody wanted to believe it could happen in a civilised society. Some accusations were met with counter allegations of a witch hunt being carried out by an ex-copper, Don Shipley, who had an axe to grind against the establishment that destroyed his career. Don Shipley was shunned as a pariah across North Wales police forces. No one was listening to him anymore. He was deemed a troublemaker who couldn't be trusted. The paranoia of child sex abuse at the time was clear in the text and interviews, as were the massive underfunding and lack of support given to the original investigation into the disappearance of the teenagers. On the face of it, the enquiry scraped the surface but didn't delve much deeper than that. It went through the motions but didn't really take the accusations of child abuse seriously.

At the back of his mind was his conversation with the Liverpool DS, Alec Ramsay. He had sounded excited by a call from a Welsh detective investigating the suicide of a John Doe in the home of a priest on Anglesey. Father Patrick Creegan. Richard had cast his mind back but couldn't put his finger on why Creegan's name was vaguely familiar. The name rang bells in his mind, but he couldn't for the life of him place it. He'd been mulling it over for days. Then he stumbled across an article which Osbourne had saved into a folder named, 'press coverage'. He read through it three times before ringing the DI. Things he'd forgotten had resurfaced and he needed to share them. He took off his glasses and called Alan.

'Morning, Richard,' Alan said. He was already at his desk. His head was foggy from the after-effects of alcohol. 'What can I do for you?'

'Have you got ten minutes?' Richard asked. 'I've come across some information that you need to hear. It could wait, but it shouldn't.'

'You sound excited,' Alan said. The fact he hadn't said hello struck a chord. 'Get the coffees in. I'm in my office.'

'I'll be there in five minutes,' Richard said, hanging up.

Alan knocked on the glass partition to get Kim's attention. She waved and picked up her cup before walking to the coffee machine and refilling it. She made one for Alan and headed into his office, just as Richard arrived.

'Is that for the boss?' Richard asked.

'Yes.'

'Good. Saves me a job.' He plonked his laptop on Alan's desk and sat down, sliding the chair noisily beneath him.

'Did you forget the coffee?' Alan asked.

'I've brought you one,' Kim said, sitting down.

'Go to the top of the class,' Alan said. 'Richard is excited about something.'

'I am,' Richard agreed. 'Wait until you hear this.'

'I'm all ears,' Alan said. 'Has this come from Alec Ramsay?'

'Yes. He sent me the files compiled by Ian Osbourne. He did a good job on the cold case, but he got nowhere with it,' Richard explained. 'Obviously, it began with the disappearance of the teenagers, Birley and Deeks, but it soon became embroiled in the wider investigation into paedophile networks. Alec Ramsay said this is why the cold case was quashed and that once the case was shelved, Osbourne was railroaded into a desk job before he died in a car crash. But that's another story.' Richard didn't speculate about the crash. 'There was no evidence about what happened to Birley and Deeks, so he focused his investigation on Don Shipley and the allegations he made. The fallout he caused is remarkable. Osbourne believed somewhere in his notes was a clue to what happened to the missing boys. We know they might have been at Bangor station and we know the jacket was recovered from lost property there, which backs up that theory. Osbourne focused on the fact that Shipley was convinced the paedophile ring was centred in Bangor. Coincidence or not it had to be looked at in the search for the teenagers.' Richard shrugged as if it made perfect sense.

'Okay,' Alan said. 'What did you find that has got you in such a tiz?'

'In among all the files are some newspaper cuttings,' Richard began. 'They start with a feel-good news piece about an aid worker priest who went to help the victims of the earthquake in Haiti in twenty-ten.'

'A priest?' Alan said, slurping his coffee. 'Our priest?'

'Yes. Father Creegan. Bear with me. The earthquake happened in January that year, and the priest had gone as part of an international relief team. The organisation was loosely affiliated to the Red Cross. Creegan went with over sixty volunteers in March of the same year. According to the article, six weeks later, twenty-two of them were deported following allegations of the sexual exploitation of local females, some as young as thirteen.'

'They were paying them for sex,' Kim said, nodding. 'I remember that on the news.'

'Me too.' Richard nodded. 'The Red Cross distanced itself from all foreign aid workers who had not been vetted by them. It became clear that other organisations were not vetting references and had inadvertently hired paedophiles and sex offenders, who took advantage of the vulnerable victims of the disaster.'

'Not the first time that's happened,' Alan said. 'It's a disgrace.'

'Quite, and the Haitians thought so too,' Richard said. 'The backlash in Haiti was violent. A minibus full of aid workers was attacked by a mob of locals and the men on-board beheaded. All except one. A priest.'

'I remember that incident, but I don't remember a survivor,' Alan said.

'No one knew he'd survived until after the news coverage had waned.' Richard showed them the article. 'According to this, the locals liked him and let him leave. They said he'd been nothing but kind to people. Creegan returned home to his native Wales and fell into obscurity and the humdrum life of a clergyman. That was until a small group went on a fishing trip from Beaumaris. Two priests and a local scout leader hired the boat. The boat capsized off Puffin Island, apparently swamped by a freak wave. Two of them died, their bodies were never recovered. A sole survivor was pulled from the sea that day. The same man who had survived the outrage in Haiti.'

'Father Creegan, no doubt?'

'Exactly. His luck was still unnoticed until he was part of a walking group who attempted a sponsored hike along the summits of Snowdonia, which was to take three days and involved them camping on the mountains for three nights. Two of the three men died in a fall when an anchor rope sheared, and they fell to their deaths from Crib Goch. The third man had to sleep exposed to the elements that night and made it down the next day, suffering from shock and hypothermia and spent a week in the ICU at Ysbyty Gwynedd. This time, his uncanny ability to survive disaster was picked up and covered in several newspapers. It was said he had a guardian angel.' Richard showed them the article. The name jumped off the page. 'Father Patrick Creegan, the luckiest priest in the UK,' the headline read. 'His story was covered in several of the red-tops.'

'I remember this now you've reminded me,' Alan said. 'There was never a hint of foul play.'

'Nothing. Creegan was praised in the coverage.'

Alan remembered reading the articles about him, but the stories had been filed in the deepest recesses of his mind for decades.

'Creegan has been very lucky,' Alan said. Alan believed there were two types of luck. Good luck and bad luck. 'Some people make their own luck, but some things have nothing to do with luck. Some things can be manipulated to appear to be lucky.'

'What do you think?' Kim asked.

'It looks like Father Creegan has avoided death a few times over the years,' Alan said. The hairs on the back of his neck stood on end as he read on about the Anglesey priest. 'My first question is, who were the men that drowned at sea and never came down the mountain?'

'I knew you were going to ask that,' Richard said. He turned his laptop around to face them. 'I have their names and details right here.'

'Good, because their relatives may be pissed off Creegan survived when their family member didn't,' Alan said. 'We asked him numerous times if there could be anyone with a grudge. Surely the fact four men died in his company would spring to mind?'

Chapter 28

The information from Alec Ramsay was split between two detective teams. Alan had a hunch the key to what happened to Ewan Birley and Chris Deeks was in there somewhere, and that it might lead them to Father Creegan's attacker. A detective constable was tasked with looking into the four men who died while in Father Creegan's company. It could be a coincidence that he was linked to two tragic accidents. Alan wanted to know as much as he could, so he could make his own mind up.

Kim was at her desk, following up on her emails. Her inbox was filling up. She opened one from a detective in charge of the evidence room at Chester. They processed and stored items from all over North Wales and Cheshire. The message was titled, 'Stolen Shotgun'. Kim read the report. The shotgun was stolen from a farmhouse in Llanberis, years prior. The text was a single line and very brief and requested a phone call for further details, which was unusual. She dialled the evidence storage facility and then entered the extension number listed.

'DS Salt,' the detective answered after a dozen rings. She sounded irritated, as if she'd been interrupted.

'This is DS Kim Davies from Holyhead MIT,' Kim said. 'I've received your email about a double-barrelled shotgun stolen in Llanberis. Can you give me the details?'

'That was quick,' Salt said. 'This shotgun must be top of your list today.' Kim could hear her typing on her keyboard. 'Let me pull up the details. Okay. The gun was recorded as stolen from a farmhouse near Padarn lake, three years ago. The make, model, and serial number match your weapon.'

'It was stolen three years ago?' Kim asked. 'Do you have a date for our files?'

'Fourteenth of January.'

'Thank you. Did you arrest anybody?'

'Yup. We arrested Tomas Adamik for the burglary last year.'

'Two years after the event?'

'He made a mistake selling some jewellery. He's of Polish origin and currently serving a three-year stretch in Wrexham. He was collared selling some ruby earrings to a jeweller in Llandudno, which were flagged by the insurance company. They were worth over ten-grand, apparently. We recovered some of the high-end stuff from the farm in a storage unit in Abergele, which he coughed to, but he denied taking the shotgun.'

'No one wants to be linked to a shotgun. Any leads on the weapon?' Kim asked.

'That's why I asked you to call me,' Salt said. 'Off the record. Adamik sold some of the antiques to a dealer from Bangor, Roger Pickford. He's got form.'

'What for?'

'You name it, he's been done for it. We quizzed him about the gun, but he denied handling it.'

'But?'

'He's a liar. His hands were shaking when we quizzed him about the shotgun. He did three months for handling the furniture, but he's been out for six months' – She paused – 'I read your query about the gun. It was used in a suicide, wasn't it?'

'Yes. It was a nasty incident. A priest was attacked and tied up during the process. It was four days before we found him,' Kim said. 'We're trying to identify the suicide victim, but there's nothing to go on. His DNA isn't in the system. The gun doesn't belong to the priest, it's the obvious place to start.'

'Speak to Roger Pickford,' Salt said. 'He's still in business in a shop unit near Bangor station. It's a cash-convertors set up, and he lives above it. Take my word for it. He's a snake. We didn't concentrate on the shotgun because it was insured, and we had the thief in the cells. Budget pressure calls the shots, if you'll pardon the pun. I'm sure you know the score. We were told to put it to bed.'

'We've all been there. Thanks for your help. We'll pay Pickford a visit.'

'You're welcome,' Salt said. 'Do me a favour and let me know what he says. I don't like that man.'

'I will do, no problem,' Kim said, smiling. 'There's nothing like a bit of irrational dislike. It's what makes us human.'

'I'll drink to that. Take care.'

Kim hung up and was about to inform Alan what had been said about the shotgun, when her phone rang. 'DS Davis,' she answered. She waved at Alan to get his attention. He gestured to the coffee pot and she nodded that she wanted one.

'Is that Kim?' a voice she recognised asked. It was Barry from the lifeboat station. Affectionately known locally as Barry Lobster.

'It is. Hello, Barry, what's up?'

'Bad news I'm afraid,' Barry said. 'We've just pulled a young woman out of the water near Rhoscolyn. She fits your description of Melanie Brooks.'

'Oh no,' Kim said, sighing. 'She's dead?'

'Oh yes. She's dead. You might want to take a good look at her, Kim.'

'Why?' Kim asked.

'She looks like she's been hit by a bus.'

'We found her car near the headland above Porth Dafarch. If she jumped from the headland and hit the rocks on the way down, I'd expect to see trauma.'

'I've lost count of how many jumpers I've pulled out of the water and not many of them undress before they jump, Kim,' Barry cautioned.

'She's undressed?'

'Down to her underwear,' Barry said. 'In my opinion, she was in bad shape before she entered the sea and there's another thing I'm not happy with.'

'Go on,' Kim said.

'Her body was floating off Penrhos Bay near the Lee caravan park.'

'And the significance of that is?' Kim asked, confused.

'If she went into the water near Porth Dafarch early this morning, she wouldn't have drifted that far with today's tide. She might be in Trearddur Bay at a push, but not that far around the coast.'

'What are you saying?'

'In my opinion, she went into the water much closer to where she was found.'

'Which is across the bay from where we found her car?' Kim said, nodding.

'Yes.'

'There's no way a current could have taken her body out there?' Kim asked.

'It's not an exact science, but in my humble opinion, not a chance,' Barry said. 'Sorry to be the bearer of bad news again.'

'No problem. Thanks for the call, Barry.' Alan approached her desk. 'You'd better sit down,' she said. 'They found Melanie Brooks, but she wasn't where she should be.'

Chapter 29

The MIT was in full flow; half of the detectives were out on the road, tracking down leads and interviewing people. Most interviews were being held virtually, but some were held indoors, using facemasks and social distancing. COVID-19 was making a difficult task harder. The information gathering was reaping useful information and building a picture which the investigation could use to move forward. It was gathering speed.

'The radio appeal on *Mon FM* has brought us two definite eyewitnesses who remember seeing a vehicle parked on the Tinto side of Penrhos, near the sand dunes,' Kim said. 'Both witnesses identify a dark coloured vehicle, possibly a Volvo or a Vauxhall Insignia. Unfortunately, neither saw the driver.'

'Another caller says he was walking his dog near the hospital and he saw a man walking towards the dunes, smoking a cigarette. He said the man was wearing a dark padded coat, gloves, and a woolly hat, but he didn't see a crowbar and he didn't see him walking back to the car park.' Alan pointed to the crime scene photographs. 'We recovered several cigarette butts and DNA may give us a hit but it's unlikely because of the sand and the rain.'

'Edward Speers hasn't regained consciousness,' Kim said. 'So, he can't help us at the moment. What we do know is Speers and Bay were attacked and left for dead. They were both originally from the Cemaes side of the island. There's a year between them, but they went to the same school in Bangor until they were sixteen. Speers went to sixth form college and further education, Bay failed his exams and dossed about for a few years. At some point, they both moved to Holyhead. Bay was married with two children and Edward Speers was godfather to both.' Images of the two men appeared on the screen. 'We know they were close friends, so they're connected. We're assuming their attacks are linked too, but we need to find out how. If we can find the answer to that, we can identify the motive and who attacked them.'

'Are we working on Jon Price being involved?' a detective asked.

'We're not taking anything off the table yet, but I think it would be a mistake to focus on Price alone.' Alan tapped the screen on the image of Luca Bay. 'Bay may have been working for Sutton but we're not certain and we know he worked for Price at the time he was arrested. Is there a connection?' Alan said, shrugging. 'That's what we need to find out.' Alan pointed to a digital image of the Anglesey coastline. 'Jon Price seems to be the linchpin in our investigations at present, including the death of a local mum, Melanie Brooks.' Alan looked around the gathering. The mood became sombre. 'At first glance, it looks to be a suicide, but we need to be thorough before we hand the evidence to the coroner. She leaves two children behind.' There was an uncomfortable silence. 'Melanie Brooks was pulled out of the water this morning off the coast near Rhoscolyn. Her car was found abandoned across the bay, above Porth Dafarch just after 6 a.m.' Most of the detectives in the room were familiar with the beaches, inlets, and coves. 'You can see the trauma she suffered, maybe as the result of jumping onto the rocks, but we'll keep an open mind for now.' Initial images of Melanie Brooks were shown, taken before she was loaded onto the vehicle that would take her body to Ysbyty Gwynedd for a post-mortem. Her face was disfigured, varying shades of purple, black, and blue merged into a sickening kaleidoscope of bruises.

'Melanie was a vulnerable adult with a history of suffering from depression and anxiety. She was arrested and interviewed yesterday by sergeants Col Gallagher and April Byfelt in regard to uploading revenge porn, featuring Jon Price and his ex-girlfriend Cristy Dennis,' he said, looking around the room. The nodding heads told him everyone was aware of the situation. 'She claimed Price coerced her to upload the videos while she was drunk and that he abused her feelings for him. She admitted uploading the content and was released pending a decision from the CPS.' Alan shrugged. 'It's a simple enough scenario. The interview was clearly upsetting for her, but I don't feel undue pressure was put on her. Col and April are experienced coppers. They don't beat about the bush, but they're competent interviewers.' The nodding heads told him the detectives agreed. 'We know she went to see Price later on in the evening at his home. This morning, her car was found here, at Porth Dafarch. The driver's door was open, engine running and music playing,' Alan said. 'We're assuming she left her vehicle, climbed over the stile here, crossed the field through the gorse onto the headland somewhere between Porth Dafarch and Porth-y-post.' He paused to look at the audience. 'She may have climbed down the cliffs or jumped into the water. Her injuries aren't consistent with her climbing down to the sea. It's unlikely. There was too much damage to her head and face. She didn't just slip into the water peacefully.' The images of her injuries appeared again. 'She's suffered severe trauma to the face and neck.'

'Do we know what killed her?'

'Not yet. We're waiting on the medical reports to tell us.'

'If those injures were inflicted before she went into the water, she may have been dead already,' Kim said.

'Which means someone else put her into the sea,' Alan said.

'So, she may have been murdered?'

'Yes. She may. Obviously, Price is the prime suspect,' Kim said.

'Price may be the obvious suspect, but we know she went to see him at nine o'clock last night,' Alan said. 'And we know she left in one piece.' A murmur ran through the room. 'Our dilemma is that we had surveillance on the Price residence, and she was seen leaving at ten-past four this morning. Very much alive.' An image came up on the screen. It was taken at a distance. 'It's taken from a few hundred metres by the surveillance team, but she looks to be unharmed. Her baseball cap and the umbrella obscure her face but there's no sign of blood or bruising. Essentially, what we have here is an image of her leaving Price's home uninjured.' Alan looked around the room. 'Any comments?'

'Are we sure it's her?'

'Good question,' Alan said. 'Here she is arriving. White Nike trainers, dark blue Levis tracksuit, baseball cap with ICON printed above the peak.' The image changed. 'This is her leaving just after four this morning, alive and well, carrying an umbrella because it's raining sideways.'

'The images are unclear, and we can't see her face,' Kim said, shaking her head. 'But they're evidence enough to make things difficult.' She pointed to the screen. 'We know they were corresponding while he was in prison, and we know he went to her house the night he was released. In her interview yesterday, she admitted they'd sex that night. Since then, he's been having female visitors at his home since he arrived there,' Kim said. 'Maybe being arrested disturbed her or maybe he's blown her out and she's heartbroken, left his house and thrown herself into the sea.' She shrugged. 'If she was in love with Price, slept with him on his release and then realised he's been entertaining other women at his house, she would be upset. She would be angry and maybe her mental health issues meant that she couldn't cope with the rejection?' Kim mused. Some of the detectives nodded their agreement. 'If I was a defence lawyer, that's what I would be saying, anyway,' she added. 'I don't think we have enough to question Price.'

'The pictures tell us she left his house unharmed. I can't see what we can do about it with what we have,' Richard said.

'The surveillance images do us more harm than good,' Alan said.

'Has he actually left his home since he got out?' a detective asked.

'Nope,' Kim said. 'He's had a delivery from Tesco and several young women coming and going, but apart from that, he hasn't moved out of there.'

'He must have CCTV in there,' Richard said.

'My thinking exactly,' Alan said. 'We need to get a warrant to bring him in and search the place.'

'On what grounds?' Kim asked, shaking her head. 'He hasn't moved since he got home. Technically, he hasn't done anything wrong. Melanie admitted uploading the porn videos and we have her on camera leaving in one piece.'

'Maybe, but we can speak to him about the Cristy Dennis videos,' Alan said. 'He might slip up, make a mistake, and give us something to apply leverage on a judge for a search warrant.'

'I'm not convinced,' Kim said. 'He's too smart. I don't see him agreeing to an interview in the first place.'

'Nor me,' Alan said. 'Ask Col Gallagher to come in, so we can go through what he had on Melanie Brooks. She said he coerced her, but she can't testify to that anymore. Let's see what he has in her statement. It might give us a way in.' Kim didn't look convinced. 'What are you thinking?'

'I'm thinking that I'm going to Bangor to find Roger Pickford and ask him about a shotgun.' she said. 'I'm sick to the back teeth of Jon Price. You don't need me here for now. I might as well do something useful.'

'That makes sense,' Alan agreed. 'Take Richard with you.'

Chapter 30

Cristy was lying on the settee, surfing Netflix for something to take her mind off reality for a few hours. Her phoned vibrated, and she replied to a text message from Rowan. He was checking in for the fourth time in an hour. The videos of her having sex with Jon Price had caused quite a stir on the Internet. Opinions were split. Most people were disgusted that someone could be humiliated in such a way but there were a few that had little or no sympathy. The camps were divided, and it appeared IQ levels had a direct impact on the type of response they gave. Rowan was trying his best to assure her that he wasn't swayed by the images and that he loved her very much. He was pragmatic about them, yet she knew deep down that they must have devastated him. She loved him, but her emotions were in a spin. Price had driven a wedge between them. She could feel it growing, forcing them apart, and she also knew that it was her pushing him away. Her barriers had come up. It was a self-defence response to feeling under siege. She was protecting her emotions by shutting them down, just as she had seven years ago. She loved Rowan, but she didn't need his sympathy. His fussing was because he adored her, but it was irritating her. It made her feel weak and unable to cope. She was coping, just about, and she needed support, not sympathy. She wanted a partner, not a nursemaid.

I'm fine. Stop mithering. Text me after work.

She reread the message and sent it. It was abrupt, but she needed him to back off. A knock on the front door interrupted her train of thought. The curtains were closed, so she couldn't see who it was. Her mum came out of the kitchen like a greyhound leaving the traps, brandishing a large stainless-steel ladle. Cristy was going to ask what she was doing with the ladle, but her mum was too quick.

'Mum, what are you doing?' Cristy asked. 'Are you going to spoon someone to death?'

Myra opened the door wide, holding the ladle at arms-length. Cristy caught a glimpse of a man wearing a mask and a baseball cap.

'Delivery for Cristy Dennis,' the man said. 'I'll leave them on the step,' he added, stepping back. Cristy stood up to get a clearer view of what was going on.

'Who are they from?' Myra asked, suspiciously.

'I don't know, doll,' the man said. 'I just deliver them.'

Cristy could see a bouquet of red roses on the step. Her mum picked them up and brought them inside. 'Is there a card on them?' Cristy asked. 'See who they're from.'

'There's a card in an envelope at the bottom there,' Myra said. 'It's got your name written on it.' Cristy took the card from the bouquet. She opened it and slid the card out.

I hope you enjoyed them. I bet it was a trip down memory lane. There are plenty more where they came from.

'What does that mean?'

'He's talking about the videos. It suggests he has more of them.'

'What? Are they from that bastard Price?' Myra said, shaking her head.

'Who else would write that?' Cristy said. 'Get rid of them.'

'I'll put them straight in the bin.' Myra walked towards the front door but stopped dead when someone knocked on it. 'What now?' she muttered. She opened the door. 'Yes?'

'Taxi for Cristy?' the man said.

'No one ordered a taxi from here,' Myra said.

'Is this Harbour View?' the driver asked.

'Yes, but we haven't ordered a taxi.'

'It's a hoax, Mum.'

'What?'

'Jon Price ordered it, no doubt,' Cristy said, sighing. Myra turned towards Cristy. Her eyes had filled with tears. She was trying to hold it together, but the barrage of harassment was relentless. 'Tell him it's a mistake.'

'I'm sorry,' Myra said. 'No one here phoned a taxi.'

'Oh. We've got a booking for Cristy Dennis from Harbour View going to Bangor hospital?' the driver said. 'Is it the wrong house?'

'No. It's the right house, but no one has ordered a taxi,' Myra said. 'I think someone is playing games. It's a hoax.'

'I'm terribly sorry to trouble you,' the driver said. 'I don't know why anyone would think that's funny. Silly buggers.'

Myra went outside and dumped the roses unceremoniously into the wheelie bin. The taxi drove away in a hurry. The driver was annoyed. She slammed the lid closed and stormed inside. 'I'm calling Col Gallagher. The useless dick-head has done nothing. Jon Price thinks he can do what he likes whenever he likes. Sending flowers here and ordering taxis. He needs to grow up, wanker.'

'Don't bother Col, Mum,' Cristy said. 'I'll call him later on after four.'

'Why wait?'

'Because he's a policeman and there are real crimes being committed. Jon Price is being childish like a kid who can't have his favourite toy. Col asked me to call and update him every day after four,' Cristy said. 'This is going to be like a game of chess. Price thinks he's clever bullying me, but he isn't. The police will collate all these incidents and send him back to jail.' Her mobile vibrated. The screen showed it was her brother Phil. 'Hello,' she said.

'Hello, Cristy?' It wasn't her brother's voice. A shiver ran down her spine.

'Yes.'

'This is Will Took. I work with your brother,' Will said. He sounded out of breath and panicked. 'Phil asked me to call you.'

'Why?' Cristy asked, her stomach tightened. 'What's happened?'

'Rowan's taken a tumble off the scaffold,' Will said. 'Phil's gone in the ambulance with him. I'm following them in the van. He asked me to call you and let you know.'

'Is he okay?' Cristy asked, holding her breath.

'No, Cristy,' Will said. 'We're working on the old Beach Hotel. He fell from the roof level, three floors up.'

'Oh my God,' Cristy said. 'What happened?'

'I don't know. I was on the other side of the building. He's in a bad way, Cristy,' Will said. 'They're taking him to Ysbyty Gwynedd.'

'I'll be there as soon as I can,' Cristy said. 'Thanks, Will.' She hung up and sat on the settee. Her hands were shaking.

'What the hell has happened?' Myra said.

'Rowan's fallen off a roof,' Cristy said, trying to remain calm. 'I need to get to the hospital.'

'Bloody hell. Is he okay?'

'No. Will Took said he's in a bad way.'

'Let me get my coat,' Myra said. 'I'll drive you there.'

'I need to put some clothes on,' Cristy said, running up the stairs. She struggled into a pair of jeans and sloppy jumper and pulled on her coat. Her UGG boots were hiding under the bed and she swore at them as she put them on. She ran down the stairs. 'I'm ready. Come on, let's go.'

They rushed out of the front door to Myra's car. 'No, no, no,' Myra shouted. 'Not again, you bastard!' All four tyres had been slashed. Cristy sat on the doorstep, her face frozen in shock. Her bottom lip quivered, like it did when she was a child. 'Cristy?' Myra said. 'What is it, love?'

'Taxi for Dennis to the hospital,' she said, shaking her head.

'What do you mean?'

'Don't you get it?'

'Get what?'

'He sent a taxi to our door to take me to the hospital,' Cristy said. 'Minutes before we got the call from Will.'

'Jesus no,' Myra said. The penny dropped. 'He did this. I don't know how, but he did this.'

Chapter 31

Pickford's emporium was a few hundred metres from Bangor station, situated on the bend at the end of the high street. The shop was situated on the ground floor of a three-storey Victorian terrace. It would have been a busy row of shops in prime position fifty-years ago. The terrace looked rundown and dated, and the only people passing were on the way to catch a train. All the big brand stores were ten minutes away, closer to the cathedral. Window shoppers didn't venture that far from the centre. There was a Chinese restaurant with dirty net curtains and a weather-beaten menu board. It looked like the type of restaurant where you wipe your feet on the way out. A fancy-dress shop displayed the most unconvincing costumes Kim had ever seen, and a cobbler was trying to survive, repairing things in a throwaway society. Next door was a greasy spoon café, which advertised a belly-buster breakfast and a pint of tea for £4.99. The window was steamed up with condensation and the smell of bacon tainted the air. The café was the only business open. The rest were closed by COVID-19.

Kim peered through the window. The shop was in darkness. The emporium was a mixture of museum and charity shop. Beyond the glass, a mannequin wearing a polka dot dress from decades ago was sitting in a red velvet armchair and dominated the window display. There was a red feather boa draped around the neck and a long cigarette holder balanced between plastic fingers. A shiny black bob framed its moulded features. The eyes were wide and seemed to look back at her. The ebony coffee table next to it was inlaid with quartz to make a chessboard. A set featuring characters from Roman mythology lined up against each other, ready to do battle. She recognised Zeus,

Apollo, and Cupid and the goddess Hera was the queen. The display was chaotic but littered with interesting items. Inside, the left wall displayed guitars and violins of every shape and size, acoustic, electric, and hybrids. On the right were ornamental swords, spears, axes, and an array of martial arts weapons. The back wall was covered with muskets, duelling pistols, and militaria of all sorts. Some were antiques, others purely decorative. A Thompson machinegun was fastened above the doorframe which appeared to lead to a storeroom at the rear. There was a *no entry* sign on the door. Kim was intrigued. A row of Welsh dressers carried a myriad of vases, tea sets, and porcelain statuettes. Some of it was probably worth something, the rest cheap imitations worth nothing.

'Is there anyone home?' Richard asked, pressing his nose to the glass.

'Just us ghosts,' Kim said.

'What?' Richard asked, confused. Kim smiled and shook her head. 'Can you see anyone?'

'Nope. The lights are off in the shop, but I can see lights on at the back,' Kim said. 'Have you tried the bell?'

'I have. No reply,' Richard said. 'Shall we have a look around the back?'

'Yes. These shops have accommodation above,' Kim said. They looked at the upper floors of neighbouring buildings. They had been converted to offices, bed-and-breakfasts, and bedsits for students. The rooms above the emporium didn't appear to be any of those things. 'There are lights on above the shop too.' Kim pointed to the first-floor windows. 'The detective I spoke to from evidence mentioned Pickford lived above his shop.' She looked down the alleyway which separated the terrace from an old cinema, which had been converted into a wine bar. Blackboards outside advertised pre-lockdown parties with half-priced shots.

'Everything has to go. The more you drink, the more you save,' Kim read. 'Make yourself sick so you can drink more. Is it any wonder they closed the pubs?'

'It's the *I'm all right, Jack*, state of mind. This is a student city, and the students think it only kills old people and they don't matter,' Richard said.

'Unless it's their grandparents.'

'Their grandparents don't live here.'

'True.' She moved away from the pavement. 'There must be a separate entrance to the flat above,' Kim said. She set off down the alleyway and Richard followed a few steps behind. The narrow alley was cobbled. There was an arched doorway on the left. The door was older than Kim and painted black. It was blistered and peeling. Kim tried the latch, and it opened. 'It's not locked. Pickford must be home.'

She stepped into an oblong shaped yard, piled high with old furniture and junk. Half a dozen rusted motorcycles leant against the rear wall. There were four sheds of different sizes, fastened with robust padlocks and bolts. 'There's the backdoor,' she said, pointing. They navigated their way through the clutter to the rear porch. A security light came on as they approached. The door was protected with a steel plate and three Yale locks. There was a doorbell fitted to the frame. 'Let's see who is at home.' She pressed the bell and stepped back to look up at the windows above. There was no sign of life. She tried again with the same result. 'I don't think Roger Pickford wants to talk to us.'

Richard tried the handle, and the door clicked open. 'Hello, Mr Pickford. This is the police. We just need a word with you,' he shouted up the stairwell. No one answered. 'Hello. North Wales Police. Is anyone at home?'

Kim stood on the first step. The stale odour of the building was tainted with something foul. 'Can you smell that?'

'I can,' Richard said. 'I think we should take a look, don't you?'

'Absolutely.' Kim heard something coming from upstairs. 'Can you hear that noise?'

'I can. It sounds like an electric motor,' Richard said. 'Let's take a look. Mr Pickford, we're coming upstairs. It's the police.'

They walked up the stairs. Piles of magazines were stored on the steps. *Railway Magazine*, *Custom Car*, Marvel comics, *2000 AD* comics,

Coin Collector magazines, and *Treasure Hunting*, a magazine for metal detectors. Each pile had some monetary value to people with a nostalgic interest in the content.

'He probably sells these online,' Richard said.

'People collect this nonsense?' Kim asked as she weaved her way to the landing. A threadbare carpet covered the floor, its floral pattern barely visible anymore. Strips of duct tape held it in place beneath the doorframes. The door to her left was open. 'Mr Pickford?'

She stepped into an oblong shaped room, which was dominated by a train set built on an old snooker table. There were four tracks and model roads and bridges, fake grass, and plastic trees. A miniature village had houses, a station, a signal box, and miniature people. Electric locomotive engines whirred around the rails towing their loads, passenger carriages, oil tankers, coal trucks, and guards' vans.

'Wow,' Richard said, stepping into the room. He walked around the set. 'The attention to detail is incredible.' He touched the transformer on the control box. It was hot. 'It's been running for a long time.' He looked around the room, which was lined with shelves that were stacked with games and picture books, annuals, and encyclopaedias. 'This is like a trip down memory lane,' he said. 'Subbuteo, Monopoly, Mousetrap, Operation, Buckaroo, Kerplunk, Jenga. And look at all these Action Men. There must be fifty or more.'

'This is like a time capsule,' Kim said. 'Kids nowadays wouldn't know where to begin.'

'This is definitely a blast from the past.'

'Why would anyone have such a collection unless it's for his own benefit?'

'I'm concerned why such a collection exists outside of a museum. There's something creepy about it.'

'Creepy is what I'm feeling,' Kim said.

'Mr Pickford?' Richard shouted, stepping back into the hallway. There was no reply. They walked along the hallway to the front of the building. A living room overlooked the high street. It was furnished with a three-piece suite and walnut sideboards. A huge globe opened to reveal a drinks cabinet, fully stocked with a range of spirits. The television was on, showing a rerun of *Bargain Hunt*. It was obsolete but still the most modern item in the room. There were two empty glasses on a copper topped coffee table and an ashtray full of cigarette stumps. 'The lights are on but there's no one home.'

'Mr Pickford?' Kim shouted up a second flight of stairs. 'That must be the kitchen,' she said, pointing to a room to their right. The door was ajar. She pushed it open and stepped inside. 'Mr Pickford?' she said. The room was unoccupied, but she noticed two mugs and two plates in the sink. A frying pan and a mixing bowl had been washed and drained. She took the lid off the bin. There were eggshells and a milk carton at the top. The odour of sour milk drifted to her. 'Someone made omelette or scrambled eggs, but it was days ago,' Kim added. She walked to the stairs and called out again. 'Mr Pickford?'

She didn't wait for an answer before climbing the stairs. The treads were worn to the underlay. An ornate bannister was attached to the wall, and the ceiling had a plaster ceiling rose and coving. Cobwebs gathered in the corners and strands of gossamer hung from the coving, out of reach of the average feather duster. The musty smell became sickly sweet, tainted with decay. It was a familiar odour for seasoned detectives. At the top of the stairs was a short hallway with three doors. The first led to a single bedroom which was a shrine to Liverpool Football Club. Posters covered every inch of the walls and the quilt cover and pillowcases were emblazoned with the club's emblems. Model war planes dangled from the ceiling. Richard recognised them from his own kids growing up. They were Second World War planes, Spitfire, Lancaster, Hurricane, Messerschmitt, Junkers-88. The painting was detailed and skilled. He wanted to look at them properly, but now wasn't the time. There were clothes on the floor. Richard nudged a pair of jeans with his foot. A jumper next to it was extra-large. A pair of size ten Nike trainers had been left behind the door.

'This room is used by a large child,' Richard said. A black-and-white photograph of a couple and a little boy was next to the bed on a small set of draws. Behind it was a brown leather wallet. Richard put gloves on and opened it with his fingertips. 'Charles Martins,' Richard said. He took out a driving licence. 'This is his address. He's thirty-nine.' He showed the photograph to Kim. She shook her head. 'The name means nothing to me either,' Richard added, putting the licence away and the wallet back where he found it. They walked back into the hallway. The second door led to a double bedroom. Kim opened it and stopped in her tracks. The body hanging from the roof beam had been there for a while. A squadron of bluebottle flies circled the corpse, taking off and landing at will. The hair above the ears was a mass of grey curls, the scalp bald and mottled.

'Roger Pickford, I presume,' Kim said, covering her nose and mouth. She stepped far enough into the room to see handcuffs were attached and the wrists were fastened together behind the back. A leather halter was attached to the face and red ball gag was in the mouth. 'We'd better call this in. Mr Pickford isn't going to tell us anything.'

'He didn't get up there by himself,' Richard said. He pointed to a set of stepladders under the window. 'Someone moved them over there and let him swing.'

'Looking at how he's dressed, I don't think that's what he had in mind.'

Chapter 32

Father Creegan let his emotions subside, pulled himself together, and took the photographs into the cellar beneath the church. He carried them as if they were as fragile as snowflakes. The people photographed were all unwilling subjects. There was no showboating, pouting, or posing. Only humiliation and suffering. They didn't know they were being photographed. Most of them were so high, they were beyond caring. The drugs made the perpetrators more enthusiastic and the victims submissive. Some of the faces were familiar to him, but not all. There had been too many to remember. Most of them were dead or dead inside, waiting to die. The years had ticked by, but the memories would not. They were an abomination from another lifetime. A lifetime he'd left behind, or so he thought. Someone was trying to suck him back down into the mire. The fragile charade he'd maintained around himself would come crashing down if it was prodded too hard.

His hands were shaking as he walked down the steps. He switched on the lights, which barely penetrated the gloom. Dust particles swirled in the air. The stone floor was dusty, and the atmosphere was dry. Old furniture was stacked against the walls, covered in dust. Chairs and pews were piled on top of each other, broken and cracked. The smell of woodworm and rot pervaded the air. He turned on another bank of lights, which lit the deeper recesses and made his way beneath the transept to the foundations at the far end. When he reached the end, the church alter was directly above him. He looked up but felt numb. It should be the heart of the building, yet he felt nothing but the ice in his soul.

The stone slabs which formed part of the footings were green with moss. There was a cold spot in that part of the cellar. It sent a shiver through him like strands of cotton touching the back of his neck. He bent low and pulled one of the stones from the wall. Behind it was a void. The priest reached inside and took a metal toolbox from the hidden cavity. It was wrapped in polythene. He fumbled in his pocket for his keys. It took him a while to find the key to the lock, and it took some persuasion to open it. The damp had rusted it. The lid creaked open. Inside it were coins, envelopes, and some smaller boxes. He lifted them out one at a time and opened them. House keys, car keys, gold rings, a chain with a crucifix, and a set of rosary beads. There were portrait photographs and letters written by them. A second box held a collection of driving licences, some credit cards, and a passport. The envelopes each held a lock of hair. Black, blond, brunette, ginger, grey, white, and all the shades between. There were dozens of them. He studied each one, savouring each memory. His heart filled with darkness and guilt. He pondered burning everything for a moment but changed his mind and put them away where they belonged. The photographs they'd delivered to him belonged there in his little box of horrors with everything else. They were tiny slices of people's lives. Each memento a snapshot in time, some happy, some tragic. Lives lived and lives lost, lives ripped from the earth violently. They were all there as evidence of what took place during those evil years.

They had no idea he'd kept the things he had. He kept them to remind him of how wrong they were to do what they did. Nothing could excuse them, and nothing could atone for them. If they knew what he'd kept, they would leave him be and let sleeping dogs lie. He was nearly dead. His secrets could die with him, but someone had set the wheels in motion once more and there would be hell to pay. Something had unsettled the equilibrium of evil between them. The past had been stirred up and there was nothing good for anyone there; it was all bad. All those involved would be scared by the events of those days, no matter which side of the coin landed. The victims and perpetrators were nothing more than puppets in a macabre play. Who they were and what they did when the sun rose in the morning was inconsequential; participation was all it took to be marked for life. Where things ended was down to the individuals. Most walked away at the first opportunity, some ran and kept running but some stayed. Some delighted in the theatre of it all, no matter how wrong it was. Someone wanted to expose the past, and maybe it was time they did. The guilt that he carried was a burden he shared with no one and he would take it to his grave if he could, maybe sooner rather than later but something told him he wouldn't have a choice. God might be there to judge him, although he doubted it.

He put the photographs into the box and locked it, before replacing the stone. The box was coming with him. There was nothing to be gained by keeping it hidden in the bowels of the church anymore. God knew it was there. Maybe that's why he had forsaken him. His time on the Earth was valueless if he kept what he had done hidden from the world. Humanity had a right to know what evil lurked among them. Not all devils had horns and cloven feet, not all demons declared their existence. Some came in the shape of men with a smiling face and a warm hand and the promise to protect. The evil in their black hearts couldn't be seen, but the carnage they left in their wake could be. Father Creegan knew they were coming for him. The truth would out. He could sit in his empty church and wait for them or he could confront them. If they were exposed, society would judge what they'd done as it would judge him. It was time to cut the head from the snake.

****

Alan was looking through information gathered on the victims killed in tragic accidents while with Father Creegan. Most of it was superficial, found with a Google search. He put the folder down, opting not to read it all in its entirety. There was too much superfluous background information.

'Okay. Summarise what we have,' he said.

'In short, we have three priests, Wilf Lawson sixty-one, Maxwell Cummings fifty-nine, Nigel Hancock sixty-four, and a local businessman Reece Moffat fifty-three.' Carmel Sheppard placed four photographs on the table. She tapped each one as she spoke. Carmel was a detective constable from St Asaph. 'The first three were career catholic priests, who served all over North Wales. Moffat was a businessman, married with three teenage children, owned a double-glazing company at Glan Conwy. He was a scout leader in his spare time and ran packs in a few towns in Gwynedd and Flintshire during the late eighties and early nineties. He went down with Hancock on the fishing boat, missing, presumed dead.'

'Boats sink all the time,' Alan said. 'Although it's unusual not to recover a body?'

'It's not that unusual around the straits, apparently,' Carmel disagreed. 'The undercurrents can take a body miles before it surfaces somewhere else where a search isn't happening.'

'I'll take your word for it.'

'I googled it.'

'It's true then. Sorry. Carry on.'

'Lawson and Cummings fell from Crib Goch during a charity hike with Father Creegan. The rope they were attached to was sheared on a rock.'

'Which happens,' Alan said.

'There's nothing remarkable about them or their deaths. None of them committed any crimes according to their records. They weren't known to us apart from a few speeding tickets.' She paused and raised her forefinger. 'What got me digging deeper was a CCJ against Moffet's wife lodged after his death.'

'His wife. Is a CCJ significant in any way?' Alan asked, looking doubtful.

'It depends,' Carmel said, shrugging. 'Which way you look at it.'

'Indulge me with your thoughts,' Alan said. He liked the young detective. She was smart and ambitious. 'I can see you have something up your sleeve.'

'Is it that obvious?'

'Yes. Don't play poker,' Alan said.

'Moffat was a regular in the local press, mostly for his work in the scout movement, raising money, bob-a-job week and the like. Most of the articles made him look like a shining example for the younger generation. He was pitched as a titan of local business and a role model as a self-made man who came from a poor background in the mountains of Snowdonia.' She showed Alan some of the newspaper articles. He was always pictured with a mayor or other dignitaries, often wearing shorts, shirt with multiple badges, neckerchief, and a woggle. 'There are dozens of press pieces over a ten-year period and beyond but when he died, his business imploded, his wife lost their house, their kids were kicked out of private schools because the fees weren't paid, and their cars were repossessed.'

'How do you know this?'

'I accessed the court records to see what her defence was.'

'Very clever. Everything was on HP?'

'Yes. It looks to me like his empire was built on debt and his reputation, but there was nothing concrete behind it. He was a fraud.'

'I can see why that would make you suspicious of him, but what exactly are you suspicious of?' Alan asked, frowning. 'Let's get to the nitty-gritty.'

'He's a fake,' Carmel said. 'He's all about his reputation, but he's a charlatan with a fascination for being around young boys. That worries me.'

'I get the feeling there's more?' Alan said.

'I crosschecked the Don Shipley files,' Carmel said.

'Good. That was my next question. Did he make accusations against any of them?'

'Not officially,' Carmel said.

'Meaning what exactly?'

'Shipley had several lists of names that he didn't give to the authorities.' Carmel tilted the screen. 'The problem is, the lists aren't titled. I can't make head or tail of what the lists are for.'

'So, we don't know if they're cowboys or Indians?'

'There may be a key to his filing system, but I can't work it out.'

'Were they made before or after he was a police officer?'

'After. They were never made public.'

'And?'

'Wilf Lawson, Maxwell Cummings, Nigel Hancock, and Reece Moffat are on all of them.'

Chapter 33

Col Gallagher and Bob Dewhurst walked into the operations room. The presence of uniformed officers was commonplace. They chatted to some detectives as they made their way to the drink station. They grabbed a cup of coffee and went to Alan's office. Alan was in a meeting with a detective they knew as Carmel from St Asaph. She was leaving in a hurry and looked pleased with herself. Alan beckoned them in.

'Afternoon, gents,' he said. 'Take a seat.'

'Is this about Melanie Brooks?' Col asked. He hadn't calmed down since he'd heard about her death. Guilt weighed heavily on his shoulders.

'Yes. It is,' Alan said. 'We know she drowned.' He held up his hands. 'This isn't a witch hunt, Col. I'm not looking for someone to blame for her death. I've heard your interview twice and I'm more than happy you and April did everything by the book.'

'Thank you,' Col said. 'That's a huge relief, although I can't help but feel some responsibility. The poor woman had issues. You know how it is.'

'She did, but she uploaded those videos knowing the effect they would have on Cristy Dennis. Don't kick yourself too hard.' He paused. 'The reason I want to talk to you is Jon Price. You both went into Price's house to speak to him,' Alan said. The officers nodded. 'Did you notice any CCTV?'

'Yes,' Bob said. 'Every room.'

'He let you into every room?'

'No. I saw the control panel in his office. Each room was labelled. It's a decent system but not the best.'

'What do you mean?'

'It's not the newest technology. I reckon he had it fitted when the place was renovated before he went down,' Bob explained. 'He's been away for seven years. Things have moved on since then.'

'I see. That makes sense. Could you tell if it was on?'

'It was on, but that doesn't mean it's recording,' Bob said. 'Or that he hasn't deleted what was on it.'

'We can recover deleted data though, can't we?'

'From some hard drives, yes.'

'I'm assuming it's Wi-Fi?'

'Yes. It's wireless,' Bob said, nodding. 'But you can't hack it, if that's what you're thinking?'

'I wasn't thinking that because I'm a dinosaur, but why not?' Alan didn't want to rule anything out.

'Those systems encrypt their signal. We'd need NASA to translate the data. You can't just piggyback into the signal.'

'Okay. It's a long shot, but did he say anything we could construe as an admission of guilt for harassing Cristy Dennis?' Alan asked. 'Anything at all we could use as leverage for a warrant?'

'No,' Col said, looking at Bob. 'He's way too clued up on the law to slip up like that. The bastard had our tyres slashed while we were in there. We know it was him who ordered it, but we can't prove it.'

'I don't recall him putting a foot out of line. I wish he had,' Bob agreed. Alan sighed. 'But I was going to come and see you anyway. I've been looking at the footage of Melanie Brooks going into the property and coming out,' Bob said. 'The images aren't clear enough to say one way or the other.'

'They're poor but her cheek and jaw are unmarked and there's no bruising to the neck. On the surface of it, she came out of there unharmed,' Alan said, deflated. 'And we can't say otherwise.'

'I'm not so sure,' Bob said.

'About what?'

'If that was Melanie Brooks at all,' Bob said.

'I'm not following, Bob.'

'There were two young women in that house when we were there,' he said, nudging Col. Col nodded but looked uncertain about what Bob was about to say. 'One of them had long dark hair just like Melanie Brooks. A bit younger and a bit slimmer but she would look similar from a distance.'

Alan stood up and walked to the window. He looked down Newry Street. It was bleak. The rain was pouring and the few shops that were there were boarded up. An elderly lady scampered by with a single bag of shopping, her hood up against the rain. He mulled over what Bob was saying. 'So, Price could have persuaded one of his visitors to dress in Melanie's clothes and drive her car to Porth Dafarch.'

'It's possible,' Bob said.

'He's a violent bully with a reputation,' Col said. 'It wouldn't be difficult to persuade a teenage girl to do what he wanted them to do.'

'How old were they?' Alan asked.

'Legal,' Bob said. 'But they were no more than teenagers and he was bossing them around while we were there.'

'They were wary of him,' Col agreed. 'If he told them to jump, they would ask how high, no doubt about it.'

'They must have been suspicious if he asked them to dress in someone else's clothes.'

'They might have been, but there's no way they're calling the police to report him. Everyone on this island is terrified of him.'

'If one of them moved her car, they may have seen what happened to Melanie,' Bob said. Col's mobile rang and Alan signalled for him to answer it. He went out of the office to take the call.

'I don't suppose you recognised them?' Alan asked.

'No, but their accents were local. Not Holyhead, probably Llangefni. I heard them chatting in Welsh, but it definitely wasn't Caernarfon area Welsh. They're from the island.'

'Okay. That narrows it down.'

'Most young women like to broadcast whatever they're doing on Facebook or Instagram,' Bob said. 'Being invited to the big house in the bay to party with Jon Price would be a splash on social media. I bet my boots there are selfies taken in his house next to the windows with the sea view behind them.'

'Good thinking, Bob,' Alan said. 'I want you to get onto the social media team and explain what we're looking for. You both saw these women, so you know who we're after. If we can find them, I want to talk to them. If we can convince them to talk to us, we may have a way into Jon Price.'

Col came back into the office. He looked pale and shocked.

'Are you okay?' Alan asked.

'That was Myra Dennis, Cristy's mum,' Col said. 'She was calling from the hospital. Cristy's boyfriend, Rowan, has had an accident at work. He fell off some scaffold.'

'Is he okay?' Alan asked.

'No. He's in ICU. He fell three floors onto his head,' Col said. 'Myra is very upset, but she's convinced Jon Price has got something to do with it.'

'How?' Alan asked.

'I'm not clear on that. She's hysterical.'

'Go and talk to her. If there's a chance we can put this joker back inside, I don't want to miss it.'

****

Cristy was sitting in the relatives' room with her mum and her brother. No one else was allowed into the hospital because of COVID-19. The doctors were planning to operate on several bleeds on the brain caused by massive trauma to the skull. A surgeon knocked on the door and entered.

'Cristy Dennis?' he asked from behind a clear shield.

'Yes. That's me.'

'I'm part of the team treating Rowan Jackson. You're effectively his next of kin?'

'Yes. I'm his partner. How is he?'

'We've stabilised him, but he isn't good, Cristy. We're taking him straight into surgery. Rowan landed on the back of his head, effectively cracking his skull like an egg. The fractures radiate out across the back to above the ears. There's severe damage to his shoulders, arms, and spinal cord, and his pelvis is shattered.' Cristy was sobbing. Her mum held her tight. 'His spleen is ruptured, and the left lung is punctured in two places by his ribs.' The surgeon had been polite but blunt. 'Before we can do anything else, we need to stop the bleeds on the brain.'

'Is he going to die?' Cristy asked.

'I'm giving him less than twenty per cent chance of surviving the surgery, but we'll do everything we can to keep him alive.'

'Will he be able to walk?' Myra asked him. It hadn't sunk in. She couldn't fathom Rowan being damaged so badly. He was so strong and fit, like indestructible. When she asked, the surgeon shook his head.

'Walking is the least of his problems. Rowan fell from around seventy feet onto rock. His injuries are similar to what we see in a car crash, but Rowan didn't have a seat belt or the protection of a car around him. His body has taken the full impact.' The surgeon paused. 'His body is broken, but it isn't the priority. The brain injury will kill him before his fractures will. All we can do is stabilise him and try to fix his brain. There's no point in thinking beyond that for now.'

Three hours later, the family were sitting in silence. There was nothing to say. Myra had called Col Gallagher and tried to explain about the roses and the taxi being sent to her house and her tyres being slashed again. She tried to explain the significance of what the taxi driver had said, but it had come out in a garbled mess. Price and his possible involvement seemed irrelevant. When Myra explained it to Phil, it didn't sink in. He said that Rowan was working on the scaffold alone and that no one else had access to that level. The idea it could be the result of foul play was shrugged off as nonsense. Phil had spoken to Rowan's parents, and they were understandably distraught. They had moved to Tenerife a few years ago and couldn't get a flight from the island because of lockdown. He promised to call them with any updates. His mobile didn't stop vibrating as news of the accident spread through the rugby club and their extended circle of friends.

He asked Cristy if she was okay and tried to give her some comfort, but she was oblivious to it. Her mind was in shutdown. She felt guilty about her last message to him and wished she'd been more affectionate. He'd reached out to her earlier. He was always looking out for her, wanting to make things normal despite the videos, and she'd rejected him. She reread her messages to him over recent weeks. Each one made her question herself. Could she have been more affectionate to him? Some of them made her sound like she didn't care. It was easy to read them and twist them into something horrid. The pressure of recent days became more intense, swelling inside her like a gas-filled balloon, threatening to burst any second. She felt sick, angry, twisted with guilt, and completely helpless. Jon Price had done it again.

'What are you doing?' Myra asked her.

'Reading his messages. He's such a softie and I'm such a bitch.'

'Don't beat yourself up. This isn't your fault.'

'My last text to him was so shitty,' Cristy said. 'I wish I hadn't sent it.'

'Send him a nice one now,' Myra said. 'He can read it when he comes round.'

Cristy smiled through her tears. She opened a text and typed.

I love you with all my heart. I'm sorry I was grumpy. Come back to me, baby. X

Cristy sent the text. Her mum wiped her tears away and squeezed her. There was a light knock on the door.

'Miss Dennis?'

She looked up from her phone to see a surgeon dressed in green scrubs. Her hair was jet black, her skin olive. She hadn't seen her before.

'That's me,' Cristy said.

'Rowan didn't make it,' the surgeon said. 'His injuries were too severe to fix. We tried everything we could, but it was too much for him. A fall like that is rarely survivable. He did well to get to the operating theatre.'

Cristy couldn't hear what she was saying anymore. She felt her tears running down her cheeks. They were hot and stinging. She felt her mother holding her, and she saw her brother embracing them both. Their words were lost on her. She felt her chest tighten, and she closed her eyes and tried to catch her breath. The pressure became too much, and she screamed for the life of the man she dared to love.

Chapter 34

Alan met Kim in the alleyway next to the old cinema. His hands were cold and buried deep inside the pockets of his wax jacket. The alley was covered by the building above, which sheltered them from the rain. His beanie hat was pulled down over his ears. Kim was animated and talking incessantly. She saw finding the body of Roger Pickford as a breakthrough. Alan wasn't so excited. He saw possibilities, which may lead to a breakthrough. They may also lead to a dead end. Experience told him that hurtling into a brick wall hurts more when you're running. He was still at a walking pace. His mind was sliding the pieces around, looking for where they fit. He wasn't ready to start fixing them yet. There were more pieces to find before he committed.

'I think we're onto something,' she said. 'This is the break we've been looking for.' Alan was studying the old cinema as he walked past. She could see he was distracted.

'Are you listening to me?'

'Yes, of course.'

'I said my legs have turned into sausages.'

'What?'

'Big fat Cumberland sausages,' she added. Alan was staring at the old cinema. 'Is something wrong?'

'No. Nothing is wrong. Just a memory burp. I was just remembering the last time I was here. Not in Bangor, actually in that cinema,' Alan said, walking towards the gate. 'It was eighty-three or eighty-four. Me, Tony Doutch, Gerard Cunningham, and Graham Humphreys caught the train from Holyhead and came here to see *Cat People*.'

'*Cat People*? I can't say I've seen that one,' Kim said, trying to hide her irritation. She wanted to get inside. 'Was it any good?' she asked, humouring him.

'I don't know. David Bowie sung the title track, 'Putting Out the Fire'.' Alan remembered. 'It wasn't his best tune, but we wanted to see it because Bowie was singing. We went to the pub first then got the train with some cans.' He chuckled. 'We were so pissed, we all fell asleep, and missed the film completely, but Bowie was singing while the credits rolled, so it wasn't all bad.'

'People are still getting pissed in there,' Kim said, gesturing to the advertising blackboards. 'No films though.'

'Make yourself sick so you can drink more?' Alan read. 'Is that an actual thing nowadays?'

'It's always been a thing,' Kim said. 'Just not encouraged.'

'I guess not. Sorry, I'm reminiscing.' Alan walked towards the back door. 'Come on. I can tell you're bursting at the seams to show me what you've found.'

'You make me sound like an old beanbag,' Kim said, following.

'Could be worse.'

'How?'

'Could be a different type of bag, but if the cap fits,' he said, stopping at the doorway. 'So, let me recap. Roger Pickford is a fence who bought antiques stolen from Llanberis, and the shotgun used at Father Creegan's house was stolen from that property at the same time?' Alan looked at Kim. She nodded. 'And he lived here with who?'

'A thirty-nine-year-old male, Charles Martins. It's a very odd setup,' she said, walking through the back door. They made their way up the stairs to the first floor.

'*2000 AD* comics,' Alan said, avoiding the piles of magazines. 'I bet they're worth a few quid.' He thought about telling her he used to buy them every week, but she wasn't in the mood to hear his memories, fond or otherwise. 'I used to read them over and over until the next one came out. Although I can't imagine they'd be the same if I read them now,' he said to no one. Kim was already at the top of the stairs. He reached the landing, and she gestured to the games room.

'Take a look in there.'

Alan stepped into the room and walked around the table, taking in the train set, games, and comics. There was a nostalgic memory on every shelf. He stopped next to the Action Men, who were standing to attention on the shelves. A Jeep, canoe, and several armoured vehicles were lined up against a bookcase; each one had an Action Man in the driving seat. 'Eagle eyes, real hair, blond hair, brown hair, fuzzy beard. They're all here,' he muttered. 'I always wanted that tank.' He turned to Kim. 'You said the train was running when you got here?'

'Yes. The transformer was hot. It had been on for a long time.'

'You think this room was a magnet?' Alan said. Kim nodded. 'If this room was a lure, it lost its attraction a long time ago,' Alan said. He studied the shelves and completed a circuit of the room. 'There's not a Play Station in sight. It's like a museum.'

'We said the same thing,' Kim said. 'Come on. The juicy stuff is upstairs.' She walked down the landing and up the second flight of stairs. Alan followed closely. They donned blue paper suits and overshoes. Harry Rankin waved hello from the double bedroom. The smell was nauseating.

'Hello, Harry. What can you tell us so far?' Alan asked.

'The ID in his wallet confirms he's the property owner, Roger Pickford,' Harry said. 'Initial observations would be death by hanging.'

'I don't know how they do it,' Alan muttered. Kim elbowed him in the ribs. 'When?'

'Approximately four or five days ago.'

Alan looked at Kim. She nodded. 'That would make it Sunday. The same day Father Creegan had his visitor,' Alan said.

'Exactly,' Kim said. 'Roger Pickford bought all the furniture and jewellery taken during a burglary in Llanberis. He did time for it. I think we can take it for granted he bought the shotgun too, although he denied it.'

'He would. An illegal firearm would have added a few years to his tally,' Alan said. He walked around the body. 'So, he bought the shotgun and kept it for himself. But it was hidden and the search following his arrest missed it.'

'Exactly.'

'Do you think he got up there of his own accord?' Alan asked.

'Sex game gone wrong?' Harry asked. 'It crossed my mind, but if it was, someone else was involved. The ladders were over there against the wall when we arrived. They haven't been moved.'

'You're getting the hang of this, pardon the pun,' Alan said. Harry looked confused, but Alan ignored it. 'I'm no expert on this type of thing,' Alan said, shaking his head. 'But he's wearing jeans and a sweatshirt, and he has his trainers on. Now, it's been a while, but I don't recall doing the business fully clothed.'

'Doing the business?' Kim said, smirking. 'Is that a codeword?'

'That's enough, Sergeant,' Alan said, regretting his choice of words. 'Don't take the piss. I'm sure you understand what I mean, perfectly.'

'Perfectly,' Kim said, nodding. 'No one does the business fully clothed, no matter what century it is.'

'Are there any signs he was coerced to climb those stepladders?' Alan asked, ignoring her. He was trying hard not to laugh. 'The bracket on the beam has been fitted a long time ago and the rope and noose look well used to me.'

'I agree,' Harry said. 'The fibres on the knot are frayed with age. The knot tied around the bolt is very tight. I think the rope and noose are a permanent fixture in here.' He pointed to Pickford's head. 'Look at the dried blood around the nose and mouth. The discolouration of the skin doesn't help, but I'm sure Mr Pickford was struck hard in the face with a blunt object before the harness was attached to the mouth and the ball gag fitted. You can see blood beneath the straps there and there. The bruise is about five inches long by two inches wide.'

'That would be the right size for something blunt like the butt of a shotgun,' Kim said. 'I think he was attacked, handcuffed, gagged, and forced up those ladders. Maybe not in that order, but the result was always going to be leaving him to hang.'

'That would take a lot of hatred and anger,' Alan said. 'Someone planned to torment him, humiliate him, and give him time to realise what was going to happen. That takes a cold, calculated mind.'

'It could be pure rage,' Kim agreed. 'This is not the type of murder you walk away from thinking there's a future. It takes the acceptance of life being over for victim and perpetrator.'

'It certainly closes the door on life as it was before,' Alan agreed.

'So does putting a shotgun in your mouth and pulling the trigger.'

'I can see how you made that jump, but it is still a big jump,' Alan said.

'There're some pieces of the puzzle missing,' she agreed. 'But the overall picture is becoming clearer.'

'Let's assume Roger Pickford is a bad man for a moment. He upsets someone who is unstable and knows where he hides his shotgun. That person snaps, Pickford ends up swinging from the end of a rope, and the shotgun he bought from a burglary ends up in Creegan's bedroom next to a dead man,' Alan said. 'Who is probably the man who did this to Roger Pickford.'

'Yes. And we don't have to look too far for a possible suspect. Pickford clearly shares his house with a younger man with issues, Charles Martins,' Kim added. 'He is surrounded by things from his youth. From what I've seen in this building, Charles Martins was a vulnerable person.'

'So, who is Charles Martins?'

'I ran his driving licence through the system. He has no record as such, but he does have a closed file held by the Child Protection Unit. It was sealed when he was eighteen.'

'Go on,' Alan said.

'He was a looked after child, originally from Towyn but was taken into care under a protection order in the late eighties,' Kim explained. 'His parents were piss-pots and drug users. His teacher at school alerted social services that he was coming to school dirty, covered in bruises, and tired. The file is comprehensive and covers several years of intervention, but eventually they removed him into care. I'm waiting on more details from child protection.'

'How long has he been here?' Alan asked.

'According to the electoral roll, he doesn't live here.'

'He doesn't?' Alan frowned. 'Where does he live?'

'He isn't registered anywhere, but if you look through his bedroom, there are letters and bills going back years. His bank account is registered here, as is a mobile phone, but we haven't found that. There are boxes of photographs going back to when he was young. He's been here since he was a teenager. I'm convinced of it,' Kim said.

'Get those photographs to the station. They could be a goldmine,' Alan said. A uniformed officer picked up the boxes and carried them downstairs. 'Tell me how this played out in your mind?'

'On Sunday, I think Charles Martins decided he'd had enough. He was angry, but cool enough to create a plan in his head. Pickford and Creegan were the focus of his anger. He took that shotgun from wherever it was hidden, attacked and killed Pickford, and then made his way to see Father Creegan.'

'Why the harness and gag?' Alan asked.

'To humiliate him. Maybe it's payback,' Kim mused.

'Okay. So, he kills Pickford then goes to see our priest. Why not kill Creegan?' Alan asked.

'Because he wanted us to find Creegan in a compromising position. He hoped we'd look into his suicide. His suicide is a signpost telling us where to look,' Kim said. 'We had no way of knowing who he was because he left his wallet and ID here on purpose, knowing we would have to investigate his death.'

'What if Creegan had told us who he was?' Alan asked.

'We would have come here anyway. I think he wanted to lead us here to this building and to connect Pickford to Father Creegan for a reason. We've said all along whoever he was, he had a plan. Nothing was random. He was as sane as you or me when he planned this, but he had clearly had enough of living.'

'Okay. I'm with you. Creegan has lied to us from day one about the identity. He knew Charles Martins. There's only one reason why he would lie to us about that,' Alan said.

'Because if he gave us a name, we would have come straight here, and he's been trying to prevent that all along.'

'Agreed. How long for a DNA report?' Alan asked Harry. 'We need to match Martins to the victim at the vicarage.'

'I've rushed it through,' Harry said. 'We have skin, hair, his toothbrush, and fluids from his bedding.' He smiled. 'It shouldn't be too long.'

'Great thank you, Harry.' Alan walked onto the landing. 'We need to crosscheck Roger Pickford with Don Shipley's files,' Alan said.

'I've already done it,' Kim said. 'Carmel Sheppard has been combing through the information we've uploaded so far.'

'Call her and see how far she's got,' Alan said. Kim rang her and put the call on speaker.

'Carmel, it's Kim.'

'Hi, Kim. I was just about to call you.'

'What have you got?'

'We've only got half of Osbourne's case files on the system, but I've found Roger Pickford's name mentioned several times. He was accused of being part of a grooming ring in Bangor in the early nineties. According to Osbourne's notes, Don Shipley gave his name to the police three times in five years. He was interviewed but never charged.'

'What was his connection to children?' Alan asked.

'He was a scout leader.'

'Reece Moffat was a scout leader,' Alan said.

'Moffat is one of the men who drowned on the boat in the straits?' Kim asked.

'Yes.'

'I've checked Pickford's police file. Only one entry was made by Bangor officers and it's blanked with a no further action marker and the information redacted. I've asked for the originals to be sent over, but apparently, they were destroyed in storage. All we have are Osbourne's files.'

'A fire in Caernarfon?' Alan asked.

'That's the one,' Carmel said. 'How did you know that?'

'Richard spoke to a detective superintendent from Liverpool. He's retired, but he liaised with Osbourne. A lot of the original evidence went up in that fire.'

Kim's phone vibrated. She looked at the screen. 'Carmel, I need to take this call,' she said. 'It's the Child Protection Unit.'

'Take it,' Alan said. He stood in the doorway of Martins' room and watched as CSI bagged and boxed belongings from the single bedroom. Charles Martins appeared to be a contradiction. He was thirty-nine, but his interests were those of a much younger man. The picture of his parents didn't match the description of the people Kim had described. They didn't look like drug using alcoholics. Maybe it was taken in better times when they weren't ravaged by addiction. Kim tapped him on the shoulder.

'Listen to this. Charles Martins was placed into care in Chester but in nineteen ninety-three they moved him.' Kim showed Alan the screen. 'He was placed in Oakland House, Prestatyn.'

'That rings a bell, Alan said, frowning. 'Why do I know that name?'

'It's the same care home that Ewan Birley went missing from.'

'Martins and Birley were both in care in Prestatyn in the nineties?'

'Yes.'

'We think Birley was last seen at the station, which is a five-minute walk from this building and Martins ends up living here all his life,' Alan said. 'That's too much of a coincidence for my liking.'

'And mine. I told you we were onto something,' Kim said, smiling.

'You did. I want everything from the initial misper case. I want to know who was working there and if they were all spoken to.'

'What if they were spoken to?'

'I want them all spoken to again, regardless of what they said first time around. We start this misper case from scratch if we have to.'

'Do we have the manpower?' Kim asked.

'One detective can do this,' Alan said. 'There's no rush. No one will notice we're straying into another case. The budget will come in and that's all the ACC cares about.' Alan thought for a moment. 'Ian Osbourne must have suspected their disappearance was linked to the home.'

'What makes you so sure?'

'Something rattled the cage. If he pointed the finger at the system, it would have rung alarm bells all the way to the top. Social Services are drowning beneath a tidal wave of cases. They have been for decades.'

'I don't get the point,' Kim said.

'Social workers need a degree, so not anyone can apply for a job. The front line is relentless and staff turnover is high. They're recruiting from a limited number of candidates in any one area. Cases are sometimes left high and dry when one employ leaves and their caseload is shared out, it causes drift and kids fall through the net. Osbourne could have been opening a can of worms. No one would want a spotlight shined in that direction. They're under too much pressure.'

'So, they shut him down,' Kim said. 'Okay. So, you're saying we don't want to rock the boat?'

'We don't have to. Things have changed since the nineties. Care homes and nursing homes were draining the system, so the government sold sections off. My bet is the care home is a private enterprise now. Its employees are not social workers.'

'Which means what?'

'It means we don't believe a word anyone says unless they can back it up. Get Carmel to search for everything Ian Osbourne highlighted around that care home. I want to know who was questioned, who was on duty, who wasn't on duty, anyone who left soon after Birley went missing. Look for employees who worked with Martins and Birley. I want the original statements torn to shreds. I want to know who did the gardens, who cooked the meals, and who cleaned the windows. Most of these people will be dead or untraceable. We need to speak to anyone who can remember that home in the nineties.'

'Do you think the home knew more than they said about Birley's disappearance?'

'I'm not saying there was a conspiracy, but someone there knew more than they said. One hundred per cent, I do.'

'Let's say they did come to Bangor. Do you think they came here?'

'I wouldn't be surprised if Birley and Deeks were in this building playing with that train set.'

'How does it link to Father Creegan?'

'I don't know. Charles Martins wants us to find the link. We need to ask him once we've put all this together.' Alan took another look around the double bedroom. The stink from Roger Pickford was becoming unbearable. The drawers had been searched and bagged up. There was an assortment of bondage and restraint equipment. None of it looked pleasant or fun in any way. 'Whoever topped Pickford did the world a favour, in my opinion. I've had enough. Let's get out of here.'

'I'm with you,' Kim said. They walked down the stairs and into the cluttered back yard. The fresh air was a welcome relief.

'Did you come with Richard?'

'Yes, but we came in separate cars. He left once we'd reported in.'

'Where is he?' Alan asked.

'He's gone to see Luca Bay's wife in Newborough,' Kim said, checking her watch. 'She called this morning and said she's well enough to speak to us. I thought Richard would be the best man for the job.'

'Is the DI out there?' a voice called from upstairs.

'Yes, I am,' Alan answered. He looked up the stairway. A uniformed officer was on the landing.

'I've got a message from Sergeant Dewhurst. He's at Ysbyty Gwynedd and says you need to call him.'

'Did he say why?' Alan asked.

'Something about Jon Price. He said he's been ringing your mobile.'

'Okay, thanks,' Alan said. He looked at his phone. Eleven missed calls. 'The bloody thing is on silent.'

'It doesn't opt to be on silent,' Kim said. 'Usually, the owner of the phone chooses if it's heard or not.'

'Sarcasm is the lowest form of wit,' Alan said. He called Bob. Bob answered on the first ring. 'Bob, it's Alan.'

'I've been trying to ring you,' Bob said.

'I've had no signal. What is it?'

'Rowan Jackson died on the operating table about an hour ago,' Bob said. 'We arrived here just after he died to speak to Myra Dennis and Cristy. They told us that a taxi was sent to their house before they knew that Rowan had fallen. It was booked for Cristy Dennis to take her to the hospital.'

'Before they knew?' Alan said.

'Yes. At least ten minutes before they received the call to tell them about the fall. When they found out, they went to drive to the hospital, but Myra's tyres had been slashed again.'

'Price is playing mind games. It's circumstantial or coincidental at best,' Alan said.

'That's what we thought until we got here.'

'That sounds ominous. Go on,' Alan said.

'The family haven't been made aware yet,' Bob said, instinctively lowering his voice. 'When we arrived, the surgeons asked to talk to us. Away from the family. They took us to a treatment room and showed us a series of X-rays that were taken on arrival. There are two lead pellets in Rowan's skull.'

'Lead pellets from an air rifle?'

'Yes. A powerful one,' Bob said. 'One of the pellets entered the corner of his right eye and entered the brain behind the forehead, and the second entered the skull beneath the left ear. The entry wounds weren't obvious following the fall because there was blood and bruising all over the place. The head X-rays show the slugs clearly. He didn't fall from that scaffold by accident. Rowan Jackson was murdered.'

Chapter 35

Richard pulled up outside the Knightly residence. It was a six-bedroom farmhouse on ten acres of woodland within walking distance of Llandwyn Beach. The mountains looked close enough to touch. A new model Defender was parked in the garage and an elderly gentleman was playing with two children on the lawn. They were all wearing wellington boots and raincoats but appeared to be oblivious to the rain. Richard waved hello, and the man nodded but looked at him suspiciously. He knew Mr Knightly had been headmaster at a boarding school in St Asaph. Headmasters were inherently suspicious of strangers. They were paid to be. As he turned off the engine, the front door opened, and he recognised Janine Bay from pictures on the murder file. She was a pretty woman with short blond hair and blue eyes, but she looked drawn and tired. Dark circles surrounded her eyes. A thin smile touched her lips. She looked haunted. Richard climbed out of the car and walked to the front door – his shoulders hunched against the rain. Strands of grey hair were ruffled by the wind.

'I'm DS Lewis. You can call me Richard. Thank you for seeing me, Janine,' Richard said. 'There's nothing to worry about. This is an informal chat if you're feeling up to it.'

'Have you caught anyone yet?' she asked. Her voice sounded gruff. He detected the odour of cigarettes. She smelt like she'd been eating them one after the other. 'Jon Price is responsible. I know he is.'

'Shall we go inside out of the rain?' Richard asked, smiling. He didn't want to debate suspects on the doorstep in the rain.

'I'm sorry. I'm forgetting my manners,' she said. 'Come in.' A new model Vauxhall pulled into the driveway and parked in the garage. The garage linked to the kitchen via an adjoining door. He heard the doors opening and closing and a glamourous looking lady in her fifties appeared in the hallway. Her forehead was smooth as silk and her smile faultless. *Botox and veneers*, he thought.

'This must be your sister,' Richard asked. Both women smiled. 'I'm DS Lewis.'

'What a charmer,' the lady said, smiling.

'This is my mother, who will love you forever for saying that,' Janine said.

'I'm Victoria Knightly. Pleased to meet you.'

'Likewise, Victoria,' Richard said. 'Victoria Knightly?' He raised an eyebrow and rubbed his chin. 'There was a judge at Caernarfon courts by that name,' he said. 'Rumour has it, she was the fairest judge that ever sat on the bench.'

'I've heard much worse said about me, Detective Lewis,' Victoria said. 'Have you ever appeared in my court?'

'I never had the pleasure, but I've never heard a bad word said about you.'

'Oh dear,' Janine said. 'My mum is famous. Pass me a sick bucket.'

'Be nice, Janine,' Victoria said, half smiling. 'If you can't be nice, be quiet.' Richard sensed anger simmering in her voice. There was a touch of resentment behind the smile. 'Excuse my daughter. She's not herself for obvious reasons.'

'Don't talk about me as if I'm not here,' Janine said. She looked at Richard and rolled her eyes. 'They treat me like I'm six-years old. Be seen but not heard, isn't that right, Mother?'

'Don't be ridiculous, Janine,' Victoria said, maintaining her smile. 'Let's not make a scene.' She turned to Richard. 'Tell me, Detective Lewis, do you work for Alan Williams?'

'Yes,' Richard said. 'He speaks very highly of you and sends his regards,' he lied. Alan couldn't stand the woman. He said she went to court on a broomstick and probably turned children into soup.

'Really?' Victoria said, frowning. 'I always got the impression he couldn't abide me or my decisions.' Richard looked surprised. 'But you're very kind to say so. Please come in,' she said. She was wearing riding gear. A checked hacking jacket and knee-length boots. Her blond hair was tied in a bun. 'Go through to the conservatory. You can talk in peace in there. Can I get you a tea or coffee?'

'Tea would be lovely,' Richard said, following the women through the kitchen. It was the size of his back yard. An island dominated the space. Dried herbs and copper pans hung from the ceiling above it. The conservatory was off to the right and tiled like a chessboard. Cane furniture and potted willow trees gave it a homely feel. The air was cooler in there. He sat down next to an onyx coffee table and studied the framed pictures on display, mostly of the grandchildren with Janine and their grandparents. There were none of Luca. 'What a lovely home you have,' Richard said. 'I can see you have an eye for interior design.'

'Thank you,' Victoria said. 'I'll make some tea and leave you to it.'

'Much appreciated,' Richard said. He smiled at Janine. 'Are you okay to have a chat about Luca?'

'Yes.' She waited until her mother was gone. 'I'm sorry about her. Is it about him selling cocaine?'

'No. Although you can tell me about that if you want to?'

'We argued about it all the time when he was working for Jon Price,' Janine said. 'I threatened to finish with him years ago. He stopped for a while and Jon gave him a shitty job working on one of his dodgy apartment sites. Of course, that ended when the bastard was sent to jail. Luca tried really hard to get another job, but you know what the island is like.'

'I do. Jobs are scarce. Good ones any way.'

'He tried taxi driving for a while but didn't make enough money. Then he worked as a commis chef for a week. The split shifts didn't suit us. We didn't see each other.'

'The hospitality industry is difficult to work in,' Richard said. 'It doesn't suit everyone. The hours are unsociable.'

'We had no money. He dabbled at dealing again without me knowing, but it wasn't long before he was working for Paul Sutton. People were queuing up to tell me he was dealing again. I gave him an ultimatum before the youngest was born. I told him I didn't want to be married to a drug dealer, and I didn't want my kids asking where their dad was when he was in jail.' She shrugged and sat forward. 'He didn't get it. My mum is a fucking judge, and my dad is a headmaster. They hate him. I don't know what I was thinking, to be honest. They were never going to accept him. I told him to pack it in or lose us.'

'I'm sure that must have been a difficult conversation,' Richard said.

'It was. I left him and came here for six months. My parents wouldn't let him near the place. He didn't see the kids for months, which broke him. He went off the rails for a while, drinking all the time.'

'When was that?'

'A few years back now. My dad hasn't spoken to him since. Not that they spoke much anyway.'

'Dads can be very protective of their daughters. I know. I have three.'

Victoria came in with two cups of tea. She put them down on the table between them. 'Can I get you a sandwich or something?'

'No. Thank you. Tea is fine.'

'I'll leave you to it,' she said, leaving.

Richard waited until she'd gone. 'You were saying your father didn't like Luca.'

'No. He couldn't stand him. He didn't want me to marry him in the first place.'

'Why was that?'

'He said he was a loser with no prospects.'

'Can I ask why he thought he was a loser?'

'He failed his exams and dropped out of school,' Janine said. 'In my dad's opinion, he didn't finish his education and had no self-respect or ambition. He wanted me to marry a barrister or accountant and be a respectable housewife with horses and Hunter boots.'

'But you saw something in Luca he didn't?' Richard said.

'I suppose so, although I'm not sure what that was now.'

'That's usually the way when we fall in love with someone. Who knows what the reason is?'

'I'm being unfair. He had a heart of gold and he was loyal,' Janine said. 'I've been cheated on by every man I've ever been with and they were supposed to be good men with good jobs and prospects.' She thought back and Richard let her talk. 'I knew Luca was different to those men. They walked around with their tongues hanging out and their dicks in their hands, trying to bed every woman on Facebook. Luca wasn't like that. He was faithful to me. He was never going to be a brain surgeon, but we had a nice house, holidays, my kids never went without anything. The opposite in fact. He spoilt them rotten. It's just a shame all he could do was supply class As. He used to say it was the only thing he'd been good at. Look where that got him.' A tear broke free and trickled down her cheek. She wiped it on her sleeve. 'Don't mind me. I'm just having a moment.'

'It's to be expected.' He paused for a moment while she settled. 'I'll be honest with you, Janine. We're not convinced he was killed because he was selling drugs.' Janine looked surprised and shook her head in disagreement. 'The killer didn't take anything from him. His wallet and phone were on him. There was a quantity of cocaine hidden in his underwear. Nothing was taken.'

'I don't see how that proves anything.'

'It doesn't prove anything but if it was a user, they wouldn't have left the drugs behind,' Richard said. Janine didn't look convinced. 'If it was a user or a rival, the money and drugs would have gone.'

'Jon Price killed him because he was working for Sutton,' Janine said. 'He's out of prison and he has a score to settle. Everyone is saying the same thing.'

'People are speculating. That's what people do. You know how they love to jangle here on the island,' Richard said, smiling. 'But there's no evidence to back that up.'

'If it wasn't Jon Price, who else would want to kill Luca?'

'That's why I'm here. We think whoever killed Luca also attacked Edward Speers.'

'How is he?'

'Not good. He's in a coma. His injuries are to the skull which is never good.'

'What happened?'

'It was what we call a blitz attack.'

'What does that mean?'

'It means he was attacked without warning. Someone knocked on his door and when he opened it, they hit him with a hammer. The attack was disproportionate to the force required to disable him or stop him from defending himself. The blows were all thrown with lethal force and the attacker fled the scene taking nothing and leaving nothing behind.' Richard paused to allow her to think. 'The attack on Luca was the same. He was attacked with overwhelming force and the attacker took nothing and fled the scene like a ghost.'

'Who would do that?'

'We don't know, but we think they're connected, don't you?'

'I don't know. I just thought it was a coincidence or Eddie pissed off Jon Price too.'

'You don't like him, do you?'

'He's rotten to the core,' Janine said. 'He came to our house once when Luca was working for him. We were struggling at the time and he knew it.' She paused. The memory appeared to disturb her. 'He offered me a way out of the debt. All I had to do was have sex with him when Luca was on site. Just a few times a week, he said. That was good of him, don't you think?'

'Very gallant. It's reassuring to know there are such caring souls around when you need help,' Richard said, sarcastically. 'I assume you told him where to go?'

'That's not quite how I put it. I was more shocked than anything,' Janine said, shaking her head. 'The sad thing is, I considered it for a moment.' She blushed and locked her fingers between her knees. 'I've never told anyone that before,' she said. Her eyes filled up. 'We were in so much debt and Luca was earning just enough to cover the bills, but we couldn't pay the debts we had. We were going backwards with the interest.'

'It happens to people,' Richard said. 'It's nothing to be ashamed off.'

'I couldn't see any way out of it. There was no light at the end of the tunnel. Jon Price is a good-looking man, and he can be charming. He actually made it sound like he would be doing me a huge favour. Just for a minute, I could see a way out for us. I often wonder how many women would have accepted the offer. It crossed my mind and then I saw sense and felt sick to the stomach. There was no way on this earth I was going to let that man put his hands on me. Not for all the money in the world. I would have robbed a bank first. Jon Price is a disgusting human being and I hate his guts and he knows that.'

'Did you ever tell Luca what happened?' Richard asked.

'No.' She shook her head. 'He felt bad enough not being able to look after us. Telling him that Jon offered me money for sex would have shattered what little pride he had left. It wasn't long after he started dealing again.' She wiped another tear away. 'Part of me was glad he was dealing. I knew we could get out of trouble if he was earning decent money again. I kept my mouth shut and looked the other way. I was torn between the devil and the deep blue sea.'

'I can see that. Do you think Price held a grudge against Luca because you refused his advance?' Richard asked.

'He's a twisted fuck. I wouldn't put anything past him. It's funny that as soon as he gets out of jail, everything starts to go to shit. People start getting killed. Shit's uploaded to Facebook about his ex, Cristy. Cristy is a lovely woman, so pretty. What he did to her was disgusting.'

'Yes. It was a cruel thing to do to someone.'

'Now Melanie Brooks has topped herself over him. She's a lovely woman with two kids. Or she was.' Janine looked angry. 'Those poor kids have been left with no mother because of that pervert. Price did this. I know he did. Everyone knows he did.' She paused to take a breath. Her eyes met Richard's. 'I bet he attacked Eddie too.'

'Eddie is godfather to your kids, isn't he?' Richard said, changing tack.

'Yes. He's a lovely guy. A bit of a loner, but lovely,' Janine said. 'I can't understand why anyone would want to hurt him.'

'Luca and Eddie go back a long way, don't they?'

'Yes,' Janine said, nodding. 'All the way to being kids. They went to the same junior school, senior school, and were in the sea cadets and scouts together. Both their parents were older when they had them, and they died while they were in their teens. They had a lot in common and helped each other through.'

'So, they were childhood friends. They must have been very close,' Richard said.

'They were. They drifted apart a bit when they finished the last year of school.' Janine shrugged. 'Eddie was clever and stayed on to do A levels, but Luca dropped out. They didn't really speak for a few years, apparently.'

'Did they fall out?' Richard asked.

'A bit. I think Luca might have resented Eddie passing all his exams. Luca's dad was a piss-head and handy with his fists. I think he expressed his disappointment a few times before he died. He fell down the stairs and broke his neck, drunk. The family were left destitute. His mother died soon after from a heart attack. Luca didn't really like to talk about his past. It wasn't a happy time for him. From what I can gather, Eddie was his only real friend. The only one he ever mentioned to me anyways. Whatever happened between them, they got over it when Eddie finished sixth form. They went travelling together for nearly a year.'

'Really?' Richard asked. 'Where did they go?'

'Thailand, Cambodia, Vietnam,' Janine said. 'The photographs are amazing. They look so happy. I think that's when they became really close again. When they came back, they both moved to Holyhead. Luca went from shit job to shit job and ended up selling coke. Eddie didn't continue his education but got a decent job on the railway. He made a bit of money on the side with his photography.'

'Wow. What type of photography?'

'Landscapes mostly. He took photographs all over the island, the mountains, and coastline. Then he uploaded them to subscription sites like Shutterstock. People pay to use the images for advertising and stuff,' Janine said.

'I know the type of sites you mean,' Richard said. 'He must have been very good.'

'Most of the pictures he took were on his phone. He just had an eye for a picture. Luca used to go with him sometimes dressed in all the hiking gear. Eddie would photograph him walking on a path or reading a map with a compass, or next to a stream or a lake. That type of thing. I think they call it stock photography. He even had me and the kids posing for family shots.'

'Really?' Richard said. 'Posing where?'

'We did dozens of places. The garden, the park, on the swings, near the beach, at the station, flying a kite, walking the dog.' She shrugged. 'People search for normal images of families for advertising and stuff. They sold quite a few every month. They didn't make much, but they made a bit.' She nodded. 'It was a second income and paid for the shopping some weeks.'

'They made pennies,' Mr Knightly said from the doorway. The children ran to their mother and jumped on her knee. Their cheeks were red and glowing. 'I think that's enough for one day,' he added. His face was stern. Richard could imagine him being a strict headmaster. 'Janine has been very tired. She needs to eat something and rest. If you don't mind, we'll be eating shortly and putting the children to bed.'

'Of course,' Richard said, standing. He smiled at the children. 'You two look like your mother,' he said. They grinned and nodded. He walked towards the door. 'Thanks for your time, Janine. If you think of anything you think might help, please call the station and ask for me.'

'Okay. I will.'

'Thank you for allowing me to speak to Janine in your home,' Richard said. Mr Knightly nodded, walking him to the front door. 'It's much appreciated. This is a terrible time for her and the children. We don't want to make the investigation process any more difficult than we have to.'

'No problem,' Mr Knightly said, although his expression said it was a problem. A massive problem. 'It's the children I'm worried about. I don't want policemen coming and going. The children ask questions. Being inquisitive is part of our DNA. They're not old enough to be told how their father died or why. That day will come, but it will be many years from now.'

'I understand. If we need to talk to Janine again, I'll call first.' Richard paused. 'You said they aren't ready to be told why he died?'

'Did I?'

'Yes. You did,' Richard said. 'Janine thinks it was because he was selling cocaine. What do you think?'

'If you swim in the gutter, detective, the rats will eat you alive. Luca Bay was a weak man. He failed at everything he did. People in that industry feed on weakness. They can sense it.' Mr Knightly puffed up his chest as if he was proud of his theory. 'I think he crossed the wrong people, and they erased him. Isn't that how it works?'

'Yes. Sometimes it is,' Richard said, opening the front door. 'Thank you for your time and your hospitality. I'll be in touch.'

Chapter 36

Alan was sitting in his office waiting to hear from Harry Rankin. They were perched on the edge of arresting Jon Price with powerful circumstantial evidence. He wasn't convinced a warrant would be granted, despite the death of Rowan Jackson. Kim knocked on the window. She pointed to his phone. The hold light was flashing.

'DI Williams,' he said, answering.

'Alan. It's Jason Marsh,' the chief constable said. Alan sat up in his chair automatically. 'Are you in your office?'

'Yes, sir,' Alan said. 'What can I do for you?'

'I need a chat with you on a very sensitive subject,' Jason said. 'It won't take long, but it's a discussion best held face to face. I'll be with you in twenty minutes.'

'Okay. That's fine,' Alan said. The chief ended the call abruptly. Kim frowned through the glass. 'What the flying flip is he coming here for?'

'What did the chief want?' Kim asked, opening the door.

'He's paying us a visit. Is it tidy out there?' he asked, sarcastically.

'You could eat your dinner from the carpet,' Kim said. 'Why is he coming here?'

'I don't know, but whatever it is, it won't be good news.'

'I reckon he's going to sack you,' Kim said.

'What for now?'

'Being an arse?'

'I'll get my coat, shall I?'

'Bribery and corruption.'

'Guilty as charged,' Alan said. His phone rang again. 'DI Williams.'

'Alan, it's Harry Rankin. Are you sitting down?'

'I am,' Alan said, rolling his eyes. 'What have you found?'

'The DNA matches. The suicide victim is Charles Martins. No doubt about it.'

'Excellent, thank you.'

'You're welcome. I'll call as the results come back,' Harry said, hanging up.

Alan stood up and walked to the window. 'The DNA matches,' he turned to Kim. 'Charles Martins is our suicide victim.'

'Shall we bring Creegan in?' Kim asked. 'I can't wait to see his face when we tell him we know who it is.'

'We don't have any proof Creegan knew him,' Alan said. 'How are we doing with his photographs?'

'They're on the second box.'

'We haven't found Martins' phone yet?'

'Nope. No sign of it. What are you thinking?'

'I want to know how Martins got from Bangor to Cemaes with a shotgun. He doesn't own a car. He didn't hire one and leave it nearby. We would have found it by now. He must have called someone.'

'He may have called an independent taxi. There are a few owner operators in Bangor,' Kim said.

'If we had his phone, we would know the answer to that,' Alan said. 'I don't want Creegan being a slippery bastard again. Let's not rush into bringing him in until we're sure we have answers. I want him squirming in that chair.'

A knock on the door interrupted them. The chief inspector and the ACC were standing outside the doorway, their uniforms immaculate, hats tucked under their arms. They were with two suited men. Kim excused herself and the men entered. Alan stood and greeted them.

'This is DI Williams,' Jason Marsh said, in introduction to the suited men. 'This is Donald Wilkinson and Geoff Lunt from the National Crime Agency.' Alan smiled thinly. When the NCA appeared in your station, shit was about to hit the fan. 'I must apologise for landing on you at short notice.'

'No problem. Take a seat, gentlemen.' Alan waited for them to sit down and decided saying nothing was better than saying the wrong thing. There was an awkward silence. 'This isn't a social call. So, how can I help you?'

'I won't beat around the bush. We're aware you're looking to arrest Jon Price on a very spurious warrant,' Geoff Lunt said.

'It's not that spurious someone needed to call the NCA,' Alan said. 'We want to arrest him so we can gain access to his CCTV system.'

'I'm afraid that can't happen.' Alan shrugged and waited for him to expand. 'Purely out of respect, we've come to tell you ourselves rather than it being passed down the ranks. That's never good practice. It only causes resentment between us and yourselves. We're trying to avoid that situation.'

'That's very considerate,' Alan said. He tried not to sound sarcastic but failed miserably. The chief constable eyed him sternly. 'A young man was shot with a high-powered air rifle at work today. He was at the top of a three-storey scaffold. He fell to his death. An X-ray showed two airgun pellets in his skull.'

'Sorry,' Lunt said. 'What has this got to do with Jon Price?'

'Price has been waging a campaign against his ex-girlfriend since he got out. Rowan Jackson was her current boyfriend.'

'Price will claim it's an unfortunate coincidence,' Lunt said, shrugging.

'Of course, he will. That's why we want to get into his house.'

'Price hasn't left his home since he arrived there,' Lunt said. 'He's not responsible for shooting anyone.'

'You know that, do you?'

'Yes. You're not the only people watching him.'

'He might not have pulled the trigger, but we all know he's capable of arranging accidents,' Alan said. The men nodded.

'He hasn't used his phone either,' Lunt countered.

'He hasn't used the phone registered to him,' Alan said. 'That doesn't mean he hasn't used *a* phone.' He paused. Lunt didn't argue. 'We also think he's responsible for the death of a young mother—'

'Melanie Brooks,' Lunt interrupted. Alan nodded, surprised. 'We're aware of her death, but I can only repeat what I've said already. Price hasn't left his home since he was released, and he won't leave it until we say he can.'

'I don't understand,' Alan said. 'We all know he has the resources to make things happen without setting a foot outside his gates.'

'Exactly. He's a resourceful man, and we're working with him on something much bigger. It cannot be compromised until he's played his role.'

'Bigger than two murders?' Alan said.

'It's a matter of national security.'

'That's a bullshit answer,' Alan said.

'I don't think that's the attitude to have,' the chief said, frowning.

'What attitude should I have when I'm being patted on the head and told to be quiet?' Alan asked. 'Either you came here to put your cards on the table and ask me to stall an investigation or you came here to tell me to do as I'm told and shut up. Which one is it?' The chief looked annoyed and was about to speak.

'Let me answer Alan's question. It's a reasonable request. The early release programme was an opportunity too good to miss.' Donald Wilkinson spoke for the first time. 'Price would never have been let out unless we arranged it.'

'We did wonder how he was released,' Alan said.

'We're aware he's a liability, but the stakes are high. Price is working for us until we are ready to cut him loose, then you can arrest him for whatever you like. We might be able to help you.'

'How is that?' Alan asked.

'Our surveillance is better than yours,' Wilkinson said. 'I think we can release our footage to you once this is all over.'

'And in the meantime, he can terrorise the island?' Alan asked. He held eye contact with Wilkinson. 'You're going to have to do better than the national security bullshit. If you want me to back off, I want a better reason than you're giving me. I'm going after Price. Once the wheels start turning, even the NCA can't stop them.' The chief looked embarrassed. 'He's hiding behind his gates, causing havoc. I can't sit here and watch him do that, I'm afraid.'

'Okay,' Wilkinson said. 'I'll give you the abbreviated version.'

'I'm listening.'

'Brexit is upon us. There will be a hard border between us and Ireland, which makes Holyhead a vital port for anyone trying to smuggle contraband from mainland Europe, Africa, and the Americas. We know Paul Sutton has the port sewn up. He's managing the payroll for a network so complex that anything can be smuggled through that harbour if the price is right. We've tried to set him up with dummy shipments, but somehow, he knows which ones are legit and which aren't. He has officers on the boats, transport police officers, border force agents, customs officers, and local uniformed officers. You name it, he has plants in there.'

'Paul Sutton has become a criminal mastermind?' Alan scoffed. 'Do me a favour. He's a conman and low-level dealer at best. There's not a chance he's developed a network like that. He's thick as pig shit.'

'He didn't develop it,' Wilkinson said. 'Jon Price did it over a decade and did a fantastic job of keeping it operating until seven years ago. He was backed by some very dangerous operators from Belfast and Liverpool. When Price went down, the powers that be drafted Sutton to play caretaker. He handles things on the ground and keeps the dogs on a leash. Things have become critical with the introduction of a border in the Irish Sea. The people at the top want Price back in play and we were in a position to do that. With Price back at the helm, we can bring down some very powerful organisations. They would take decades to recover if they can at all.'

'So, you're setting a thief to catch a thief?' Alan said. The men nodded. He thought about it for a minute. 'How long is this going to take?'

'Two to three weeks,' Wilkinson said. 'I think that will give you enough time to gather your evidence and make sure he can't wriggle out when you arrest him.' Alan shrugged and nodded. 'We're not protecting the bastard, Alan. We are using him to get control of that port. It's absolutely vital to the rest of the UK. Once we have our targets in the bag, you can have Price.'

'You're not offering him a deal?'

'He thinks we are.'

'So, he thinks he's protected, but he isn't?'

'Yes. You have my word.'

'This must be a very lucrative operation. What makes you think Paul Sutton will let go of the reins?'

'We know how these people operate,' Wilkinson said. 'He won't be an issue.'

'Three weeks?' Alan said to Wilkinson. Wilkinson and Lunt both nodded. 'And you're okay with this, sir?' The chief nodded. 'Okay. I'll play ball.'

'Obviously, this conversation never happened.' Wilkinson stood up. 'I won't shake your hand. Hands, face, and space and all that palaver.'

'I appreciate your honesty,' Alan said. 'Thank you, sir.'

The men filed out, much to the amusement of the MIT detectives in the operations room. They pretended they hadn't noticed the strangers arriving. The chief constable and the ACC rarely made an appearance on the island, especially together. Once they'd gone, the volume went up.

'What's the chief doing here, is he lost?' Richard asked. Laughter rippled around the room.

'Did you see how shiny his buttons were?' another voice called.

'I reckon we're all getting a medal.'

'What are you getting a medal for?'

'Turning up.'

'The only medal you're getting is a chocolate one at Christmas.'

'Have you been promoted?' Kim asked.

'You're not getting a medal and I haven't been promoted. Calm down,' Alan said. 'I'm not supposed to say anything. It's all top secret.'

'Come on, spill the beans. Are we getting a pay rise?'

'We might do if we can pull it off,' Alan said, seriously. The laughter stopped.

'Pull what off?'

'I can't tell you yet.'

'Come on, Alan. What did they want?'

'I shouldn't be telling you this yet. It isn't official.' Alan put his hands on his hips and shook his head. 'This goes no further than the people in this room,' Alan said. The volume dropped. Silence descended. 'Okay. If this gets out, I'll be shot. I need a firm promise from everyone in this team that this will not be repeated outside of this room.' Nodding heads all around the room. 'We're all aware how COVID-19 is affecting our operations.' More nodding heads. 'The force wants to identify ground-breaking teams of detectives to trial the newest test and trace measures. The chief inspector nominated us as the force's best team. We'll be trialling this, but it is top secret. If the press gets hold of this, the country will be in uproar. No one else is aware of this. It could be a game-changer.' He paused to allow the news to sink in. 'Each of you will partner up with a COVID-19-buddy of the same sex. At the start and end of each shift. You will test your partner to see if they're infected or have been infected during the shift.' He paused again. 'There will be a new piece of equipment distributed at the end of the shift today. It's not to be taken home under any circumstances.' He held up a box of latex gloves. 'Take one each. Under no circumstances are they to be reused, understood?'

'A latex glove. What do we have to do?' Richard asked, confused.

'At the start and end of your shift, put on a latex glove, bend your partner over your desk, and perform an internal examination of your partner's back passage. If their temperature is raised, tell them that they need to get tested.'

'Oh, fuck off!'

'I was listening to that all the way, dick-head!'

'I knew it was bullshit when he said the chief thinks we're the best team.'

'So, is that a wind up then?'

'What do you think?' Alan said. 'That serves you right for being a bunch of nosey coppers,' Alan said. A barrage of abuse was hurled at him.

'On a serious note,' Carmel said, gesturing for his attention. 'I think you might want to see this.'

'You're not going to bend over are you, Carmel?'

'Bugger off,' Carmel said, smiling.

Alan and Kim walked over to her desk. The laughter died down and everyone got back to work. 'What is it?' Alan asked. Carmel was looking at a payroll list from Oakland House in Wrexham.

'It's a payroll report. They were part of the local authorities back then, and their records are online. They were uploaded years ago to save space storing them.'

'When is that report from?'

'December ninety-three. It's a twelve-month summary. I've downloaded the reports for ninety-three to ninety-five.'

'Excellent. What have you found?'

'Look at this name here,' Carmel said. 'He's there for all three years. The surname jumped out at me. Alister Pickford.'

'Pickford?' Alan said, staring at the screen.

'Related to Roger Pickford?' Kim asked.

'Look at his date of birth,' Carmel said. Alan frowned. 'It's the same as Roger Pickford. I've checked Roger Pickford's birth registration. Bangor registry office has Roger and Alister recorded as twins. Identical twins.'

'Find out where he is,' Alan said. 'We need to speak to him.'

Chapter 37

Cristy sipped her Honey Jack Daniels and enjoyed the sweetness and the burn at the back of her throat. It was smooth and drinkable without ice or mixer. It was beginning to numb her emotions. Her mind was in a state of shock. Rowan had been in her life since school. Phillip and Rowan were like brothers. They went everywhere together as kids and ended up as partners in their roofing business as men. He'd loved Cristy since school but never crossed the line. She was Phil's sister, Myra's daughter, and out of bounds. It was years after Price went to jail that he confessed how he felt. They were in the Driftwood in Trearddur Bay, drinking shots and watching football. Rowan blushed purple while he spat out the words in a garbled sentence, as if he had revealed the world's biggest secret. Cristy nearly choked on her drink and laughed. She thought he was going to cry. He was so embarrassed. It had taken years of suppressing his emotions and finally he had the opportunity to express them and she laughed. Cristy cried at the memory. She wanted to hold him and tell him how much she'd loved him, even if she didn't always show it.

Of course, she hadn't laughed in a cruel or callous way. She had laughed because it had been obvious how he felt about her. Her mother had been teasing her about Rowan since their school years. Phil did too, although not as much. He was protective of his sister and he loved his best friend. Them dating could lead to someone getting hurt and then he didn't want to take sides. She remembered his face when she laughed at him. He looked so young and sad and confused. She had taken all the confusion away when she kissed him on the lips and told him she knew how he felt. She didn't tell him that everyone knew how he felt. The poor man was struggling as it was. They started dating that day and had stayed together ever since. It had been a long, slow process, but Rowan respected her feelings and was patient.

She thought she'd never love another man after Jon Price had abused her, raped her, and destroyed her confidence. Her trust was trampled into the dirt, and she couldn't find it in her to give anyone a chance. Until Rowan made his feelings clear. She let him in, slowly. One day at a time and days turned to weeks, and then months and years and their love grew. She knew he was going to propose at Christmas, and she was going to say yes. They talked about it often. She wanted to be married at the Trearddur Bay Hotel, so all their friends and family could be invited. Their life was planned out. Married, four children, two boys and two girls, and grow old together watching their family become adults and have their grandchildren. Rowan said he wanted dozens of them, the more the merrier.

That was all gone. He'd been shot in the eye, stumbled blindly in a panic, frightened and in pain, and tumbled over the safety rail to his death. She tortured herself about how scared he must have been. The last minutes of consciousness would have been traumatic. Pain, fear, confusion. She wondered if he would have known he'd been shot. If he did, he would have known it was Jon Price who was responsible. She knew he was responsible. He'd ruined her life once and now he'd done it again but this time, she didn't think she was going to survive. She couldn't live without Rowan. The pain was too great to bear. She wanted to die. There was a bottle of tramadol in the bathroom. All she had to do was swallow them and wash them down with the Jack Daniels and she would sleep forever, away from the pain and anguish. Away from Price. She simply couldn't cope without Rowan. He'd brought her back from the brink and made her strong again. Without him, she was nothing. Her hopes and dreams were dashed. She emptied her glass and went upstairs to the bathroom.

****

The MIT was dwindling. Most of the detectives were chasing leads on the Rowan Jackson murder. There were only so many places a shooter could have hidden. The air rifle used was high powered but only over a short distance. Someone must have seen something. It was getting late and Alan had sent the stragglers home to get some sleep. Carmel was still sifting through employment records and Kim was helping two detectives with the photographs taken from Pickford's home in Bangor. She opened a bulging envelope of photographs developed by Kwikprint. Four strips of brown negatives fell onto the desk. The first photograph caught her attention. Father Creegan was standing next to two men in scout uniform. In front of them was a group of beaming young boys, standing proudly in their uniforms, holding up certificates for the world to see.

'Bingo,' Kim said. She waved the photographs. Alan and Carmel came to the desk. 'That is Creegan and Pickford,' she said. 'They're much younger, but it's unmistakably them. That's Roger Pickford.'

'Look at the teenager there,' Carmel said. 'That could be Charles Martins.'

'And that scout leader is Reece Moffat,' Alan said. 'Let's see the others.'

Kim dealt the photographs onto the desk in rows and columns. They all showed faces they were familiar with, younger but recognisable. Priests, businesspeople, and scout leaders all mentioned by Don Shipley and Ian Osbourne.

'Every single photograph in this packet shows Creegan or the Pickford brothers with Moffat,' Kim said, shaking her head.

'I think these men here could be Father Hancock and Father Lawson,' Alan said, pointing to another image. 'And that's Father Cummings with Moffat.'

'Charles Martins put all these photographs into one packet for a reason,' Kim said. 'They're taken years apart, yet he's bundled them together.'

'Look here,' Alan said. 'The Pickford twins together with Charles Martin and another scout troop. Look how alike the twins are. That's freaky.' He took off his glasses and cleaned them on his shirt. 'Father Creegan can't deny knowing them now, can he?'

'These photographs are taken over a decade at least.' Kim selected two. 'Look here. Charles Martins is a scout here. Late teens maybe?' she said. 'Here he is in a leader's uniform. Ten years older at least. Look how grey Pickford has gone.'

Richard walked over to the desk. He was carrying two sheets of paper with figures on them. 'They used the scouts and sea scouts as recruiting grounds,' Richard said.

'Sea scouts?' Alan asked.

'Yes. And church choirs,' he said, putting the papers on the desk next to the photographs. 'When I talked to Janine Bay earlier today, she told me that Luca Bay and Eddie Speers were childhood friends. They were in the scouts and the sea scouts, and they both lost their parents at a young age and spent a short time living with other relatives. That would have made them very vulnerable,' Richard said. 'Something she said made me think.'

'What was that?' Alan asked.

'She said they went travelling when Eddie finished sixth form. Both of them were eighteen at a push. They travelled for over a year. Cambodia, Thailand, Vietnam.'

'And?' Alan asked.

'Both sets of parents had died, and they had no money,' Richard said. 'They were from poor families. They inherited nothing, yet they had the money to travel across south-east Asia for over a year at eighteen. It didn't sit right with me, so I pulled their bank records.'

'We've looked at them,' Kim said. 'There was nothing out of the ordinary.'

'We have looked at them, but we didn't look back far enough,' Richard said. 'They were both paid a sum of ten-thousand pounds in two-thousand and eight.'

'From whom?' Alan asked.

'A double-glazing company in Glan Conwy. Snowdon Glass owned by Reece Moffat,' Richard said.

'You've got to be kidding me?' Alan said beneath his breath. 'That is good work, Richard. We need to get a warrant for Moffat's accounts. All of them, business and personal.'

'No wonder he was broke when he died,' Carmel said.

'He was broke?' Richard asked. 'How do you know?'

'We found a CCJ lodged against Thelma Moffat after his death,' Carmel said. 'His wife lost everything after his accident. Now we know why there was no money left.'

'He was shelling out hush money,' Alan said.

'Bay and Speers fit the profile as vulnerable boys,' Richard said. 'No direct family to tell what was happening to them. They were loners, and they stopped talking for a few years when Luca dropped out of school. I think they were traumatised and dealing with it independently of each other. Then they received a ridiculous amount of money for a teenager to have and went to the airport and ran away.'

'It adds up,' Alan said.

'That means Jon Price has nothing to do with their attacks. Their deaths could be linked to Creegan and Pickford and Moffat and all the other paedo scum.' Richard paused to take a deep breath. He was angry. 'Sorry,' he said. 'That's not very professional.'

'Maybe not, but that's what they are,' Alan said. He patted Richard on the back. 'That's good detective work. Charles Martins may have started a sequence of events which will expose historic abuse on a huge scale. That means someone might be trying to silence the victims of a paedophile ring which operated a long time ago. Maybe Charles Martin decided it was time to out them all,' Alan said, rubbing his eyes. 'Right, people. Go home. Get some sleep. Tomorrow morning, we'll bring Creegan in. I want everyone refreshed and fed and sharp.'

'What about Jon Price?' Kim asked.

'He hasn't moved out of his house and he hasn't used his phone,' Alan said. 'Cristy Dennis is being tormented and her boyfriend is dead. Someone else is out there doing that. Tomorrow, we'll concentrate on finding out who that is.'

****▢

Paul Sutton drove across the island towards Porth Wen brickworks. It stopped making fire bricks in the forties, but the buildings were still there like sentinels perched on the cliffs above the sea. He'd been summoned to a meeting he couldn't be arsed going to, but they'd insisted. They weren't the type of people you said no to. Not that he'd met them. They were like ghosts. It was getting on for midnight and he wanted to be at home in bed watching a film and drinking brandy. He parked his car as close as he could. It was a five-minute walk down a narrow path to the brickworks. He reached into the glove box for his torch and opened the door. A full moon hovered above the black sea, reflecting silver on the waves. The wind cut through him.

'Are you struggling to get out, fatty?' a voice asked. The accent was Northern Ireland. Harsh and guttural, probably Belfast.

'I'm fine,' Sutton said, angrily. 'Who the fuck are you?'

'That doesn't matter,' the man said. He was wiry with a shaven head and broken nose like a boxer. There was a jagged scar across the bridge of his nose. His eyes were focused on him. Sutton sensed he was a very dangerous man, probably ex-paramilitary. If he wanted to call him fat, that was fine. 'Shamus sends his regards.'

'He said he would be here.'

'He got called away on business.'

'Business?' Sutton said. 'What is this, Monopoly?'

'Shamus calls the shots. I do as I'm told.' The man shrugged. 'So do you.'

'He could have told me that before I drove out here at stupid o'clock. I've got better things to do with my time.'

'Have you brought the memory stick?'

'Have you brought the money?'

The man turned around and waved his torch in the air. A dark panelled van approached, its headlights off. Sutton heard a door slide open.

'Give me the account details,' the man said. Another man appeared, dressed in black combat gear. He carried a laptop. 'As soon as we have the files loaded, the money will be transferred wherever you like.'

'I said cash. Shamus always gives me cash.'

'No more cash. All transactions will be digital from now on. Things are changing.'

'How am I supposed to pay people?' Sutton said. 'Everyone wants cash. It's not rocket science. Bank transfers leave a footprint.'

'I'll need the files,' the man said, holding out his hand. 'It is what it is.'

'No cash, no files. This is not what Shamus said. Tell him to get in contact with me when he's finished fucking around,' Sutton said. He turned and walked towards his car. A crossbow bolt pierced his right shoulder blade. The tip exited beneath his collarbone and glinted silver in the moonlight. He stared down at it, mouth open, shocked by the excruciating pain. A second bolt pierced his left thigh and protruded above his knee. He fell heavily to his knees. 'Stop!' he gasped. 'What the fuck are you doing?'

The man stood over him. 'Memory stick,' he said, holding out his hand. Sutton reached inside his coat and gave it to him. 'Why didn't you do that in the first place?'

'I need to go to the hospital,' Sutton said, trying to stop the bleeding with his hands. He heard footsteps approaching. The man walked behind him, out of sight. 'Help me, please.'

'Get him into the van and torch the car,' the man said. 'We've got what we came for.'

Chapter 38

Sean Bannon stormed into the interview room and thumped his briefcase onto the desk dramatically. Father Patrick Creegan followed him quietly in comparison. The priest sat down and steepled his fingers on the desk. He sat back and closed his eyes, as if in silent prayer. Alan and Kim walked in and sat down. Bannon remained standing and glared at them, his hands on the desk like an angry teacher facing a classroom of unruly students.

'I'm ready to file a formal complaint when we leave here. This is crossing all the lines and is turning into a harassment suit,' Bannon said. Alan and Kim looked at each other and shrugged.

'Sue me,' Alan said. He looked at Kim and smiled. 'I've always wanted to say that.'

'Cross it off the bucket list,' Kim said.

'Is that it?' Bannon snapped. 'You'll be laughing on the other side of your face when NWP gets landed with a lawsuit.'

'Sit down, Mr Bannon,' Kim said. 'Before you give yourself a heart attack.' Bannon looked at her defiantly. 'We have a lot of new information to discuss, which may result in some serious charges being pressed, so I suggest you sit down and do your job.'

'What type of charges?'

'Sit down, Mr Bannon.'

Bannon sat down and huffed as he took out his laptop.

'This is a total waste of my time,' he said, angrily.

'You don't have to be here. You can leave at any time you like,' Alan said. 'I assume you're being paid handsomely for being here.'

'What I get paid is none of your concern.'

'No. It isn't but today I guarantee you're going to earn every penny,' Alan said, smiling. Bannon looked worried for a second. 'I need to remind you, Father Creegan, you're now under caution and we will be recording the interview and whatever you say may be used at a later date. Understand?'

'Yes,' Father Creegan said. He looked worried. His tongue licked at his thin lips repeatedly. Alan could feel how nervous he was. It was cool in the room, but there was perspiration on his forehead. 'Have you identified him?' he asked. Alan nodded. 'Who was he?'

'Do you know who Charles Martins is?' Alan asked.

'Oh, dear lord. Was that who it was?' the priest asked. He shook his head slowly and looked down at his hands. His fingers were trembling. 'Poor, poor Charles. I did wonder if it might be him.' The priest shrugged. 'Charles has been vulnerable all his life.'

'So, you do know him?'

'Yes. Or I should say I did know him many moons ago,' Creegan said. He closed his eyes. 'It feels like a lifetime ago.'

'When was the last time you saw him alive?'

'I don't know,' Creegan said, thinking. 'Ten years ago. Maybe a bit less. Did he leave a note?'

'Sort of,' Alan said. Creegan looked confused. 'He left enough for us to connect him to you.'

'I don't understand.'

'Tell us how you know him?'

'I met him many years ago when Donald Shipley began running around accusing everyone of being a paedophile,' Creegan said. 'We first met in the nineties when Charles Martins was a vulnerable teenager in care. He was befriended by an employee at the care home he lived in. Unfortunately, that friendship led to him being groomed by a group of men from Bangor that I was familiar with. I tried to help Charles, but it was a losing battle.'

'You tried to help him how?' Kim asked, frowning.

'I befriended him and told him I was there to talk to if he needed to,' Creegan said. 'I saw him as often as I could and tried to get him to open up to me, but he was under their spell. He was too scared to say a word.'

'Who were the men he was scared of?' Alan asked. The priest was very calm considering the topic of conversation. His voice was stable and balanced.

'Roger Pickford and his brother, Alister. They were twins and had an unhealthy interest in teenagers,' Creegan said. 'Alister worked at the home where Charles was residing, and it was his influence that brought Charles to Bangor. That was where the group operated from. It took me years to comprehend the scale of their influence, but the twins and a man called Reece Moffat were at the centre of the web.' He stared at Alan, analysing his expression. 'You've heard of Moffat?'

'We're aware of him, yes.'

'The Pickfords and Moffat were the driving force behind the group. Moffat had influence in the business community. Don Shipley tried to warn people what was going on, but no one listened,' Creegan said, calmly. He looked saddened by the memories. 'There were dozens of others surrounding them, supporting them and helping to cover things up. And there were even more on the periphery. Some of them were my colleagues from the church. That was a paradox for me.'

'A paradox how?' Kim asked.

'The choice between exposing a fellow priest and damaging the reputation of the church and men of the cloth was torment for me.' Creegan looked down and reflected. 'Paedophile priests have become almost old news. The damage done to the church has been irreparable. At that time, we were trying to deflect accusation after accusation worldwide. I was reluctant to add fuel to the flames.'

'Did you know the Pickfords and Reece Moffat personally?' Alan clarified. Creegan nodded. 'And you knew they were abusing teenagers?' Alan asked. Creegan nodded again. 'For the tape please, Father.'

'Yes. I knew that they were abusing teenagers.'

'How did you know for sure?' Kim asked.

'Don Shipley told me,' Father Creegan said. Alan sat back as if the statement had pushed him backwards. 'He had detailed evidence.'

'Shipley told you directly?' Alan said, surprised. 'My understanding is he didn't trust priests. I think you'd better expand on that.'

'He didn't trust priests at all, but I wasn't part of the click. My work abroad sct mc apart from them. Don Shipley trusted me.'

'You worked abroad before where?' Kim asked.

'Africa and South America, mostly. I was stationed abroad for the best part of twenty-years on and off before I settled in North Wales. Many of the priests here started at the same time as I did, but my time abroad made me a stranger on my return. The trust they had with each other didn't extend to me. I think Don recognised that. He knew I was different. Don and I became good friends.' Alan and Kim exchanged glances and tried not to look shocked. Creegan looked troubled. He shook his head and pinched the bridge of his nose. 'I'm very sad that Charles took his own life. I feel a terrible guilt weighing on me.'

'Why do you feel guilty?' Alan asked.

'Perhaps I could have done more to help him. I tried.' Creegan's eyes filled up. His bottom lip quivered. He looked genuinely upset.

'Perhaps we should take a break?' Bannon said.

'No, please.' Creegan held up his hand. He took a deep breath. 'What I'm going to tell you is nothing new. I told people twenty-years ago, as did Don Shipley, but people were too concerned about the damage it would do to important men with reputations. And they had to protect the church, you see. Don and I were a thorn in the side of the organisation. I will tell you the truth about what happened. Everything I know.'

'I think we should have a break while you run this by me,' Bannon said. 'I must insist. This is going way beyond knowing who committed suicide in your home. We're venturing into the realm of serious crime.'

'It's now or never, I'm afraid,' Creegan said. 'The truth has been buried for long enough. If I tell you what happened, maybe this time people will listen.'

'You need to remember I'm acting on behalf of the church, Father Creegan. They pay my bill. My job is…'

'To protect the church. I've heard it all my life. People like you helped to keep it buried. You helped the paedophiles walk free to re-offend. You're as bad as they are,' the priest said to his brief. Bannon looked angry. 'You can stay, or you can go. I'm not bothered either way, but I won't be silenced any longer. I don't need you to protect me as I haven't done anything wrong.'

Bannon looked defeated.

'I must insist on a break,' Bannon said. 'I'm concerned about my client's mental wellbeing. I think he may be suffering a breakdown due to the trauma he's suffered. What he's saying could be taken out of context.'

'He seems fine to me,' Alan said.

'And to me,' Kim agreed. 'Are you feeling unwell, Father?'

'Not at all. I'm of sound health and sound mind,' Creegan said. Bannon went to speak, but the priest held up his hand. 'Be quiet or leave. You're making me feel quite nauseous.' Bannon sat back and put his pen down with a clatter. 'I'll start at the beginning, shall I?'

'Please do,' Alan said.

'My first introduction to Don Shipley was during the investigation into what happened to Ewan Birley and Christopher Deeks. He was already campaigning against certain members of the church in the area. When those boys went missing, it seemed to trigger something in him. Several unconfirmed sightings of the boys indicated they'd been on a train. Another put them at Bangor station. The police couldn't substantiate either. There was a meeting at the university, arranged by a local neighbourhood watch group. It was well attended by the police and community leaders. Roger Pickford and Reece Moffat were there too. I was sitting next to Don, and he was incensed. It was the first time we'd met, and he made it clear his superiors had gagged him for the meeting. Their focus was simply to engage the public to help find the teenagers or find out what happened to them. I got the distinct impression they wanted to prove the boys had never been in Bangor, but Don wanted to start a witch hunt. He would have named and shamed his suspects right there if he was allowed to. His superior officers watched him nervously. I think they were concerned Don was going to embarrass the Bangor force.'

'What did you think about what he said?' Alan asked.

'Back then you mean?' Creegan asked, frowning.

'Yes. What were your feelings at the time?'

'He didn't outright tell me his concerns in detail, but the implication was clear. I was both a stranger and a priest. He was understandably cautious. I remember being disturbed by the level of his conviction, and I gave him my number and address. There's very rarely any smoke without fire,' Creegan said. 'At the break, he mentioned Pickford's name in a hushed conversation with another uniformed officer. I was aware of Pickford as a shop owner and local scout leader. When the meeting ended, I went back to my normal business, but I made a point of seeking out the local scout groups, youth clubs, church choirs, and the like. I identified sixteen out-of-school groups where teenagers gathered under adult supervision and I offered my time to each one.'

'To do what, exactly?' Alan asked.

'To see for myself what was going on,' Creegan said. 'I wanted to prove to myself that there were good people out there doing good things for the young and vulnerable in our society, especially the church.' He shrugged and sighed. 'I wanted my presence to be a warning to those considering anything untoward. I would turn up unannounced and observe. Sometimes, I was asked to participate, especially in the choirs. Over the next few months and years, what I discovered rattled my faith in God and the church. The more involved I became, the more evidence I saw of organised abuse. Don was right most of the time although it was many years later when I believed him completely.'

'What do you mean?' Alan asked.

'I was forever the optimist. I was so focused on finding the good in people, I couldn't believe Don was correct about everything he said.

Not all the time. It was too much to take in. Of course, by the time I was convinced, Don was long gone. Don disappeared in ninety-seven, I think. If we'd listened to him then, we could have stopped years of abuse for dozens of children, but we didn't.' The priest closed his eyes again. 'Don came to see me a week before he disappeared with all his evidence,' Creegan said. Alan and Kim looked surprised. 'He gave me copies of his research. I had lists of the people he suspected and the places where youngsters were being selected and groomed. He told me to read it and said we would meet the week after and discuss the information. He was ready to go to the national press because the local avenues were closed. I studied it in detail of course, but we didn't get the chance to meet again. He vanished and left me with the vilest information anyone could have in their possession. I debated what to do with it for weeks.'

'Why you?' Alan asked.

'Pardon?'

'I mean why did he choose you to disclose his evidence to?'

'Because I wasn't on any of his lists, inspector,' Creegan said, shaking his head. 'I wasn't involved in any of the groups or organisations he accused of being involved. He needed help on the inside, but needed someone he could trust. It's my belief they knew he was going to disclose his findings and recruit an insider and that's why they got rid of him.'

'You think he was murdered?'

'Yes. I would love to think he was sunning himself somewhere far away from here but I don't believe a man with such conviction would run away.' Creegan shrugged. 'Plus, there were the threats I received.'

'What threats?' Alan asked.

'Phone calls telling me to be quiet or they would cut my tongue out, letters made from newspaper cuttings, all sorts of shenanigans,' Creegan said. 'I ignored them. Don Shipley is dead. I have no doubt in my mind of that.'

'He told you the Pickford twins and Reece Moffat were the ring leaders?' Alan asked.

'Yes.' Creegan nodded. 'I spoke to them all at length.'

'You spoke to them about what?'

'About being paedophiles, of course.'

'How did those conversations go?'

'Badly at first,' Creegan said. 'They were wary. I approached the subject as a priest struggling to understand our vow of celibacy.'

'So, you didn't confront them about being paedophiles?' Kim asked, confused. 'You baited them to invite you in?'

'Yes. I didn't confront them. What was the point in that?' Creegan shrugged. 'Don had already shouted their names from the rooftops and the police had investigated them and nothing was done. At that time, several of my colleagues in the cloth had been spoken to and slapped on the wrist, and the issue brushed under the carpet. Don's evidence wasn't enough, as convincing as it was. Any witnesses he had were stifled quickly. No one was prepared to come forward and give evidence. I tried to infiltrate. I needed proof. Cold, hard proof.'

'Did you find any?' Kim asked.

'Plenty,' Creegan said, nodding. 'I had procedures to follow. Every time I took the evidence to my superiors, they said it would be dealt with. I was given a pat on the back and told to go back to my church and tend to my parishioners. The offenders were shuffled about here and there, but nothing of any substance happened. No one was prosecuted. Eventually, I contacted the head of the scout movement myself and bypassed my superiors. I gave them the evidence I had directly, and they finally acted.'

'What happened?' Alan asked.

'They banned Moffat and Roger Pickford from being members and closed the packs in the North Wales area while they investigated.'

'They closed them?' Kim asked, searching for the notes. 'What year was that?'

'Twenty-ten,' Creegan said.

'Thirteen years after Shipley went missing?' Alan asked, shocked. 'It took you thirteen years to close them down?'

'This is what I'm telling you. No one listened,' Creegan said. He sat back and raised his hands in the air. 'I was stuck between identifying offenders and protecting the church and the church wasn't listening.'

'So, what did you do?' Kim asked.

'I decided to act myself,' Creegan said.

'How?'

'I threatened to expose the individuals themselves,' Creegan said. 'I confronted more men than I can remember, and I threatened to expose them to their wives and families. Most of them stopped immediately. Threatening to tell their wives did the trick most times.'

'That was very brave,' Kim said.

'There was no other option open to me.'

'Why were Moffat and Pickford not charged if the scout movement banned them?'

'There were no criminal proceedings. They stopped them operating, but Moffat started his own organisation. Snowdon Adventure Scouts. He was up and running again six months later.'

'You're joking?' Kim asked, shaking her head.

'No, unfortunately not. I made contact with as many parents as I could, anonymously, but some of them weren't interested. Moffat was very plausible. People liked and respected him.'

'You knew all this and went on a fishing trip with Reece Moffat and Father Nigel Hancock,' Alan said.

'I heard them talking about fishing and went home and did some research. Then I engaged them in conversation about sea fishing and that's how we came to rent a boat.'

'Tell me how that came about?'

'It was a long time ago, detective.' The priest sighed and sat back. 'I needed to get Moffat and Hancock to trust me. I was on the edge of their seedy little world, but they didn't trust me enough to let me in. I suggested the trip, hired the boat, and stacked it with booze.' He shrugged. 'When we reached Puffin Island, they were drunk. We all were. I got them talking by telling them I was having fantasies and struggling with my vows of celibacy. They believed me. It worked, but they were drunk and feeling seasick. They went into the cabin for a lie down, leaving me at the helm. I made the fatal mistake of turning the boat sideways against the waves. I was drunk and panicked. Of course, the boat was swamped within minutes. It tipped onto its side for a while. Moffat and Hancock were trapped inside. It capsized completely and sank very quickly. I'd managed to make an SOS call on the radio, but there was no way to recover them. The sea was too rough. I managed to swim to the island and clung to a rock. I was lucky they found me.'

'So, Moffat and Hancock admitted to you that they were abusing teenagers?'

'Yes.'

'And then they died?'

'Yes. Karma perhaps, detective,' Creegan said.

'Karma indeed,' Alan said. 'We know Moffat made two payments of ten-thousand pounds to sea scouts from the island,' Alan said. 'Not long before he drowned. Coincidence, Father?'

'The lord moves in mysterious ways,' Creegan said. 'I wasn't the only crusader searching out the filth within our society. Don Shipley began something in the nineties, which is still rolling today. People will not tolerate our children being abused by paedophiles. Any sign of predators nowadays brings swift and violent responses online and in real life. If Moffat paid money to those boys, then good for them. Someone may have threatened him with exposure. He portrayed himself as an honourable family man with a wife and children. He was a high-profile businessman. Anyone could have pointed a finger at him. They would have been queuing up to expose him. Remember that a lot of their victims would have been older by then. The young boys would have grown into young men with sharp memories, social media accounts, and a lot of anger.'

'Luca Bay and Eddie Speers,' Alan said. 'Do their names mean anything to you?'

'No. But there have been so many over the years. My memory isn't what it was.'

'Tell me about the priests who died on Snowdon,' Alan said. 'Wilfred Lawson and Maxwell Cummings.' Creegan's eyes seemed to glaze over. 'Were they involved in the ring?'

'Yes. They were very close to Alister Pickford,' Creegan said. 'Alister was the linchpin in all of it.'

'Are you telling us Alister Pickford was the leader of this group?' Alan asked, frowning. 'Not Roger.'

'Roger was an angel compared to his brother,' Creegan said. 'Alister is the evilest man I've ever had the misfortune to meet. He's the devil incarnate.'

'But Charles Martin lived with Roger?' Kim said.

'As Charles got older, he became of no interest to Alister, but Roger and Charles had developed a bond. They were unusual soulmates, but soulmates they were,' Creegan said. 'I'm assuming they were still together before Charles committed suicide?'

'Roger Pickford is dead,' Alan said,

'I read an article online,' Creegan said, 'About a shopkeeper found dead in suspicious circumstances on the high street but it didn't name him. Was that Roger?'

'Roger Pickford was tied up, gagged, and hung from a beam in his bedroom,' Kim said. Creegan looked shocked. 'We think Charles Martins did it. Maybe they weren't soulmates after all.'

'Oh, no. You're so wrong. Charles would never have killed Roger,' Creegan said. 'He was a very quiet child. There was no violence in that boy. Roger and Charles loved each other. They became even closer when Alister went to prison.'

'When did he go to prison?' Alan asked, surprised.

'Nine years ago,' Creegan said.

'You seem sure about that.' He nudged Kim. She opened the door and instructed the uniformed officer to tell Richard Lewis to check the prisons for Alister Pickford.

'I'm absolutely certain.' The priest paused, choosing his next words carefully. 'He was arrested when some photographs and videos were found in a house in Manchester. That's where he lived, you see.'

'Whereabouts?' Alan asked.

'Stockport somewhere,' Creegan said. 'He married a girl from the island, and they moved away. She was pregnant, and it was clear he'd been seeing her while she was underage. That's why they left. Anyway, they had a son. It didn't last long, and she moved back to the island with the child. Alister stayed there but travelled to his brother's often. Roger knew he made recordings, and I told GMP where they could find them. The evidence was damning and combined with the statements from Charles and Roger, he was sent to prison for twenty-years.'

'Twenty-years?' Alan asked. 'His brother testified against him?'

'Yes. Roger told me where to find the evidence, and it was the opportunity I'd been waiting for. Putting Alister in jail was the final nail in the Bangor group's coffin,' Creegan said.

'It's one thing pointing you to the information but testifying is another. Something must have nudged him to give evidence?' Alan said.

'Yes, me.'

'You?'

'Yes. I made him testify,' Creegan said. Alan looked shocked. 'I told him if he didn't, I would implicate him, and Charles, and they would be sent to prison too. Splitting them up would have broken both of them. I'd uncovered a box owned by Alister. It holds powerful evidence going back years that would have sent them all to prison for a very long time.'

'Did you give it to the police?'

'No.'

'Why not?'

'There was enough to send him to prison. I kept the box as protection. If anything happened to me, it would be sent to you here,' Creegan said. 'That box has kept me alive.'

'You're telling me that you've been on a one-man crusade to shut this abuse down?'

'Yes. Don Shipley was the catalyst in me. I've spent years telling the perpetrators to stop doing what they were doing.' Creegan sat forward and tapped the desk as he spoke. 'Wilfred Lawson, Maxwell Cummings,

Nigel Hancock, Reece Moffat, the Pickfords, and many others stopped doing what they were doing. I made them stop.'

'Four of those men died in your company,' Alan said.

'They had accidents,' Creegan shrugged. 'There were enquiries into their deaths. There was never any suspicion of foul play. Just because they were evil men doesn't excuse them from having an accident. The mountains and the sea are not theme parks. They're deadly playgrounds. They were unfortunate.'

'What if they hadn't had accidents?' Alan asked. 'What then?'

'I would have found a way to persuade them to stop. Just like I did with Alister and his cronies. They all stopped for their own reasons, but they stopped. Charles killing himself has raked it all up again and I can only guess the reason why.'

'And what would your guess be?' Alan asked, frowning.

'I've heard about the early release scheme because of COVID-19,' Creegan said. 'It's been on the news. Alister's son was released, and he's not a very popular man. I've seen his name in the news.'

'Who is that?' Alan asked.

'His name is Jon Price. I've seen it online. He was doing fifteen years,' Creegan said. 'I believe he's as bad as his father. They say victims of abuse often become abusers, don't they?'

'They do,' Alan said, rendered almost speechless. 'Do you know Jon Price?'

'I know of him,' Creegan said. 'Roger mentioned that his brother had made contact with his son. That wasn't long before he was arrested.'

'What was his mother's name?'

'Polly Price,' Creegan said. 'She was from Menai, I think. She became a nurse.' Alan wrote it down and Kim took the note to the door. 'You're missing the point I'm making, inspector.'

'What point am I missing?'

'If they let a violent man like Jon Price out early on this release scheme, then maybe they let Alister out too.' Alan nodded and contemplated the news. 'You've asked me several times how Charles

Martins came to the vicarage carrying a shotgun.' Alan nodded. 'How does a man cross the island carrying a double-barrelled shotgun without being seen?'

'You're suggesting Alister Pickford brought him?' Alan asked.

'Yes, but more than that. I'm suggesting Alister Pickford killed the men who sent him to prison. Roger Pickford and Charles Martins. I think Charles came to my house to kill me because Alister told him to.'

'You think Alister Pickford killed his brother then forced Charles Martins into his vehicle and brought him to your house?'

'Yes. That's exactly what I'm saying.' The priest shrugged and shook his head. 'Charles Martins didn't kill himself and he didn't kill his lifelong partner. He loved Roger.'

'Assuming Alister was released,' Kim said.

'Obviously, we'll look into where Alister Pickford is,' Alan said, standing up. 'I need the whereabouts of the box you spoke about too,' he added.

'It's hidden in my workshop at home,' Creegan said. 'I'll take you to it.'

'Okay, thank you. You need to wait here while we look into what you've said.' The priest nodded. Alan looked at Bannon. The brief looked like he'd been slapped across the face with a fresh mackerel. 'You've been quiet for a change,' Alan said. 'You look like you need a cup of strong coffee. I'll have some sent in.'

Chapter 39

Myra Dennis put her ear to the door and listened. Cristy was still sleeping. She twisted the handle and pushed the door open a few inches. Cristy was lying on her back. There was vomit covering her chin and neck. It pooled on her pillow. Myra panicked and burst into action. Her mind was working at a million miles an hour. She wanted to scream, but her voice wouldn't engage. Her throat was constricted by fear. She spotted the empty bottle of pills on the floor and the Jack Daniels on her bedside cabinet. The bedroom smelt of sick. Her brain told her Cristy was dead. Suddenly, her body reacted.

'Cristy!' she screamed, opening the door and pushing inside. She ran and knelt next to the bed. Cristy wasn't breathing. Her eyes were rolled into the back of her head. 'Phillip. Help me!' she screamed as loud as she could. 'Cristy isn't breathing!'

'What's going on?' Phillip shouted. She heard the sound of heavy footprints stomping up the stairs, and Phil entered the room in a panic. He took in the scene quickly. 'Call an ambulance, Mum,' he said. Myra didn't react. Her mouth was moving, but no sound coming out. 'Mum!' he snapped. She looked up at him. 'Call an ambulance, now!'

He shook Cristy and put two fingers into her mouth. She dribbled, and he cleared the vomit. She felt warm and supple, not dead and stiff. He turned her onto her side and smacked the palm of his hand between her shoulder blades. A gurgling sound came from her throat. He pushed a finger to the back of her mouth and smacked her again. Her eyes flickered and projectile vomit spewed from her mouth. She coughed and spluttered and tried to speak. Her eyes couldn't focus, but she was breathing. Phil grabbed a towel and cleaned her mouth and lips. Her hair was matted with vomit. He could see partly dissolved tablets in the puke. 'How long will they be?' Phil asked, sobbing. 'The silly cow has tried to kill herself.'

'They're on the way,' Myra said from the doorway. 'Is she dead?'

'She's breathing,' Phil said. 'She's taken a load of pills.'

'She's taken an overdose,' Myra said. 'My girl has tried to kill herself because of that bastard Price. I'm going to kill him.' Myra sobbed. They waited fifteen long minutes watching Cristy breath. Her skin was so pallid she could have been dead.

'I want the bastard dead,' Myra kept muttering. The ambulance arrived and they let the paramedics take over. Phil watched as they loaded his little sister into the back of the ambulance. His mother climbed in next to her, too upset to speak sense. 'Kill him, Phil,' Myra said. 'Break his fucking neck.'

The ambulance pulled away and a police car pulled up. The plumber from down the road slowed down to wave from his van. He was having a good nosey at what was going on. An ambulance and a police car outside a neighbour's house. Always a bit of gossip to be had. Carmel Sheppard and April Byfelt got out of the car and walked towards him. He turned and walked into the house before they reached him.

'Phil,' April called after him. 'How is Cristy?'

'Great,' Phil said. 'Her boyfriend is dead, and she's swallowed a bottle of pills. How the fuck do you think she is?'

'We know this is hard for you and the family,' Carmel said.

'Do you?' Phil said. 'We were fine a week ago. Everyone was happy and healthy. Jon Price is let out of jail and we're turned upside down.' He clenched his fists. 'That's my little sister in the back of that ambulance. He raped her seven years ago, and I did nothing. I left you lot to it. More fool me. I should have done him when I had the chance.'

'I understand how angry you must be,' Carmel said.

'I doubt that. My sister is in the back of an ambulance and my best friend is lying on a slab in the mortuary and do you know what we can do about it?' He shrugged. 'Fuck all because you lot can't do your jobs.'

'We're going to put him away,' Carmel said. 'I can promise you that.'

'What, like you did last time?' Phil scoffed. 'Remind me how that one worked out, will you?'

'Phil, we need to ask you if those cameras you put up are switched on?' April said. 'You were putting them up when I dropped Cristy off from work last week.' Phil looked up at the cameras. His brain wasn't functioning properly. 'Are they working?'

'Yes. They're working. I haven't got time for this,' Phil said. 'I need to get to the hospital. My sister tried to kill herself because you lot are fucking useless.'

'Someone slashed your mum's tyres the morning Rowan was killed. Cristy told us that,' Carmel said.

'So what?' Phillip snapped.

'Jon Price hasn't moved from his house,' Carmel said. 'Someone is working for him. He didn't shoot Rowan, but he had someone else do it.'

'We might be able to find whoever is stalking Cristy, if we can look at the footage,' April said.

'Come in,' Phil said. He went upstairs and grabbed his laptop. 'I think it's a bit late to be doing the detective work, don't you?' He put the laptop on the table and inserted a memory stick. Opening the app, he transferred everything the cameras had captured. It took less than a minute. 'Here you go. Knock yourselves out. Although, I won't be holding my breath. Price walks on water as far as you lot are concerned. He's fucking untouchable. If you've got what you need, I'll be going to Bangor hospital to be with my sister. The last time I was there, it didn't end too well.'

Chapter 40

Alan and Kim walked to operations in silence. There was too much to ponder. Richard was sitting at his desk, trawling through information. He saw them coming.

'It's true,' he said, cheerily shaking his head. 'It's bloody true.'

'Which bit?' Alan asked. 'I'm in a state of disbelief about the entire story, but it makes sense where there was none before. Charles Martins has blown the lid off a can of worms like we've never seen before.'

'There's a lot to consider,' Kim said.

'Granted,' Alan agreed. 'What can we verify, right now?'

'We can verify Alister Pickford was jailed at Manchester Crown Court for a series of crimes including online grooming and the abuse of two teenagers, one male, one female. Their identities are hidden, but I'm guessing they're from that area. He was also convicted of the historical abuse of Charles Martins,' Richard said. 'Martins and his brother were key witnesses in the case.'

'He said it was Alister Pickford who befriended the teenagers in the care home,' Alan said.

'The police acted on a tipoff from an informant who directed them to a cache of photographs and videos stored on three mobile phones and several storage devices. His brother and Charles Martins gave evidence remotely about historical abuse. He received an indefinite sentence pending behavioural and psychological reports, but the judge recommended twenty-years because of his age. Pickford claimed he was innocent, and that someone set him up. He said the photographs and videos had been doctored but it didn't wash with the jury.'

'Please tell me Creegan is wrong, and he's still banged up,' Alan said. Richard shook his head. 'When was he released?' Alan asked.

'He's been out for nearly two weeks,' Richard said. 'He's under license and can't go back to Manchester. Nor can he approach his brother or Martins.'

'It's a bit too late for that,' Alan said. 'Father Creegan was telling the truth. Alister Pickford is at the centre of this.'

'Do you think Pickford killed Martins and made it look like it was a suicide?' Kim asked.

'It's not beyond belief,' Alan said. 'It would be a very strong warning for Creegan to keep his mouth shut.'

'Well, that hasn't worked, has it?' Kim said. 'Now he's started talking, there's no shutting him up. As for Pickford being Jon Price's father. WTF?'

'I found Polly Price,' Richard said. 'She moved back to Menai when Jon was eight months old. There were accusations made to social services at the time, although Pickford was never charged with anything. It was a case of he said, she said. Jon Price was over a hundred miles away and deemed to be safe. Polly was given an injunction, and that's all we have.' Richard brought up another file. 'She hanged herself when Jon was sixteen.'

'Any suspicious circumstances?' Alan asked.

'There's nothing on file,' Richard said. 'Jon Price inherited the property they lived in. He got a job, mortgaged it, and started his property business.'

'Did Ian Osbourne know Don Shipley and Father Creegan were friends?' Alan said. He shook his head. 'Did we get him so wrong?' He looked at Kim. She sighed. 'We've had Creegan pegged as a liar all the way through this when he was actually the good guy in it all.'

'Can we be sure of that?' Kim asked.

'Everything he said is true,' Alan said. 'Shipley listed Lawson, Cummings, Moffat, and Hancock. Along with the Pickford twins. No matter how we look at this, they all stopped offending because Father Creegan threatened to expose them to their families.' Richard and Kim nodded. 'Granted, four of them died in suspicious circumstances, but they stopped, and Father Creegan stopped them. He stopped all of them. The man is a fucking hero.'

'Do you think he killed those men?' Kim asked.

'I don't know,' Alan said. 'I don't know what to think. If I put myself in his shoes and I'd tried to tell my superiors they were abusing youngsters and they ignored me and the abuse carried on, would I cut the rope they were attached to on Crib Goch and let them fall a thousand feet to their deaths?' He shrugged. 'Probably.' He sat down and rubbed his temples. 'Would you?' Alan asked Richard.

'Hypothetically, I would be quite happy to push them off.'

'As for the fishing trip, he could have locked Moffat and Hancock in the cabin and then capsized that boat easily. Without inspecting the vessel to see if that door was locked from the outside, we'll never know. It's way too deep. He may have killed them all, we can't say otherwise and what if he did?'

'He destroyed an active paedophile ring and had the ringleader jailed,' Richard said. 'From where I'm sitting, he saved a lot of children from a lot of grief.'

'What are we going to do with him?' Kim asked.

'Nothing. He hasn't done anything wrong. I want the box of evidence he says he has, and we let him go home,' Alan said. 'In the meantime, we need to find Alister Pickford before he kills anyone else. That bastard needs to go back inside rapid.'

Chapter 41

Bob Dewhurst looked at the pictures on Facebook. The two girls were pouting like champions. One of them was blond, the other brunette. He recognised both of them from Price's house.

'That's them,' he said.

'Definitely,' Col agreed. 'Angela Parry and Bev Jones.'

'Go back through their timelines for me,' Bob asked. The tech scrolled down both profiles. 'They're prolific on there until they went to Jon Price's house. Look there. She's a dinner lady.'

'Dinner ladies were different in our day,' Col said. 'This is where she goes to visit Price. Bev Jones posted fifteen selfies from inside and then nothing for days. Assuming she's alive and kicking, something has happened to stop her posting.'

'It's the same for Angela Parry,' Bob said. 'Dozens of selfies on a daily basis and then a handful since leaving Price's. Something happened in that house which has disturbed them enough to stay offline. Maybe he threatened them. He might have told them to keep a low profile. We saw them there, and he knows that. Let's get their addresses,' Bob said. 'You track them down. I'll tell the DI we've identified them. He's going to want them spoken to today.'

****

Jon Price was standing on his balcony smoking and listening to music. He cleared his throat and spat phlegm onto his lawn. His cough was getting worse. KLF were on the last train to trans-central. 'All aboard, all aboard,' he sang along. The waves were crashing onto the rocks and the boats anchored in Porth Diana were pitching perilously against the tide. The view was amazing, but he was becoming impatient. The NCA officers had been very specific. If he did what they said, he would keep his freedom. If he didn't, they would lock him up and he would do his full-term. They were monitoring his phone and told him not to use it under any circumstances unless it was one of his contacts from Ireland or Liverpool. He was to wait for them to make contact with him. They would do the rest. It was a simple deal to make. He wasn't a grass because he wasn't giving the dibble any evidence or information. They had all the information they needed. They were the National Crime Agency. They knew everything. Waiting was driving him insane. He couldn't leave his house. That was part of the deal. They would tell him when he could leave. Until then, he could drink, smoke, and fuck to his heart's content. He was contemplating which one of his hareem to message on Facebook when he heard a message arrive on his phone. He flicked his cigarette into the garden and went inside.

The message icon on the screen flashed. He opened it and read the message.

Hello. It's me. I need some cash and a vehicle. I wouldn't ask, but it's an emergency. Can you help, please?

Jon smiled and shook his head. 'Of course, I can, Dad,' he said to himself. He sent a reply and went into the kitchen. It was time to eat something before he decided what he wanted to eat later. Blond, ginger, or brunette, or the really dark-haired girl from Caernarfon. Decisions, decisions. He coughed again and felt clammy and hot. Ginger. He was going to eat ginger, he decided. She would love every minute of it.

****

Phil Dennis and Myra were sitting in the same relatives' room they'd been in the day before. They had to mask up and wear gloves and aprons. The hospital was struggling with COVID-19 patients. The doctors had pumped Cristy's stomach. There wasn't much left inside her. They said she'd vomited hours ago, which had saved her life. She hadn't had time to digest a lethal dose of the drug. The effects of the whisky and the drugs had made her sick and sedated. They'd run blood tests and were waiting for results. The door opened and a young doctor walked in. She was black and looked too young to be out of school.

'I'm Doctor Oruche,' she said. 'We've had the results of Cristy's blood tests. There's no permanent damage to her liver or kidneys. We've got her on a drip for now and we'll monitor her while she recovers from the effects of the alcohol. She shouldn't be drinking at all in her condition.'

'What do you mean?' Myra said.

'She's pregnant,' Dr Oruche said. 'Did you know?'

'No,' Myra said. She hugged Phil and cried. 'We didn't know.'

****

Richard was eating fish and chips from Price's chippy, which was ironic, but the chippy had been called Price's long before Jon Price became a household name. He was convinced the fish were getting smaller, the older he got. Or the trays were bigger, making the fish look smaller, but that was unlikely. They still tasted good although he wasn't allowed to put his own vinegar on his food. Health and safety gone mad. He shovelled another mouthful in and savoured the flavours. His phone rang, and he emptied his mouth quickly, almost choking.

'DS Lewis,' he answered. Washing the fish down with a mouthful of coffee.

'Richard, it's Rob Wilkinson,' the caller said. 'You asked me to go through the photographs uploaded from the Samsung Galaxy belonging to Edward Speers.'

'I did,' Richard said. 'His wife told me he sold them on Shutterstock and the like.'

'He did,' Rob said. 'He has thousands of images on sale and he did quite well out of them. I think you're going to want to take a look at some of them though.'

'That sounds interesting,' Richard said.

'That depends on whatever floats your boat,' Rob said. 'I think he was branching out recently. Not in a good way.'

'Branching out how?' Richard asked.

'Come and take a look,' Rob said. 'You'll see what I mean.'

****

Bernice was walking her dog along the Rocky Coast. It was a stretch between the breakwater at Holyhead and the base of the mountain by the quarry. She walked her dogs, Star and Layla, there every day, sometimes twice a day. Walking kept her fit and in shape. She walked for miles with her dogs and she walked for miles with some of the online groups on the island. It was always quiet along the Rocky Coast, which suited her as she was paranoid about the virus. Avoiding people was top of her list.

The weather was cold but clear. She was sheltered from the worst of the wind by the mountain. There were no fishermen on the breakwater today. It was too rough. The waves crashed over the wall and would sweep a man away in the blink of an eye. As she walked, she watched the waves hitting the rocks below her while the dogs ran in circles, chasing each other. Something caught her eye. There was something floating in the water. At first, she thought it was a big seal. They frequented the island and weren't strangers along the coast or even as far out as the Skerries lighthouse. Sometimes they got hit by a boat and torn up by propellors. As she neared the inlet where it was floating, she realised it was way too big to be a seal. Even the big ones weren't that size. It was a man. A big man. He was face down in the water, arms and legs bound together. She could see something glinting from metal shafts at the shoulder and thigh. She was fifty feet above the body, at least, but she could make out flights like those on a dart or an arrow. He was clearly dead. She took out her mobile and dialled the emergency services.

Chapter 42

Carmel and April watched the CCTV footage. They rewound it to the point they needed. April pressed play, and they slowed it down. The camera angles covered the front and side of the house, including the driveway where Myra parked her car. The quality was decent and the images clean and clear.

'Okay. There's the flower delivery. The van is there. The logo and phone number are genuine,' April said.

'Are you sure?' Carmel asked.

'Yes. The shop is in Valley, in the square, next to the Indian.' April flexed her biceps. 'I used to go to a personal trainer there.'

'Jamie Hollinshead?' Carmel asked. 'I heard he's good?'

'I wouldn't go anywhere else,' April said. 'Look there. It's the taxi arriving. Zoom in on that plate.'

'Got it,' Carmel said. She entered the plate into the system. 'It's a silver Toyota Prius hybrid. A lot of the firms are using them nowadays. Keeps the fuel costs down.'

'Okay, let's see what he does. He knocks on the door has a chat with Myra and then goes back to his car.'

'Then Myra comes out of the house and throws the flowers into the bin. She looks proper pissed off there. The tyres are okay on that shot,' Carmel said. 'Wind it on.'

'There,' April said. 'The flower shop van goes by. He must have gone to the end of the cul-de-sac, turned around, and then driven out but where is the taxi?'

'He hasn't gone through the shot yet,' Carmel said. 'He could be parked up waiting for a job.'

'No. They go to the station rank and wait there. They're not licensed to pick up anywhere else but the station and the cenotaph,' April said. 'He hasn't driven out of the street.' They continued to watch. 'There's our phantom tyre slasher. Hood up, mask across the face, boiler suit on.' They watched the figure move quickly from tyre to tyre, stabbing each one in turn. Then he vanished from view again. 'Wait for it,' April said. They forwarded the images to a few minutes later. A silver Toyota Prius came into shot, heading out of the cul-de-sac. 'It's the taxi driver. And that there, is our tyre slasher, delivery man, sniper, and whatever else we can find on him.'

'When they found Melanie Brooks' car, it was called in by a taxi driver, wasn't it?'

'Yes. It's all adding up now. Whoever dumped Melanie's mini had to have someone waiting to take them away from the scene.'

'The taxi is owned by Stewart Lodge, thirty-five years old from Thomas Street,' Carmel said. 'Let's tell the DI and arrest the wanker.'

****

Richard knocked on the door and Rob Wilkinson waved him in. He was sitting in front of a bank of monitors that were showing images of Janine Bay, Luca Bay, and their children. They looked like the perfect nuclear family.

'Take a seat,' Rob said. His accent gave away his roots on the outskirts of Liverpool. 'As you can see, Edward Speers used Luca and his family as subjects for stock photography. Luca is in hundreds of outdoor shots. Speers uses a lot of people in his photography. There are hundreds of images in and around the railway where he works, on trains, in the buffet cars, ticket offices, platforms, and newsagents. He must have had his phone or a camera in his hands permanently. I don't know who these people are, but the family are featured the most. You can see hundreds of shots of them, all innocent and all very saleable to advertisers looking for stock images. Playgrounds, roundabouts, swings, seesaws, football, bicycles, you need a family shot, Speers has one for sale.'

'You haven't dragged me all the way up here to see these,' Richard said. 'Show me what you've found.'

'These,' Rob said. Images of Janine appeared. Hundreds of them. 'They start out as mysterious, alluring even but as the clothing becomes more sexualised, she looks less comfortable.' He changed the images again. Janine was restrained and looked frightened. 'They get too raunchy for Shutterstock. But there are sites where you can sell this kind of stuff.' The images became more bondage orientated. Richard sat down and shook his head. 'I had a funny feeling something more was going on when she mentioned the photographs. When were these uploaded?'

'About a month ago. They've been downloaded dozens of times,' Rob said. 'Speers would have been making decent money from them. Did you recover any memory storage from his flat?'

'I'm not sure,' Richard said. 'Why?'

'The images become more sexualised. But the date stamps on the images stop two weeks ago and there's nothing on his phone since then, which tells me he's using another device to take pictures. Photographers like Speers don't suddenly stop taking pictures, they just use something else to do it. There will be storage somewhere in his property or he has an online storage site, like Dropbox or iCloud.'

'If they were selling well, he might be encouraged to push the boundaries,' Richard said, nodding. 'I think I need a chat with Janine Bay. She's not been telling me the whole truth.'

Chapter 43

Alan and Kim walked either side of the priest as he led them through the vicarage garden to his workshop at the rear of the garage. The trees were bare and swayed gently in the wind, and a light rain was falling. Leaves the colour of burnt amber tumbled across the lawn. The light was grey, neither bright nor dark. It was difficult to tell what time of day it was. Bannon walked behind them, eager to ensure Father Creegan didn't dig a deeper hole than he already had, although he'd been on the phone most of the time since leaving the station. Alarm bells would be ringing around the Catholic Church, which made Alan smile. Let the brimstone and eternal fire eaters panic for a change. Redemption wouldn't be good. God couldn't make them appear any less guilty for covering up decades of abuse. The atmosphere was strange. Alan felt guilty for mistrusting the priest. He put that down to his personal prejudice.

'What's in the box, Father Creegan?' Alan asked, making conversation.

'Evidence of a misspent life,' the priest said, looking up into the trees. 'One man's mission to create havoc and confusion wherever he could. Fear and loathing drove him. Seeking to make others suffer was his only goal in life. Evil incarnate. There're no other words to describe him.' The priest nodded and smiled. 'It's time. I'm sure you'll be very interested in what you find. It's been hidden away from the light for too long. Now is the time to expose him for what he is. The world needs to know what went on. What my fellow priests did and what the church didn't do to stop it. Shame upon them all.'

'Maybe you should have handed it over sooner,' Alan said.

'Maybe. I haven't always got everything right, although I've tried,' Creegan said. 'The balance has tipped and now is the right time.' He paused. 'You don't like me do you, inspector?'

'Not really,' Alan said. 'Although I don't like many people, so don't take it personally.' The priest smiled. 'Religion is my pet hate.'

'Really?'

'Yes. My favourite book is, *God isn't Great.*'

'I've read it.' Creegan smiled and chuckled at the memory. 'It amused me no end. I could imagine Cardinal Vincent frowning and muttering at the content, although he's on his own planet most of the time.'

'You think so?'

'Yes. He sits on a cloud next to God, looking down at us sinners. They lost touch with the people decades ago. The church became all powerful and the people don't matter anymore. I got lost in there somewhere and so did my faith,' Father Creegan said. He looked sad again. 'It used to be about good versus evil, helping the weak, and protecting the innocent, but not anymore. Evil has come to the fore. Sex and violence reign. I feel religion has lost its way.'

'Me too,' Alan said, nodding. 'My dislike of religions causes my distrust of all things religious, including yourself. One thing enables the other.'

'And why do you think that is?'

'Because it's all nonsense.'

'Oh, please indulge me. How so?'

'How long have you got?' Alan said. The priest shrugged and smiled. 'The Bible is a compilation of writings chosen by a Roman to quell the increasing number of Christians in the empire. Controlling them required a rulebook. Enter stage left, the Bible along with ten commandments and the promise of eternal damnation if they weren't adhered to and bingo, control reigns.' Creegan smiled as he listened. 'I think it's the most incredible work of fiction ever created.'

'Then there is no hope for you, inspector,' Creegan said, laughing. 'In this world or the next.' They reached the workshop, and the priest stopped in front of the door. 'Here is the key,' Father Creegan said. He offered a bunch of keys to Alan. 'The box is stored safely in here. It's dry in there, so the contents will be intact.'

'Please open it,' Alan said, refusing to take the key. Creegan opened the door and reached inside to switch on the light. 'After you,' Alan said. The priest stepped inside. Alan followed him. The smell of sawdust hung in the air. It was a pleasant smell. He noticed the half-made coffee table and the woodworking tools. 'Are these yours?'

'Yes,' Creegan said. 'I used to spend hours in here when I had spare time.' He looked sad again. 'That was before I met Don Shipley, of course. After that, all my spare time was spent trying to stop the Pickfords and their followers. In hindsight, it took over everything.' He walked to another door to their right and unlocked it. 'This is my storeroom. It is where I stored all my valuable tools. I had a break-in many years ago and they took my drill and my favourite saw. They weren't worth much, but I was so annoyed. I had this lock fitted and a steel plate fixed over it, so they couldn't break-in again.' He stepped inside and picked up a heavy object, wrapped in polythene. It was dark in the storeroom. Alan felt uneasy. 'Here we are,' the priest said. A powerful odour tainted the air. Alan could see a metal toolbox through the plastic. 'This is it, inspector. I've only ever looked inside twice. Once when Richard Pickford told me it existed and then once a few days ago. I couldn't bear to look at the contents for long.'

'You've looked inside recently?' Alan asked. 'Did you touch anything?'

'No. I'm acutely aware of the chain of evidence. What is in that box belongs to Alister Pickford and I'm desperately sorry that it's taken this long for me to hand it over to the police, but I was convinced the animal would be caged for the remainder of his days or at least until sex was beyond him. I hoped age would castrate him.' Creegan closed his eyes and shook his head. A tear broke free from the corner of his left eye. 'This terrible virus has descended on the planet and unwittingly caused the release of something much worse.' The priest wiped the tear from his eye. Alan blinked. The odour was becoming stronger, making his eyes water. 'They've inadvertently released evil upon us again. Alister Pickford is the devil himself and I failed to protect people from him.'

'You had him put away,' Kim said. 'You did more than anyone else did.'

'It was too little too late,' Creegan said, wiping away another tear. He handed the box to Alan. 'All I can say is I'm desperately sorry. Goodbye, inspector,' the priest said. He stepped back into the storeroom, closing the door behind him. They heard the lock closing. 'Find Pickford and lock him away, inspector,' the priest said through the door. 'Make sure he stays away this time.' Father Creegan stepped onto an old shower tray, which he'd adapted. The liquid covered his shoes up to his ankles. He opened three of the valves on the shelf.

'Father Creegan open this door,' Alan shouted. 'See if there's another way out,' he said to Kim. Kim ran through the workshop and outside. 'Father Creegan. Open this door!' Alan put the box down on a workbench and kicked the door with the heel of his foot. The shock sent a shooting pain up his leg into his knee and hip joint, but the door didn't budge. The metal plate made the door impregnable. 'Father Creegan. Open this door!'

He heard a whooshing sound and Father Creegan screamed. The sound of flames devouring timber crackled, becoming a steady roar.

'Father Creegan!'

Smoke billowed from under the door, thick and cloying. Alan could smell petrol burning. The smoke was hot and choking. The heat from the door was so intense, he could feel his skin glowing and his hair sizzled.

'Get out,' Alan shouted. Bannon stumbled through the workshop. Alan was close behind him. 'Move it,' he shouted. A butane gas bottle exploded in the room where the priest had locked himself. His scream was cut short suddenly as the others caught and the resulting explosion rocked the building.

Chapter 44

Stewart Lodge was sitting in his taxi, listening to the radio. A body had been found near the breakwater which was interesting. He would have to find out who it was. It could be a fisherman, swept away by a wave, or it could be a tourist tipped out of his canoe. The idiots come to the island determined to put their boats into the water no matter what the weather. Some of them don't make it back to their cars. Better still, he hoped it was someone from the island, someone he knew. The gossip mongers would be out in force if it was, and they could have a bloody good jangle about who it was and why. The juicier the better, as far as he was concerned.

The Irish ferry was docking, and the London train was due in, and he was second on the rank. He was due a good job; the work was drying up since lockdown. Driving with a mask on was a pain in the arse too. If it wasn't for the extra work he was getting from Jon Price, he'd be skint. Jon getting out early had saved his bacon, no doubt. Scaring the shit out of little Cristy Dennis had been fun. She was asking for it anyway. Walking around in skintight leggings that clung to her arse. What did she think blokes would want, a fucking good conversation? Jon was obsessed with her, but he was a strange man at the best of times.

Flashing lights caught his eye in the mirror. Two police interceptors were on the station approach. Something must have gone off in the custom sheds. They weren't heading to the port they were hurtling towards the rank at speed. It took a few seconds for his brain to function. A third vehicle joined the convoy. The marked vehicles stopped either side of his, the third directly behind him. Armed police exited the vehicles, weapons raised and pointed in his direction. His hands were on the steering wheel. He felt a warm sensation as his bowels let go and the smell of excrement filled his car. The door opened, and he was dragged out and unceremoniously dumped face down on the tarmac.

'Fucking hell!' he shouted. 'I haven't done anything!'

He heard the officers shouting at him. Others searched his taxi. The boot was opened, and he heard a female voice.

'Bring him here,' she said. He was forced to the rear of the vehicle. 'Are these yours?' she asked. Stewart stared at the holdall. Inside was a boiler suit, mask, and knife.

'I don't know where they came from.' He shook his head. 'A customer must have left them by mistake.' The clothes and holdall were bagged. The officers folded back the carpet to reveal his air rifle.

'That's a BSA Meteor with a telescopic sight,' a firearms officer said. 'It's a two-point-two. The same calibre used to kill Rowan Jackson.'

'Hold on a minute. I didn't mean to kill him,' Stewart said. 'It was just a laugh shooting a few pellets at him. I didn't know he would fall off. How could I? Jon Price told me to annoy him. It was just a laugh.'

'A laugh?' Carmel snapped. 'I bet the judge finds it fucking hilarious. Stewart Lodge, I'm arresting you on suspicion of the murder of Rowan Jackson. Take him away,' Carmel said. 'He stinks. I think he's shit in his pants.'

****

Bob Dewhurst knocked on Alan's door. Alan waved him in. Bob was surprised by how rattled Alan looked. He was wearing a blue tracksuit which buried him.

'What on earth are you wearing?' Bob asked, frowning.

'My clothes were singed,' Alan said. He pointed to the clothes he'd been wearing. 'They stink of petrol.'

'That was a close shave,' Bob said. 'You were lucky. Col said there were Calor gas bottles in there. They explode with some force. I can tell you from a misspent youth.'

'Look at my eyebrows.'

'They look better burnt,' Bob said. 'It's got them under control. I might try that on mine. Eileen says they look like big grey caterpillars. Perhaps being caught in an explosion is the answer.'

'Thanks, Bob,' Alan said. 'Your concern is touching.'

'You know what they say about sympathy,' Bob said, nodding. A wry smile on his lips. 'It's between shit and syphilis in the dictionary.'

'Sympathy is not your forte, Bob,' Alan said. 'Anyway, I'm feeling fine apart from having to wear the tracksuit. It was in lost property.'

'It doesn't fit,' Bob said. 'You look like a chav.'

'Was there a reason you're here doing my head in?' Alan asked.

'There is, now you mention it. We've got a problem talking to Bev Jones and Angela Parry.'

'The girls from Price's house?'

'Yes. We found them on Facebook without too much trouble.'

'Do we know where they live?'

'We do, but they're not at home. That's the problem.'

'Where are they?'

'Hospital,' Bob said. 'Ysbyty Gwynedd.'

'What?' Alan asked. 'What's wrong with them?'

'They both have COVID-19,' Bob said. 'Angela Parry is being ventilated. She's in a bad way. The doctors won't let us anywhere near the ward.'

'How long have they been in there?'

'Three days, both of them,' Bob said. 'And you know what that means, don't you?'

'Jon Price will be infected,' Alan said. 'Maybe there is a God.'

'If there is, he didn't stop Father Creegan having a barbeque in his workshop,' Bob said, chuckling. 'You'd think he would look after his own, wouldn't you?'

'I don't believe you just said that,' Alan said. His phone rang. He answered it. 'DI Williams.'

'Hello, Inspector Williams. This is Geoff Lunt, NCA.'

'Hello,' Alan said, frowning. 'How can I help you?'

'You can't but I can help you,' Lunt said. 'I'll be very brief. We've been monitoring Jon Price's communications. He's received a text message asking for cash and a vehicle. It's from a burner phone, but it's not from anyone we're interested in. But you will be.'

'How do you know?' Alan said.

'Because Price replied, "no problem, Dad." *Dad* being an individual called Alister Pickford. We believe you need to speak to him.'

'We do,' Alan said. 'Price is aware you're monitoring his phone messages.'

'Yes. He knows we've seen it.'

'So, he's tossing his father to the wolves?'

'It certainly looks that way,' Lunt said. 'They corresponded a few times while they were away, but it was always strained. Price wasn't receptive to say the least. He clearly wants Pickford lifted for whatever reason.'

'Where will he be?'

'Price told him to be at the Four Crosses roundabout at five o'clock.'

'Thank you. I owe you one,' Alan said. He checked his watch. They had two hours to set a trap.

'One more thing. There's been a development on our side of things,' Lunt said.

'Paul Sutton being killed?' Alan asked.

'Well, it wasn't unexpected to be honest. He was always going to be collateral if he resisted. It would appear our targets are changing their plans,' Lunt said. 'Liverpool has become their favoured port. Holyhead will be a secondary consideration.'

'I see. Where does that leave Price?'

'Standing naked in the dark with his dick in his hand,' Lunt said. 'The organisation will have no need of a caretaker on the island. They will cut the network to shreds and cherry pick the ones they want to keep. Price is surplus to requirements.'

'So, you're off Price?'

'We've pulled our surveillance already, but he doesn't need to know that.'

'That is good news.'

'I'll see to it our footage of Melanie Brooks leaving his house is sent to you. We have no interest in Price any longer. Feel free to do as you please. Good luck.'

The call ended and Alan smiled. 'Game on,' he muttered.

****

Alister Pickford parked his hire car at the Pringle Mill. The car park was empty. He'd never seen the place so quiet. Everything was closed. Except the chip shop across the road, which didn't surprise him as it opened every day of the year including Christmas Day. The owner was an elderly lady with silver hair, who always wore immaculate white socks over her tights. Her jumbo sausages were his favourite, but he didn't have the appetite to eat today. Things had unravelled dramatically. Being released from prison was an unnerving event. He was paranoid people would be waiting for him outside, seeking revenge for what he'd done or more to the point, what they thought he'd done. His brother and that fucking priest had done a number on him. They'd conspired against him and taken nine years of his life. It seemed only fair he wanted to repay them with something equally devastating. He wasn't sure what would happen when he went to see Roger and Charles. Nine years is a long time and personalities warp. Charles had changed from a passive man into being volatile and unpredictable. It hadn't taken much to push him over the edge. The police would jump to conclusions, but it wasn't how it looked. What had happened was beyond his control. The whole thing got out of hand very quickly, and now he needed to run before people twisted everything on him. His son, Jon, was the only person he could ask for help. To everyone else, he was a pariah. He'd asked for help and his son had come through. One day, he would thank him.

Alister walked along a path from Llanfair to Four Crosses. It was about a mile and took him ten minutes or so. The roads were quiet, which was good. He planned to take the vehicle Jon had arranged and head through Snowdonia and keep on going until he reached the south coast. Brighton would be good or Dover. Somewhere with access to the ferries to France. He needed to leave the country indefinitely. Hopefully, Jon would payroll his getaway until he could find the money to support himself. There was money stashed, and he had a good idea where it was. Roger had a ton of cash stashed for a rainy day, and right now, it was pissing down.

He caught sight of a red Vitara Jeep. It was parked at the Four Crosses hotel. There was one other vehicle there, but it had been abandoned. The tyres were flat. The Jeep was most likely his escape route. Alister jogged the hundred yards across the roundabout and looked inside the vehicle. He tried the door, but it was locked. The alarm started blaring. Suddenly, all hell broke loose. Vehicles screamed from the side roads and boxed him in. Armed police surrounded him, and he was handcuffed and bundled into the back of a police van before he could make sense of what had happened. It was all a confusing whirlwind of sounds and colours.

Events had escalated and brought him to this place. Despite everything, he could take pride in the fact his estranged son had tried to help him. At least he could be thankful for that. It meant a lot to him.

Chapter 45

Pamela Stone and Harry Rankin were standing either side of an evidence table. The contents of the toolbox were spread out on it. Alan and Kim circled the table, examining the items one by one.

There was tension in the air. Alan could feel it, and it wasn't a good feeling. Pamela was unusually subdued. Her recovery from the virus had been easier than for most. Her symptoms had remained on the milder side of the disease. She'd come back to work and walked into a maelstrom of historic evidence.

'This is quite a collection,' Pamela said. 'It's unparalleled to anything I've seen before.'

'In what way?' Alan asked.

'It's a memory box of sorts,' Pamela said. 'Everything is referenced and organised.' She shrugged. 'There is so much to crosscheck. I wanted to go through what we know for certain. The rest is over to you to investigate, but it's going to take time. The items here go back to the eighties.'

'Okay,' Alan said. 'Where shall we start?'

'The IDs are the most obvious place to begin. We have referenced them straightaway,' she said. She pointed to a driving license. 'Susan Kershaw. Her address was in Blackpool.'

'Who's she?' Alan asked.

'She's been a missing person since ninety-eight. She was seventeen when she went missing from care. She was living in private accommodation paid for by social services,' Pamela said. Alan got a nasty tingling down his spine. 'We have her licence, and we have an envelope attached with paperclips. This envelope is dated, March twenty-third, ninety-eight and labelled as 'Susan Kershaw'. It contains a lock of blond hair and two fingernails.' Pamela pointed to the contents of the envelope. 'They're painted red and they're not false. Some of the finger is still attached to this one. Obviously, we need to check the DNA, but I think we have the perfect trophy collection here.'

'Jesus,' Kim said. She looked along the table. 'How many envelopes are there?'

'Twenty-two,' Pamela said. 'All containing locks of hair, some pubic, fingernails, toenails, some eyelashes, and earrings. Each envelope is labelled neatly, dated, and stored in chronological order. The names are male and female, and some of the names are just the Christian name. Like this one says Peter, August two-thousand and three, and is a single lock of brown hair. No more detail and the handwriting is different on this one.' Alan looked confused. 'At the opposite end is this passport for instance, belongs to a Trudie Littler. We found her on the system. She was eighteen when she went missing in twenty-ten. Her envelope has two teeth in it and some red hair, which matches her photograph. She went missing from a refuge in Wigan. Her two-month-old baby was found in its pram outside a café near the rugby ground. It's been stored in the column relating to that decade. This is eighties. This is the nineties. These are two-thousands.'

'Are they all missing persons?' Alan said.

'The ones we have searched so far are missing or dead,' Pamela said.

'Which ones are dead?' Alan asked.

'There are six in this line here. All six are suicides ranging from the early nineties to nine years ago. There're locks of hair, nails, teeth, jewellery, all dated when the suicides were recorded.'

'Begging the question if they were suicides?' Alan asked.

'That's your job, but I'm not sure how you can investigate historic suicides from twenty-years ago. Or missing persons.' She paused. 'One thing stands out.'

'What?'

'There is nothing in this box dated from after nine years ago.'

'Alister Pickford went to prison nine years ago,' Alan said. 'Father Creegan said he was the devil himself. Looking at this, I'm tending to agree with him. Have you identified everything in here?'

'We've hardly started,' Pamela said, shaking her head. 'I just wanted to give you the heads up on what you're dealing with. This will take three to four days, at least. I know you don't have that long to hold him, so you have what we have so far.'

'Thanks, Pamela,' Alan said. 'Can we prove this box belongs to Pickford?' he asked.

'It's engraved on the clasp with the initials, *AP*. We're running prints from the envelopes and there may be DNA in among the workings. I'll update you as we go, shall I?'

'Yes, please,' Alan said. He looked at the photograph of Susan Kershaw. 'She looks like an ordinary teenager who went missing and was never found.'

'How many of them are there going back to the eighties?' Kim asked.

'I don't want to think about it,' Alan said. 'Hundreds probably. We'll find out what happened to you, Susan.' Alan looked at the driving licence and shook his head. 'Let's take a run at Pickford. I'm just about ready to rip his head off his shoulders.'

Chapter 46

Alister Pickford was a slightly built man, bald on top with a swathe of curly grey hair above his ears and thick glasses which magnified his eyes. His forehead was wrinkled beyond his years, making him look like he was constantly frowning. He hadn't shaved for days and his eyes were bloodshot. He looked tired and nervous. Alan sat opposite him and immediately wished he hadn't. Pickford stank. Kim sat next to him and wrinkled her nose. His solicitor was a local brief, lured by the seriousness of the charges. There would be a bumper payday for whoever represented a potential multiple killer. Alan sat down and ran through the legal necessaries. Alister confirmed he understood.

'We want to talk to you about the death of your brother and Charles Martins,' Alan began. 'What can you tell us about them?'

'I don't have to speak to you,' Pickford said, pointing a finger. 'Let's get that straight before we start.'

'You can either answer our questions or you can choose not to,' Alan said. 'The choice is yours.'

'I know that.' He paused and frowned. 'First of all, how did you know where I was?' Pickford asked. 'That's been bothering me.'

'I'm sure you can work that out for yourself,' Alan said. 'You asked someone for help. Unless you told anyone else where you would be, then you can narrow it down.'

'I messaged my son, Jon Price?' Pickford said, disappointed. 'I've tried to build bridges, but he's a bit of a cold fish. I bet they were monitoring his phone. Or did he turn me in?'

'Jon Price isn't why we're here. We want to ask you about what happened to your brother,' Alan said, closing the topic. 'He was murdered. What do you know about it?'

'My brother. The lovely Roger Pickford. He was a freak of nature,' Pickford said. He frowned and the lines on his face deepened. 'As far back as I can remember, he was bad. They say twins can be polar opposites. We were. I'm not surprised someone killed him. I'm surprised it took him so long.'

'Someone being who?' Alan asked.

'Charles Martins,' Pickford said. 'He was another empty head.'

'Charles Martins killed Roger?'

'He killed our mum, you know?' Pickford said, ignoring the question.

'Who did?'

'Roger the Dodger,' Pickford said. 'Do you remember him from the *Beano*?'

'I do,' Alan said. 'His real name was Roger Dawson.'

'Roger Dawson.' Pickford looked blank. 'Who knows shit like that? No one would have read it if they'd called him Roger Dawson. That would be a proper shit name for a comic strip. Roger the Dodger is a proper cartoon character. That's what I used to call my brother. He was always coming up with a plan to avoid chores or homework or eating sprouts. He could wriggle out of most things but not a noose, eh?'

'What happened to him?' Alan asked again.

'I can distinctly remember him killing our mum,' Pickford said. He looked like he was going to cry. 'Sorry. But it brings back such terrible memories,' he said, his voice breaking a little. 'I loved her so much. Can you imagine watching your twin brother kill your mother?'

'How did he kill her?' Alan asked. He wasn't really interested in the family history, but if Alister was in the mood to talk, so be it.

'He drowned her. It was terrible.'

'Drowned her?' Alan asked, taken aback.

'We were at the Miner's Bridge, Betws on a day out,' Alister said. 'Do you know it?'

'Yes.'

'It was a lovely day, but it had rained earlier. Dad went to get some ice creams. We ran along the path to the bridge as fast as we could. She'd told us off for jumping in puddles and dirtying our new shoes. Roger got a clip around the ear hole. He was always getting a clip around the ear hole. Anyway, he was really angry. Roger waited until we got to the rocks near the bridge. She was close to edge and then he ran up behind her and pushed her in,' Alister said, matter-of-factly. 'Dad came back and gave us the ice cream and asked where Mum was. Roger pointed to the rapids. Dad got in a panic and then set off trying to catch-up with her as she hurtled down the river.' Pickford became animated, talking with his hands. 'It was like slow motion. Dad kept slipping on the rocks and falling on his fat arse, and Mum was flailing about in the water like a windmill in a hurricane. She would sink and then bob back up again. Roger cheered every time she went under and booed every time she popped back up.' He shook his head at the memory. 'Hurrah, when she sank. Boo, when she popped up. Hurrah, boo, hurrah, boo, hurrah, boo. Fucking madness.'

'What happened?'

'Dad chased her but was falling over every couple of minutes. Roger could hardly breathe he was laughing so much.' Alister shook his head and tapped his finger against his forehead. 'He was cracked in the head. A proper fucking fruit-loop. Can you imagine a kid laughing at that?'

'Not really,' Alan said.

'Not fucking likely. He wasn't normal,' Alister said, nodding. 'Roger was a psychopath. My poor old mum. They pulled her out of the river a mile downstream in the village, all banged up by the rocks. Of course, there were tourists everywhere. They were made up. Some of them were taking pictures. It's not every day you go on a day out to Welsh Wales and see a woman drowned.'

'Your mother was dead when they pulled her out?' Alan asked. He glanced at the reflective glass. The detectives on the other side were listening.

'Dead as a dodo. Dad had to stay in Betws and talk to the police. They thought he might have pushed her. Roger thought that was hilarious too. We got a lift home to my nan's in a police car. That was a laugh. Roger wanted the sirens on. They got so sick of him asking, they put them on in the end. All the way to Valley.' He paused as if thinking. 'That's where my grandparents lived. They were upset of course. I was dumbstruck. It was very disturbing for me. I was never the same after losing my mother like that. It was very disturbing. Very disturbing indeed.'

'I'm sure it was,' Alan said, nodding. 'Did they find out Roger had pushed her?'

'No. Everyone thought it was an accident. Roger was the best liar I ever met, second best liar in the world. Roger the Dodger.' Pickford chuckled. 'We were ten. No one thought he was capable of that. Except me. I knew. I think my dad knew too, but he never said anything. As we got older, Dad became disabled and couldn't get out of bed. Richard used to hurt him when no one else was around. Dad was petrified of him and he tried to tell the nurses who came to change him, but Roger was such a good liar, no one believed Dad. They thought he was losing his marbles. He was carted off to the funny farm in the end. That's where he died, sitting in a chair watching *Bargain Hunt*.' He chuckled again. 'Second best liar on the planet, my brother. Roger the Dodger.'

'Second best?' Alan said. 'Who is the best?'

'That evil bastard Father Creegan,' Pickford said. He sat forward, his expression a mask of hate. His hands became fists and his eyes dared anyone to contradict him. 'That man can look you in the eye and lie to your face without blinking. He killed my brother.'

'Father Creegan killed Roger?'

'Not in the real sense of the word, but he's responsible for it.' Pickford said, nodding. 'You mark my words it was his fault.' He paused. 'I hear he's dead?'

'Where did you hear that?'

'On the radio. They didn't say his name, but I knew it was him. There aren't many priests on that side of the island. They said there was a fire?' Alan ignored the question. 'Suspicious circumstances, they said on the radio. I bet it was fucking suspicious. Everything about that nonce was suspicious.' He waited for a response, but the detectives remained poker-faced. 'He was a raving paedo, you know?'

'Tell me what happened to your brother,' Alan said, bringing the topic back on track.

'Changing the subject, are we?' Pickford said. 'Okay. I can do that. My brother was a bully and Charles was sick of him and hung the bastard,' he said, nodding. The frown deepened again. 'Roger ruined that boy's life, that's why.' He shook his head. His eyes darted to and fro, magnified by his lenses. There were moments when he looked insane. 'There's not a day goes by when I don't regret taking Charles to Bangor. It was a day out from the home. I carry a lot of guilt for that. I didn't know what my brother was at the time. I suspected he was on the other bus, but I had no idea what he'd become.'

'And what was he?' Alan asked.

'A dirty paedo,' Pickford said. He looked disgusted. 'He used to make me sick. As soon as he saw Charles, I knew what he was thinking. Charles was sixteen and didn't know any better. He was gay but didn't know it then. Everyone else did but him. Roger swooped on him like a rat up a drainpipe. Charles didn't know what hit him. I distanced myself from him. I felt responsible, you see. I worked at the home where he was living. If anyone had found out I took him on a day out, I would have been for the high jump. Charles left care soon after he met Roger, and then it didn't matter so much. I still wasn't happy about it, but they were in a relationship and Roger told me to back off and mind my own business.' Pickford wagged a finger. 'I had no idea Roger was pimping him out. Not then anyway.'

'Pimping him out?' Alan said. 'Tell me about that.'

'Roger had a circle of weirdo pals, all dirty paedos. They were into teenagers,' Pickford said, lowering his voice. 'He said they were becoming sexually active at that age and all they were doing was encouraging them to explore. I told him he was a dirty paedo. He didn't like that. We had a punch up about it. That priest was at the centre of the whole thing. There were six of them from the church. Dirty bastards. Men in frocks. What does that say?'

'When you said the priest was at the centre of it, you mean Father Creegan?' Alan asked.

'Yes. Him and the rest of the God squad. Men in frocks, says it all really, doesn't it? What that man did was disgusting. I hope he rots in hell. Roger was at fault, but Creegan pushed them to do stuff they wouldn't have done otherwise. He had them all dancing to his tune. I don't know what kind of hold he had on them, but everyone did what he said.' Pickford paused, recalling memories. 'I told him to piss off and leave my brother alone, but he laughed in my face. He told me my brother was his own man. My brother had a go at me for interfering. That was when I moved away. Roger was being sucked deeper and deeper into their filth, and I couldn't watch. That priest and his cronies were to blame. They changed my brother and turned him into a pervert.'

'And you had no part in any of it?' Alan asked.

'What, messing with teenagers?' Pickford scowled. He tried to stand up, but the cuffs were fastened to the desk. A uniformed officer moved closer to the table. 'Are you calling me a paedo?'

'I'm asking you if you took part in the abuse. You've just been released from prison after serving nine years for historical abuse,' Alan said, shrugging. 'If it wasn't for the virus, you would still be inside, so I don't think I'm being harsh asking you if you were involved.'

'I'm not a nonce. I was set up,' Pickford said. 'Haven't you been listening?'

'I'm listening, but I'm not clear on events,' Alan said. 'You're telling me Creegan and your brother were grooming teenagers and Charles was part of it, willingly?' Alan asked.

'When he was young, he was. They were in a relationship. As he grew older, he became withdrawn. It's as if it was all catching up with him.' Pickford sounded sincere. 'In hindsight, I think he could see he was groomed and abused. He became resentful. I think he began to realise what Roger was.'

'And what was that?'

'Roger was a control freak.'

'Tell me what happened to your brother,' Alan said.

'You're like a broken record.' Pickford looked at Kim. 'He does sound like a broken record, doesn't he?'

'If you answer the question, he won't have to ask it again,' Kim said.

'Oh, fucking hell,' Pickford said. 'Excuse me for breathing. What happened to your brother, what happened to your brother, what happened to your brother,' Pickford said, in a childlike voice. He smiled, and then the smile vanished just as quickly. 'Okay. Let's be serious.' He took a deep breath. 'I was released from prison and I went to confront them about planting evidence at my home,' Pickford said. 'I hired a car and drove to Bangor. They were surprised to see me, and I could tell it wasn't a nice surprise.' He shook his head. 'Not for them anyway. They didn't look pleased to see me. Nine years and not even a smile. We had a lot to drink, and I confronted them outright. They denied it. I think it pushed Charles over the edge,' Pickford said. 'I went out for some food. I bumped into an old mate and got chatting. That's when Charles flipped and got the gun. He made Roger put the gag on. That was to embarrass him. He wanted to humiliate him. Then he made him climb up the ladders and then kicked them away and let the bastard dangle from the ceiling. Dodge that Roger, hey?' Pickford laughed. 'Roger didn't dodge that. It was payback time.' He stopped laughing and became deadly serious. 'I felt sorry for Charles. I'm surprised he didn't do it years ago.'

'How do you know he had a gag on?'

'I saw him hanging, Sherlock,' Pickford said, shrugging. 'I was very upset. He was my twin after all. It was terrible seeing my brother hanging like that. I haven't been the same since. It was very disturbing.'

'So, Charles killed Roger while you were out.'

'That's what I just said.' He looked down at his hands. 'I'm surprised Charles didn't kill him years ago.'

'Why do you keep saying that?'

'Roger was cruel. He set up his twin brother for a kick-off. My brother tried to deny it was him who set me up, but I could tell he was lying. Roger the Dodger up to his old tricks again. Liar, liar, pants on fire.' He laughed. 'Not any more, Roger the Dodger. I knew it was him.' Pickford winked at Kim. 'Sometimes, you just know.'

'What made you so sure it was him?' Alan asked. Pickford leant forward as if to share a secret.

'I'll tell you why I was so sure. Because the pictures the police found weren't me. They were him. Those pictures were of my twin brother. We're identical,' Pickford said. Alan frowned and shook his head. 'You don't believe me, do you?'

'No.'

'Have you seen the images?'

'No. We're not here to question the validity of your conviction,' Alan said. 'We're way past trying to prove your innocence or guilt. That's been done. You were sent to prison on the back of that evidence and whatever we think, doesn't matter.'

'You should be questioning that evidence because it's all connected. You don't see what's going on here, do you?' Pickford said. 'Everyone of those pictures is taken from the righthand side. Do you know why?'

'No. I don't know. Tell me why?'

'Because my angelic brother has a tattoo on his left arm. Roger the Dodger, you see. At his old tricks again. He couldn't let the tattoo show or people would know it wasn't me.' He sat back to let the information sink in. 'I don't have any tattoos. Now then, that has got you thinking, hasn't it?' He smiled. 'Now you can see what a miscarriage of justice this was.'

'Not really, no. I'm sure the police checked your version of events,' Alan said.

'The police were involved in the cover-up, stupid.'

'Greater Manchester Police are involved in a cover-up with your brother, to have you locked up for something you didn't do?'

'Yes. Dirty pigs.'

'Why would they do that?' Alan asked, shaking his head.

'That's what they do. Everyone knows the police are bent. Bent as a nine-bob note, all of them. You included. Everyone knows it.'

'Do they?'

'Yes. They do. How did all those paedo priests stay out of jail?' Pickford asked, shrugging. Alan shook his head and sighed. 'Because they're all in it together. The police, the church, the masons all dancing around in the dark bumming each other and telling lies about ordinary people.' He looked angrily from Alan to Kim. His brief looked bemused. 'I'm telling you, Roger and Charles hid those photographs in my house and called the police and told them where they were.'

'But why did they do that?'

'Roger, Charles, and the priest wanted me silenced. Creegan wanted me locked away and anything I said discredited so I couldn't testify against him.'

'I don't understand why Father Creegan would do that?'

'Because of the recent stink about catholic priests. It's all over the news, not just here, everywhere. Victims are coming out of the woodwork and they were shitting themselves that the police would re-investigate old cases.' Pickford pointed his finger at Alan. 'Look at the evidence. Creegan made them all stop kiddie-fiddling years ago when it started to come on top. He tried to stamp it all out. Some of them did as they were told, but some didn't. Look into it, Sherlock. Some of them died,' Pickford said, whispering. 'Creegan killed four of his nonces. Check it out.'

'We're aware of that,' Alan said. 'There were enquiries into those deaths and there was no evidence of foul play.'

'Bollocks,' Pickford said, sneering. 'That shithouse Reece Moffit was having a crisis of conscience. He started paying some of the kids off to shut them up. Him and that pervert priest Hancock wanted Creegan to ask the church for money to recompense victims. They were going to confess and suddenly, they're dead in a fishing accident.'

'How do you know Moffit paid victims?' Alan asked, frowning.

'My brother told.'

'Roger told you about Moffat?'

'Yes. Creegan was panicking. He knew it was going to come out, and he knew everyone would point the finger at him. He'd gone too far,' Pickford whispered again. He looked around as if people may be listening. 'Lawson and Cummings were as thick as thieves. They wouldn't listen to Creegan when he told them to pack it in, and then they took a tumble off the mountain. Shock, horror, what a surprise.' He shrugged and shook his head. 'You're not listening to me.' He whispered again, 'He went too far, and he knew he was going to get found out, so he shut them up. That bastard Creegan took those boys. Everyone knows he did. Him and Roger the Dodger took them.'

'What boys?' Alan asked. Kim sat upright.

'The kids from Prestatyn. Ewan Birley and his friend Cristopher Deeks,' Pickford said. 'Ewan Birley was at the same home as Charles was and I worked there. He and Charles were a bit more than friends.' Pickford winked again. 'They kept in touch and Charles told Ewan how cool my brother's shop was. It was like a toy shop and there was booze and motorbikes. Roger had a couple of fifty-cc bikes and he let them ride them. The kids loved them. Ewan and Deeks came to Bangor to meet Charles and Creegan saw them.' He shrugged. 'They were just thirteen. Exactly what he liked. Pretty boys. They were vulnerable, and they disappeared. Everyone knows Creegan was responsible, but he'd fucked up because one of them wasn't in care. Christopher had parents. Those boys were all over the news and people started to whisper. Suddenly everyone was pointing the finger at perverts in the community. There was nowhere to hide anymore. Creegan knew he was going to be found out.'

'That's quite an accusation, Alister,' Alan said. 'You're telling us Father Creegan and Roger Pickford abducted Ewan Birley and Christopher Deeks?'

'Genius,' Pickford chuckled. 'Welcome to the party, inspector. This is what I'm trying to tell you. Father Creegan and Roger the Dodger were very bad men.' He smiled thinly, his eyes piercing as he spoke.

'There are good men, there are bad men, and there are pure evil men. They were the latter.'

'We found semen on the sleeve of Birley's jacket,' Alan said. 'It belonged to Charles Martins.'

'He was there. They were teenagers, and they were exploring their sexuality. They did stuff together. Roger and the priest encouraged them. I'm sure of that, but he didn't expect Creegan to take it as far as he did. He tried to interfere, and he didn't expect him to react the way he did.' Pickford shook his head. 'When I found out, I was very disturbed,' he added.

'I bet you haven't been the same since?' Alan said.

'Are you taking the piss?'

'Heaven forbid,' Alan said. 'Carry on.'

'That was the beginning of the end.'

'What do you mean?'

'That was when that copper got onto Creegan. He was all over him like a rash, followed him everywhere taking pictures of him. Everywhere Creegan went, that copper was behind him.'

'You mean Donald Shipley?' Alan asked.

'Yes. He was all over it. Roger told me Creegan was losing his shit. The copper was getting too close, harassing Creegan and the next thing, the copper disappeared. How much of a coincidence is that?'

'We have Shipley's evidence,' Kim said. 'Father Creegan isn't mentioned in any of the lists of suspects.'

'That's because Creegan got to his evidence before you lot did, idiot.' Pickford shook his head in despair. He put his head in his hands. 'You're not listening to me. Creegan was a paedo, but he wasn't stupid.'

'Tell me what happened to Ewan Birley and Christopher Deeks,' Alan asked. He sat back and folded his arms. 'If what you say is true, what happened?'

'How would I know?' Pickford said. 'Ask the paedos where they are. I keep on telling you, I had nothing to do with them and what they did.'

'So, how do you know Father Creegan had anything to do with their disappearance?' Alan asked.

'Roger told me.'

'We spoke to Father Creegan before he died,' Alan said. He stared into Alister's eyes. 'His version of events is very different.'

'Oh, I bet it is,' Pickford said, nodding. He nudged his solicitor with his elbow as if they were drinking buddies sharing a joke. 'The paedo priest gave them a different version of events. That's a fucking cracker.' He scoffed. 'I bet he did. I bet he told you he rode around on a unicorn handing out rainbows and chocolate saving the planet.' He stopped smiling. 'Tell me, did he blame Roger the Dodger for everything?'

'No,' Alan said. He paused for a second. 'He blamed you.'

'Me?' Pickford pointed to himself and feigned shock.

'Yes, you.'

'Listen to yourself.' Pickford rolled his eyes. 'Father Creegan is the most fucked up individual, I've ever met,' he said. 'He killed himself because you were digging and do you know why you're digging through all this?'

'Enlighten us,' Alan said.

'Because of me. I confronted what they'd done. Charles killed Roger following a lifetime of abuse at his hands and then he went to see Father Creegan because he couldn't cope with what he'd done.'

'How do you know that?' Alan asked.

'Charles told me,' Pickford said. 'Roger had given him a black eye, and a broken nose during one of his sessions.' A detective walked into the room and handed Kim a note. 'You see, it was all about control for Roger and that's why Creegan and him gelled. When I turned up and rocked the boat, I raked up the past and made them look at what they'd done. Charles had enough and lost his temper. He got drunk, took out the shotgun, and hanged Roger from the beam he forced Charles to hang from most of his life. Roger was dead when I got there.'

'But you said you had a lot to drink with your brother and Charles, and he denied setting you up?' Alan challenged. 'You said he wasn't pleased to see you and that he denied setting you up. And he was alive when you went for something to eat.'

'Did I say that?'

'Yes. You did. You said he was dead when you got back.'

'I made a mistake.' Pickford shrugged. His eyes looked from Alan to Kim. 'I get mixed up. It was very disturbing. I haven't been the same since that,' he said, shaking his head. He started to weep. 'He was my twin brother.' They waited for him to settle. 'When I got there, Roger was dead. Charles was drunk and in a real state. He was holding a shotgun, crying into a bottle of whisky. He told me everything that had happened to him over the years. All the parties and all the priests and their friends. He'd been passed around like a toy. Charles said he was going to kill Father Creegan, so I gave him a lift.'

'He'd already murdered your brother, and you gave him a lift to commit another one?'

'Yes. I hated my brother. Dirty paedo.' Pickford shrugged. The tears were gone. 'As for that bastard Creegan, I would have killed him myself given half the chance, so giving Charles a lift was a no-brainer.'

'That's two different versions.' Alan shrugged. 'I'm not convinced, Alister,' Alan said. Kim showed him the note. Alan read it and nodded. 'You're lying to us.'

'If you can't see the truth when it's dangled in front of your eyes, you shouldn't be a detective,' Pickford said, shrugging. 'All I can do is tell you the truth. If you choose not to see it, you should retire and become a security guard or something less taxing on the brain. You're clearly past it.'

'You wouldn't know the truth if it ran up behind you and bit you on the arse,' Alan said. Pickford frowned. He looked bemused.

'That's a bit rude.'

'Your mother didn't drown in Betws. She died from lung cancer at a hospice in Wrexham,' Alan said, holding up the note.

'Roger killed her,' Pickford said, shaking his head. 'It was terrible. I haven't been the same since.'

'We've checked, Alister.'

'Roger pushed her into the river.'

'And your father chased her?' Alan asked, sarcastically.

'Yes.'

'He didn't chase your mother, and he didn't go into a home. Your father died of a heart attack driving an HGV to Coventry when you and your brother were babies. You didn't know him, apparently.'

'Not my dad. My dad was a cabbage at the end.' Pickford shook his head. 'I used to read the *Sunday Sport* to him.'

'And your grandparents lived in Dublin, not Valley,' Alan said. 'They were Irish.'

'A diddle-dee-dee. Top of the morning to ye,' Pickford said, smiling. He became serious again. 'You've made a mistake. Check your facts.'

'There's no mistake,' Alan said. 'And your brother doesn't have any tattoos.'

'He doesn't?' Pickford looked disappointed.

'No. I don't believe a word you say, Alister,' Alan said. 'You're the liar, not Roger. I believe Father Creegan. I believe you were at the centre of the wheel.'

'More fool you. Idiot.'

'Father Creegan gave us your memory box before he died,' Alan said. 'Forensics are going through it.'

'The toolbox?' Pickford said. He took off his glasses and cleaned them on his sleeve. Alan nodded. 'You have the toolbox. Bugger'

'Yes. Roger gave it to Father Creegan as insurance,' Alan said. Pickford looked shocked. He looked at the table and shook his head. 'You know what I'm talking about, don't you?'

'Roger the Dodger never gave Creegan that box,' Pickford said.

'He did. And Creegan gave it to us before he died.'

'Creegan is a fucking liar. I can see where this is going,' Pickford said, shaking his head. 'I'll get the blame and he'll get away with everything.'

'Who will get away with what?' Alan asked. Pickford went quiet. He was deep in thought. 'Creegan is dust,' Alan said. 'He isn't getting away with anything, Alister. You need to start telling the truth.'

'Okay. But you won't like the truth.'

'I think I should talk to my client alone,' the brief said.

'Shut up,' Pickford said. 'It doesn't matter anymore.'

'Why is that?'

'The box is full of the past. Bad things from the past. Susan Kershaw for a start,' Pickford smiled, thinly. 'And Trudie Littler.'

'What do you know about them?'

'Everything,' Pickford said, sighing. He stared at the ceiling. 'They are a blast from the past. Just like Christopher and Ewan.'

'If you know what happened to Ewan Birley, Christopher Deeks, and Susan Kershaw and Trudie Littler, now is the time to tell us.'

'Do you really believe Creegan is innocent in all this?' Pickford asked, frowning.

'His version of events is far more plausible than yours,' Alan said, nodding. 'All you've done today is lie to us. Father Creegan told us you're the catalyst behind everything. If you know different, then tell us.' Pickford looked angry. 'If Father Patrick Creegan is guilty of something, tell us.'

'Creegan is as guilty as sin itself,' Pickford said.

'Prove it to us,' Alan said. 'Give us something we can prove.'

'Tell me where Creegan died and I'll tell you everything,' Pickford said, calmly.

'He died in his workshop,' Alan said.

'In the storeroom at the end?'

'Yes.'

Pickford smiled. 'I don't want history giving that bastard a pass,' Pickford said. 'He doesn't deserve a pass.'

'Okay. Tell us the truth.'

'If you walk through Creegan's garden, there's a path which leads into the woods. After a hundred yards or so, it leads to a clearing, although the last time I was there, he'd planted it with thorns and brambles.'

'What about it?'

'Ewan Birley and Christopher Deeks are buried there, next to Don Shipley.' Alan opened his mouth to speak but Alister held up his hand to stop him. 'When you've finished digging there, check the graveyard at his church. Susan Kershaw and Trudie Littler are there. Look for the graves marked, Wilson and Broom. There are some extra bodies in them too. I don't remember all their names, but they'll be in the toolbox.' Kim stood up and left the room.

'How do you know Birley and Deeks are buried there?' Alan asked.

'Creegan couldn't carry the bodies on his own. Don Shipley was a big man,' Pickford said. 'Roger the Dodger and Charles helped him carry Shipley and Deeks and Birley. They were terrified of Creegan.' Kim came back in and sat down. 'They did as he told them.'

'We've found your fingerprints on the envelopes in the box,' Kim said. Pickford smiled. 'Yours and Father Creegan's.'

'Well done. Took your time.'

'We found your prints on some photographs in there too. They were sent recently to the church,' Kim said. 'Images that clearly show you and Father Creegan and others.'

'They've been doctored.'

'Of course, they have. How do you know your brother helped Creegan to bury the bodies?' Alan asked, frowning.

'He told me when he realised what I was going to do,' Pickford said. 'I had the shotgun pointed at his balls. He spilled the beans before he died. I just wanted the box. He had me sent down once, I wasn't going to let him do it again. I wanted the toolbox.'

'So, you killed Roger?'

'No. Haven't you been listening?' Pickford asked. 'Charles pulled the ladders away.'

'I don't believe you, Alister,' Alan said. He shook his head. 'We ask you a question, you blame the others. You know they helped bury the bodies because you were there, weren't you?' Alan asked. There was a long pause. 'It's finished, Alister. You're going away for life this time.'

'We did some bad shit, but no one could prove any of it. I wanted the box, so I could walk away from them. Away from the past,' Pickford said. He shrugged and sighed. 'Roger wouldn't tell me where it was but eventually, he said he'd given it to Creegan, then I killed him.' He shrugged. 'I went to see Father Creegan. I told Charles we were going to trick him. We agreed he would pretend to be frightened, that I was threatening him with the gun. I told Charles to strip, and he did as he was told. He had done as he was told all his life. I asked Creegan where the toolbox was, and he wouldn't tell me. I tied him up and threatened to blow Charles's head off. Charles went along with it, but Creegan called my bluff. He wouldn't tell me. So, I blew Charles Martins' fucking head off.' Pickford laughed. 'The silly old fucker passed out on me. Couldn't tell me anything. I knew he would retrieve it sooner or later, so I planned to go back.' He shrugged again. 'You lot got to it first and here we are.'

'You needed somewhere to carry out your abuse, Alister,' Alan said. 'Where did all this go on?' Alan asked. Pickford smiled.

'Enough is enough. I'm not saying anything more,' Pickford said. 'No comment.'

Chapter 47

Richard and Carmel arrived at the Knightly residence. They parked up and climbed out of the vehicle. Carmel looked around at the gardens.

'Nice house,' she said. 'They must earn a fortune between them.'

'I'm sure they do,' Richard said, nodding. 'Expect a frosty reception from the father. He's a bit prickly to say the least.' He looked into the garage. The Defender wasn't there. The front door opened. Janine was standing there. She looked nervous but smiled hello and let them in. 'Thank you,' Richard said. 'This is my colleague, DC Sheppard. You can call her Carmel. She's not as scary as she looks.'

'Hello, Carmel.' Janine nodded and looked at Richard. 'I wasn't expecting you today,' Janine said. 'You didn't call.'

'We were passing, and I wanted a chat. You look a bit brighter,' Richard said. 'How are you doing?'

'I'm okay,' Janine said. 'I have good days and bad days. My parents have taken the kids to the beach to collect shells.' She closed the door behind them. 'Please go through to the conservatory. You know the way.' They walked through the kitchen. 'Would you like tea?'

'Yes, please,' Richard said. 'Milk and one sugar.'

'I'll have the same please,' Carmel said. 'This place is beautiful.'

'Thank you,' Carmel said. 'I can't take any credit for it. I just live here with my children and spend my inheritance.' She laughed. 'That's how my dad would put it. He loves having the kids here. They say the love for a grandchild is different to loving your own. I didn't understand what that meant until I had mine. He's like a different person with them.'

'How do you mean?' Carmel asked.

'He was always super strict with me, but he lets them get away with murder. They idolise him, so it works,' Janine said. 'It's a good job really. We'd be in trouble otherwise, rotting in a refuge or something.'

'Do you own your own house?' Carmel asked.

'Yes, but I can't bear to be there. I don't feel safe there anymore. Whoever killed Luca is still out there.'

'That's understandable,' Richard said.

'Have you come to tell me you're arresting Jon Price for murdering my husband?' Janine asked, putting the tray of tea on a table. Richard grimaced. 'Looking at the expression on your face, I guess not.'

'We've come to talk to you about Edward Speers and his photography,' Richard said.

'Eddie and his pictures?' Janine said. 'What on earth has that got to do with anything?'

'I don't think you were totally honest when we spoke last time.'

'I wondered why you mentioned it at all, to be honest,' Janine said. 'The photography was just an income stream. We needed the money.'

'I think it was an income stream to begin with,' Carmel said. 'Speaking as a woman, I'm always amazed at what drives men. It's obvious. They're sex mad. The images Speers took of you being restrained are different to the stock photos of your family,' Carmel said. 'The boundaries were clearly moving, and we don't think you were comfortable with that.' Janine blushed red. 'They're not on Shutterstock. We found them on some less reputable websites.'

'Oh God,' Janine said. 'How embarrassing. I didn't think much of it at the time. We were broke, again.' She shrugged. 'Luca said it was an easy way to build a residual income. He bought some lacey stuff online, and I didn't like to say no. I was always moaning at him about money and the bills. He said it was our responsibility as a couple to earn money, not just him all the time. I felt a bit guilty, so I went along with it.'

'There are a lot of photographs, Janine,' Richard said. 'But he stopped taking them a few months back. When did you leave Luca?'

'Six weeks or so.'

'Eddie stopped taking pictures,' Carmel said.

'I don't know anything about that,' Janine said.

'Did Luca try to get you to go further?' Carmel asked. Janine sipped her tea but didn't answer. She blushed again and couldn't make eye contact. 'You can be honest with us. It's very important you are.'

'We think there are more photographs we haven't found,' Richard said. He heard a diesel engine arriving. Doors opened and slammed closed and children giggled. 'Photographers like Eddie don't just stop taking pictures, which make us think the most recent ones are missing.'

'Eddie had all sorts of equipment. I don't know if he stopped taking pictures or not. How would I?' Janine asked.

'You wouldn't know, and it's not your place to speculate either. I think you've said enough,' Mr Knightly said from the doorway. The children ran to their mother and climbed on her knee. 'I asked you to inform me if you needed to speak to Janine again,' he added.

'And we like to be flexible when we can, but under the circumstances, we don't need your permission, Mr Knightly. This is a murder investigation.' Richard met his gaze with his own. Mr Knightly looked uncomfortable, his eyes on the adjoining door. 'We can always continue this at the station if it's a problem?' Mr Knightly looked angry but bit his lip. 'Shall we book an interview room, and you can contact a solicitor if you would rather?'

'There's no need for that,' Janine said. 'Is there, Dad?' Mr Knightly shook his head. 'We won't be long. Take the kids upstairs. I'll be along in a bit.' She hugged the children. 'Go on with Grandad. I'll make you some dinner shortly.' The kids ran to their grandad, and he reluctantly went towards the stairs. 'He's very protective of me,' Janine said.

The back door which led to the garage opened. Victoria Knightly stepped into the kitchen, followed by a man in his thirties. They were wearing walking gear. Victoria had a fleece hat and gloves on and a lambswool scarf around her neck. The male was wearing a black Stone Island beanie and a Canada Goose jacket. Richard knew the beanie cost over a hundred pounds. The jacket nearer a thousand. He was a handsome man.

'Here's Nathan,' the kids shouted. They ran down the stairs and hugged his legs. He bent down and scooped them up in his arms, kissing them on the cheeks. 'We beat you into the house. Where have you been, slowcoach?' William said, laughing.

'Are you staying for tea again?' Charlotte asked.

'Oh, no, not more tea. I can't stay for tea. Not again,' Nathan joked. 'I'll be as big as an elephant.'

'Yeey. Stay for tea!' the kids sang in unison.

Victoria was laughing, and Nathan was focused on the kids. They saw the detectives in the conservatory and stopped talking. Mr Knightly ushered the children towards the stairs.

'Come on now, children,' he said. 'Nathan will still be here when you're changed.'

There was an embarrassing silence. Janine blushed red again. This time, she verged on purple.

'Detective Lewis,' Victoria said. 'I didn't know you were coming. We weren't expecting you.'

'It's not a problem,' Richard said. 'Janine has been looking after us.'

'Good. We've been to the beach with the kids,' she said. 'This is Nathan Hunt, he's a friend of the family.'

'Good afternoon, Nathan,' Richard said. 'Nice to meet you.' He stood up and finished his tea in one swallow. Carmel followed suit. 'We were just about to leave, so we won't take up any more of your time.' Janine looked confused. 'Maybe we can continue this another day,' Richard said. 'If we find any more photographs, that is.' Janine nodded but didn't speak. Victoria and Nathan looked sheepish. Richard walked towards the door and they said an awkward goodbye. He opened the front door and turned back to Nathan.

'I like your boots,' he said. 'Doc Marten's, aren't they?'

'Oh, thank you,' Nathan said. 'They're comfortable.'

'They look it,' Richard said. 'What size foot are you?'

'I'm a ten, why?'

'Where were you the night Luca died?' Richard asked.

'How dare you?' Victoria Knightly said. 'Detective Lewis. Do I need to remind you what I do for a living?' She shook her head, angrily. 'Nathan was here with us, all night.' Richard looked at Janine. She looked away.

'Of course, he was. Apologies. Just asking,' Richard said. 'Thanks again for the tea. We'll be in touch.'

Chapter 48

Jon Price was struggling to breathe. His temperature was through the roof and his cough was dry and painful. He was weak as a kitten. The virus had a grip of him. He knew one of the women he'd invited round had brought the disease with them. His mother had always warned him about sleeping with easy women. She said he would catch something, but she didn't mean a deadly virus. Polly Price had no idea how poignant her words would be. She had no idea her son would catch COVID-19 by shagging a fangirl. That's what they were. Fans. He was rich and notorious. A handsome rogue. One of them had infected him. He could cope with a dose of the clap, but this would need more than a course of antibiotics. Breathing was becoming more difficult. The breeze from the balcony door was cooling him slightly, but the sweat was running from his head. His hair was matted. He coughed, and it felt like razor blades at the back of his throat.

He closed his eyes and mulled things over. His dad had asked for help. That was a laugh. He smiled at the thought of him thinking he was going to drive off into the sunset, instead being surrounded by armed cops, cuffed, and thrown into a meat wagon. Fuck him. The man was a raving paedo. His brother too from what he'd found out. The news said a shopkeeper in Bangor had been found hanging. The cameras had focused in on a second-hand shop. There had been rumours about that place being used by a paedo ring years back. It was all linked into the inquest into the Catholic Church. They could all fuck off and die. He hadn't had a father growing up, and he didn't need one now. The time for playing happy families was long gone. His mother had tried her best, bless her, but the best thing she had done for him was to top herself. The house gave him the start he needed. Wherever dead people went to, she would know he'd done well. His success was eye watering and when the Irish corridor came online, he would be receiving money with six zeros after it. He hadn't heard from them yet, but they would be in touch when the details were ironed out. Sutton was dead, fat lump that he was. He was the only hurdle in reclaiming his crown.

The breeze touched his skin and soothed him. He tried to open his eyes, but he couldn't. Exhaustion gripped his entire body. His chest felt as if someone was sitting on him. He simply couldn't suck in enough air. His oxygen levels were dropping, and he considered phoning for an ambulance.

Something struck his head with an almighty bang. A blinding light went off in his brain. The pain was incredible. He opened his eyes in time to see a figure swinging an axe for the second time. The blow severed tendons, ligaments, and muscle, sending him into a convulsion. His muscles jack-knifed violently. He was aware but immobilised when the third blow severed his head from his neck. His head rolled off the bed onto a sheepskin rug. The attacker kicked it across the room like a football. It went between the patio doors onto the balcony. A light rain began to wash the blood from the tiles.

Chapter 49

Alan watched as a green JCB cleared the brambles and thorn bushes from part of the clearing. The land to his right had been cleared and ground X-ray machines had been brought in to search the area. There were two false alarms already. One was a tree root the other a dead goat. What a dead goat was doing there was beyond him. The exhumation at the church was underway too. They were starting with the plot marked Broom. The Wilson plot was owned by a local family and there were legalities, which needed to be dealt with. The family was quite rightly reluctant to allow their loved ones to be dug up. Alan was tired and felt deflated. The entire saga was draining. Paedophile clergy were one thing, but this was way beyond explainable or comprehensible. The Catholic Church was throwing as many obstructions in the way as they could, although to be fair to his superiors, their protestations were being ignored. The time for excuses and cover-ups was gone. No one was listening anymore. History would show thousands of vulnerable young people were abused by priests and their cohorts, and the abuse went all the way to the Vatican. The activity ranging back decades was only the tip of the iceberg. Alan felt the weight of the victims on his shoulders. They had evidence that missing teenagers were no longer missing. They were dead. The sad fact was most of them had no families to tell. Being alone and vulnerable was what made them targets in the first place. Their innocence was like blood in the water to the sharks wearing dog collars and the others who hid behind the uniforms of trust. He felt sick to the stomach. Uncovering their remains brought some conclusion but didn't negate the sadness he felt.

'Over here,' a tech wearing a blue paper suit shouted. He marked the spot.

'What is it?' Alan asked.

'An object about six feet long,' the tech said. 'The density is consistent with human bone.'

'Dig it up,' Alan said. 'Let's see who it is.'

****

Kim was in operations when she took a call from the switchboard. It was Col Gallagher. He was the police contact with the local chamber of commerce. He'd been contacted by a local business.

'Hello, Col,' she said. 'What's up?'

'Tesco have been on the phone,' he said.

'Have you been fiddling your club card points again?'

'No. I shop at Morrisons,' he said in his monotone voice.

'Good for you,' Kim said, shaking her head. 'What do they want?'

'They've set up an alert system for customers who live alone,' he said. 'If they get a delivery order from a single occupant, they book a time slot and if they don't answer, they alert us. Just in case they're sick or have had an accident.'

'Okay, that's commendable. I'm sure there's a reason for you telling me this,' she said.

'Yes. There is,' Col said. 'They took a delivery to Jon Price's house, but he didn't answer the door. We know two of the women who visited him are in hospital with COVID-19. He's more than likely infected and can't answer the door.'

'They must have a contact number for him,' Kim said.

'They have, but he's not answering. Hence me calling you.'

'Have you checked if he's in hospital?' Kim asked.

'Yes. I've already called them. He's not in Ysbyty Gwynedd.'

'The DI will be pleased,' Kim said. 'He's been trying to get in there for weeks. Let me give him a call. Get uniform to look for an entry point. He may have left a door or window open. If not, get a breach team ready. I'll get back to you.'

Chapter 50

Alan drove through the gates onto Jon Price's driveway. Uniformed officers were cordoning the house off from the public. It was quite apart from the odd jogger and a couple of dog walkers. He could see the beach and the Black Seal, the patio area deserted. Tourists were still barred from crossing the border, although the policing of the bridges onto the island was non-existent. He stopped the vehicle and turned to Kim.

'Let's go and see Mr Price,' he said. 'I feel a bit nervous about this,' he added.

'There's a nervous anticipation to it,' Kim agreed.

'Jon Price has been a massive pain in the arse for years, but the fact someone has taken it upon themselves to cut off his head is disturbing.'

'Very disturbing,' Kim said. 'You won't be the same after this.'

'Funny,' Alan said, grinning. 'He left the patio doors open at the rear?'

'The bedrooms are on the ground floor, living room is on the first floor.' Kim climbed out. 'The gates were locked, but a reasonably fit person could scale the fences easily enough. There's access from the sea and a mooring at the bottom of his garden, but it's been rough the last few days. Crossing the bay and tying up a boat would be impossible. Whoever got in climbed the walls in and climbed them out,' she said.

They entered the front door and donned forensic suits. CSI had arrived and were dusting the house. Photographers were at work upstairs on the mezzanine floor. They walked through the atrium to the corridor which led to the bedrooms. The stench of death was in the air. Kim smeared Tiger Balm beneath her nose and passed the jar to Alan. They walked into the bedroom. Harry Rankin was processing the body.

'Good afternoon,' he said, without standing up. 'I'm going to assume you know the cause of death.' Alan nudged Kim. Harry was catching on. 'Three or four heavy blows, probably a felling axe. Looking at the blood patterns, the head landed here and then rolled across the room onto the patio,' he said. 'It's unlikely it rolled under its own steam.'

'The killer kicked it?' Alan said. 'Killing him wasn't enough.'

'I'd agree with that,' Harry said. 'I thought the head was missing at first.'

'Where is it?' Alan asked, looking around.

'Take a look in the bathroom,' Harry said.

Alan walked to the en suite. He walked into a slate and marble bathroom, finished in chrome and mosaic. Mirrors covered most of the wall space. His eyes followed the blood trail to the toilet. Price's head had been placed in the pan, forehead showing above the seat, his eyes rolled back into his head.

'Someone didn't like Jon,' Alan said. 'There should be a clear suspect, but unfortunately, there's a queue as long as your arm.'

'Who is at the front of the queue?' Kim asked.

'Someone strong and fit enough to get over the fence unseen, carrying a felling axe and take off his head with a few well-aimed blows?' Alan said.

'Maybe a roofer who plays rugby,' Kim said. 'His sister has been terrorised and his best friend murdered. He has to be top of the list.'

'My thinking exactly,' Alan said. 'Although, I don't know whether to arrest him or give him a medal.'

'How are they getting on at the dig?' Kim asked.

'I think we've found Don Shipley, but there's no sign of the boys yet,' Alan said. 'Alister Pickford is a pathological liar. We can't rely on what he said. Those boys could be anywhere.'

Chapter 51

Myra Dennis opened the door. She frowned and shook her head. Alan and Kim stepped inside. Cristy was sitting on the settee, covered with a blanket. Phillip was in the armchair across the room. He looked rough. There was a smell of alcohol in the room. Phillip was holding a tin of Stella.

'I wondered how long it would take you lot to come here,' Myra said. 'Where were you when Price was hounding my daughter and murdering the father of her baby?' she asked. 'That baby will never know its father because of that bastard. No one wanted him dead more than us, but you're looking in the wrong place.'

'Do you know who killed him?' Cristy asked. She sipped a cup of coffee.

'Who gives a fuck?' Phil said, raising his tin. 'Hats off to him. That's what I say.'

'Look, we have to ask the obvious question, Phil,' Alan said. 'Price was murdered sometime between eight o'clock and midnight yesterday. Where were you?'

'At Rowan's funeral, along with forty other people. Most of us came back here, and I didn't go to bed until about four this morning,' Phil said. He shrugged. 'I'm glad someone beat me to it. I was thinking about killing him myself, but they've saved me a job and a spell in jail. I was always going to be top of the list, wasn't I?'

'You have good reason to hate him,' Alan said. 'More than most people. We had to ask.'

'Well, now you've asked your question, piss off and leave us in peace,' Myra said, opening the door.

'Good luck with the baby,' Kim said. They walked out and Myra slammed the door behind them. They walked to Alan's BMW, taking in the view of the harbour and the breakwater beyond it. The waves were crashing over it, dwarfing the lighthouse. 'Sometimes, I wonder why we do this,' she added.

'What else would we do?' Alan asked.

Chapter 52

SIX MONTHS LATER

Richard knocked on the door of Edward Speers' flat. He'd been out of hospital for months but had avoided every attempt to contact him. His employers were still paying him sick pay and had no idea when he would be well enough to return to work. Richard had his suspicions as to what had happened. The Knightly family were up to their necks in it, but he couldn't prove a thing. Janine had point blank refused to talk to the police, and the honourable Victoria Knightly was flexing her muscles whenever she could. Nathan Hunt lawyered up immediately. He had an alibi from a Crown Court judge. Every single image of Janine and her children had vanished from the Internet. He knocked again. The next-door neighbour opened their door.

'Are you looking for Eddie?' she said.

'Yes. Is he in?'

'Nope.'

'Do you know where he is?'

'I do,' she said, smiling. 'Would you like to know?'

'Yes. That would be helpful.'

'How much is it worth?'

'Would you like to be arrested for obstructing an investigation?' Richard asked. The woman shook her head. 'Where is he?'

'Vietnam,' she said. 'He gave the keys back last month. He said he'd come into some money and was off travelling. I asked him when he was coming back and he said, when hell freezes over.'

'Okay, thank you,' Richard said, walking away.

'Fuck you, dibble,' the woman said, flicking her middle finger. She slammed the door closed.

****

Jason Marsh, the chief constable, was sitting across the desk from Alan. They were expecting a visit from the Diocesan Bishop. The chief was fussing about trying to calm Alan down, but it wasn't working.

'You need to be professional,' the chief said. 'The man wants to make amends.'

'Have you seen him on television?' Alan asked. 'He walks as if he has a pole up his backside and talks to people as if they're an annoyance.'

'Keep the conversation grounded.'

'I'm reluctant to meet with the bishop for a number of reasons but mostly because his appearances on the television have shown him to be a sanctimonious twat.'

'Keep that opinion to yourself please,' the chief said, shaking his head.

The bishop arrived and was shown into the office by an aid. He was short and stout. His scalp was a patchwork of freckles and eczema.

'Thank you for your time, inspector,' Bishop Hanson said. 'I'm aware of how difficult this investigation must have been. I want to apologise on behalf of the church. Patrick Creegan brought shame on us all.'

'He did indeed,' Alan said. 'As did Father Lawson, Father Cummings, and Father Hancock and all the other priests on the lists we gave you.'

'Yes, they have,' the bishop said, straightening his fingers. He bowed his head slightly. 'We're very grateful for the information.'

'Have they been removed?' Alan asked.

'I'm sorry. Have who been removed from where?'

'The other priests on the lists compiled by Donald Shipley and Ian Osbourne, of course,' Alan said. 'Have they been removed while you investigate?'

'I'm not in possession of where the investigation is up to,' the bishop said, clearing his throat. 'But I can assure you if there's any wrongdoing we will deal with it severely,' he said with a thin smile.

'Like you did with Father Creegan?'

'We weren't aware of what Patrick Creegan was doing. Had we known, action would have been taken.'

'I've been digging through the records. Creegan was reported to you in the early eighties and you did take action,' Alan said. The bishop looked irritated. 'You sent him to South America and Africa and let's not forget Haiti. You sent the problem abroad. God only knows how many victims there are in those countries.' The bishop didn't reply. 'I don't need your apologies, those children do. Investigate what he did properly, find all of his victims and apologise to them.'

'We must be realistic, inspector.'

'I couldn't be more real if I tried.'

'It would be impossible for us to find all the people he came into contact with,' the bishop said, frowning.

'You haven't tried,' Alan said, becoming frustrated. 'Run a social media campaign asking for victims to come forward.'

'I think it would be counterproductive.'

'You could run adverts, *Where there's shame, there's a claim,*' Alan said. The priest looked at the chief for support. That annoyed Alan further. '*Was your priest a beast? If so, call 0800,* try something.'

'I'm not sure this is helpful,' the chief said. 'Inspector Williams is disappointed with the way the church has handled this historically. We all are.'

'That's why I'm here,' the bishop said, shaking his head. He looked offended. 'We can't change the past, but we can change things going forward.'

'The recent enquiry into historical abuse singles out the cardinal personally, yet he's still there doing the same job.' Alan shrugged. 'The

Vatican has ordered him to stay in post and therein is the problem. You pay lip service where you can, but you change nothing. Ewan Birley, Christopher Deeks, and Donald Shipley would tell you what happens when you shelter evil men in your churches. Don Shipley was buried in your vicarage by your priest. A priest who had come to your attention decades before. A predator who you sent abroad. He was a trophy hunter, and we can link him to over twenty missing youngsters of various ages, but we don't know where they are.' Alan raised his hands in question. 'How many are there, really?'

'I think I should probably go,' the bishop said, standing. 'I think it's unreasonable to take the actions of a psychopath and paint the church with them.'

'Unreasonable?' Alan said. 'Allowing your employees to abuse our children for decades and doing nothing about it is what I would call unreasonable. Is it unreasonable to hope our children are safe when they're in the company of other adults?' Alan asked. 'Is it too much to ask that when a paedophile is exposed, he is sent to jail where he belongs and is never allowed to work with children again?' The bishop walked to the door and opened it. 'This isn't over, Bishop Hanson. Not by a long way. Once we have a full list of the victims and the dates and location they went missing from, we'll be investigating each and every one of them. Or is that unreasonable?'

The bishop left and closed the door. The chief inspector looked tired. 'That went well,' he said. 'I wouldn't expect a Christmas card from him.'

'Fuck him.' Alan said. 'I need a drink.'

****

Gethan watched his grandchildren playing on the sand. They were happy there, filling up their buckets and making sandcastles. Each castle had a doorway and windows made from shells. The waves were creeping up the beach towards them. They built a gulley for the advancing sea to fill and form a moat. Their mother had done the same when she was a little girl. Looking at them was like looking at her but it broke his heart. She would never see them grow up and have children themselves. That had been stolen from them by Jon Price. He looked up at the path which led to the stile where her Mini had been found. It was still raw. Tears filled his eyes. The kids were calling for him to help them dig their moat. He wiped his eyes and looked towards the headland where they'd walked when she was a little girl. She loved the sea so much. He missed her more than he could explain. The aching gap in his soul could never be filled, nor the pain in his broken heart dulled.

There was a life ring standing near the cliffs above Porth Dafarch. That was the point he'd hurled the axe from. The axe he'd used to behead Jon Price. He remembered how it sounded when it hit the sea and disappeared beneath the waves. Killing Price hadn't numbed the pain and anger he felt. Nothing could do that. He'd stopped him from hurting another man's daughter. That felt good. Melanie Brooks was the last woman he would hurt. There would be no more.

Epilogue

A year later

Alan and Kim were driving to the vicarage. It was pouring with rain and the mountains were hidden by clouds. Over the last twelve months, the Father Creegan case had blown up and been reported worldwide, causing a tsunami of silent victims to speak out. The church was reeling from the backlash. Alister Pickford was sentenced to five life sentences but remained tight-lipped.

'I saw Cristy Dennis yesterday,' Kim said, turning into the driveway. 'She had a little boy – called him Rowan after his dad.'

'How was she?'

'She seemed okay on the face of it, but there's a haunted look in her eyes,' Kim said. 'I guess time will tell if she can move on. Myra was with her. She couldn't get away quick enough, but Cristy was nice and talked for a while. She's back at work, so things are starting to get back to normal for her.'

'That's good,' Alan said. 'There's Richard.'

They pulled up and climbed out of the BMW. Richard was sitting on an ornamental step that led to the side of the building. His face was glowing red from the wind. He stamped his feet and rubbed his hands together.

'It's bloody freezing,' Alan said.

'You're not kidding,' Richard said. 'What is so important you have to drag us out here?'

'I went to see Pickford again yesterday,' Alan said. 'He's stringing us along with one story after another. The guy is a lunatic. I challenged him about Christopher Deeks and Ewan Birley, and he smiled. Just like he smiled when we first interviewed him.'

'He smiled a lot,' Kim said. 'Although not when he should have been.'

'Exactly,' Alan said. 'Do you remember he asked where Father Creegan had died?'

'Vaguely,' Kim said, frowning.

'I said in the workshop,' Alan said.

'And?'

'He said, "In the storeroom at the end",' Alan said. 'Then he smiled. When I was talking to him in the prison, he did it again and something clicked.'

'I'm lost,' Kim said.

'I was looking at the drone footage of the dig last night,' Alan said. 'It flies from the clearing where we found Don Shipley, down the path, over the workshop, and back again. Come and see this,' he said. They walked to the shell of the workshop. The roof was gone and there was no glass in the windows. The remaining wall around the storeroom was hip height and all the doors were missing. Alan pointed to the floor of the workshop. 'Look at the floor there,' he said. 'There's three inches of water covering it.'

'At least,' Richard agreed.

'Now look here,' he said, pointing to the storeroom. 'There's no water at all.'

'The water is running somewhere?' Kim said, nodding.

They stepped into the shell and looked through the charred debris. Alan pulled at the remains of a shelving unit and it disintegrated into blackened fragments. He kicked the base away with his boot and exposed an oval-shaped hole in the concrete, about three-feet long. The rainwater was running down into it. Alan cleared the rubble from around it and used his torch to peer down into the pit. There was a hollow void. Two yellowed skulls grinned at him from the darkness. The skeletons were lying side by side. He stepped back to let the others see.

'Christopher and Ewan, I think,' Alan said. 'Let's get CSI here. It's time they went home.'

Author's Notes

If this is your first Anglesey book, Alan Williams wasn't a detective in real life. He was an architect, but stories about architects don't sell. He was my brother-in-law and lifelong friend, and he died too soon. Using his name keeps him close a bit longer, and I'm sure he would be amused wherever he is now.

The characters in the book are made up, but some names are real people from the island. Bob, Kim, April, and Richard all know who they are. Kris, Dan, Jack are Alan's sons, my nephews, and lovely men. Tony D is mentioned in there and the trip to cinema in Bangor was real. Tony left us a few years back, and he was a good friend. I miss him and often think of him, hence he sneaks into my books from time to time. The other characters are purely fictional, and the incidents completely made up.

I hope you enjoyed the novel. Thank you for reading it. There are twenty-four other novels to enjoy if you're new to my writing. The next one will be out early 2021 and it would be nice to do a few signings.

Maybe we'll be able to meet and greet again soon.

Until then, take care, good luck, stay safe. x

Printed in Great Britain
by Amazon

54908571R00173